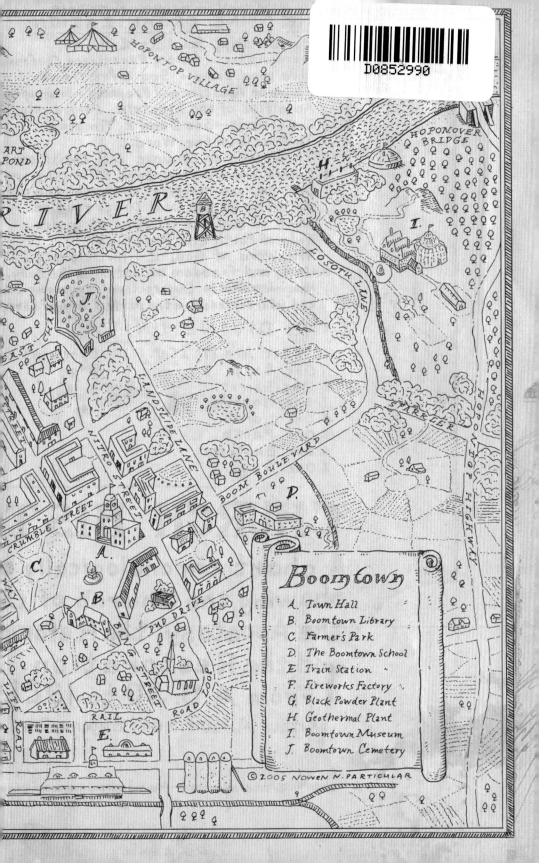

HOPONTOP VILLAGE

HOPONOVER BRIDGE

ART POND

RIVER

H.

I.

LOSOTU LINE

J.

EAST GANG

SPARKLER

LANDSZIPE LANE

NITRO STREET

HOPONTOP HIGHWAY

BOOM BOULEVARD

D.

CRUMBLE STREET

A.

C.

B.

BANG STREET

PND DRIVE

WAY

RAIL

ROAD LOOP

LIFE ROAD

E.

Boomtown

A. Town Hall
B. Boomtown Library
C. Farmer's Park
D. The Boomtown School
E. Train Station
F. Fireworks Factory
G. Black Powder Plant
H. Geothermal Plant
I. Boomtown Museum
J. Boomtown Cemetery

© 2005 NOWEN N. PARTICULAR

EST. 1894

BOOMTOWN

EST. 1894

BOOMTOWN

On behalf of the business owners and community organizations
the Welcome Wagon cheerfully welcomes you to Boomtown.

BOOMTOWN COMMUNITY ORGANIZATIONS

Boomtown Town Hall
Boomtown Library
Boomtown Museum
Boomtown Power Plant
Boomtown Fire Station
The Boomtown School
Boomtown Train Station & Telegraph
Boomtown Chamber of Commerce
VFW Hall Local #1214
FFA, Future Farmers of America
First Presbyterian Church

St. Bernard's Lutheran Church
Boomtown Church
Boomtown Cemetery
Lavatube Landfill
Public Pool - Chang Park
Farmer's Market - Farmer's Park
Boomtown Arts League
The "Lions" Club
Boomtown Historical Society
Men's & Women's Rotary Club

CHAMBER OF COMMERCE MEMBERS

Chang's Famous Fireworks Factory
Chang's Black Powder Plant
Bank of Boomtown
Boomtown Grain & Feed
Rexall Drug Store - Post Office
Fannie's Fleece & Feathers
Guenther's Gun Corral
Mabel's Diner
Walt's Barber Shop
Gertrude's Beauty Parlor
Wayne's Warehouses
Boomtown Curiosity Shop
Gus's Gas-N-Go, Towing & Repair
Greyhound Bus Station
Mitterand's Boarding House
Dr. Emil Goldberg, M.D.
Candice Oldham, Midwife, R.N.
Dr. Xu, D.D.S.
Dr. Don Haydinger, D.V.M.
Brown & Son Red Bird General Store
Martin's Mercantile
Boomtown Music
Boomtown Hobby Center
Boomtown Books

Rocket Ridge Gold Mining Co.
Soisson Winery
Tebs's Salvage Yard & Thrift Store
Carpenter King, Fine Furniture
  & Upholstery
Straightline Lumber Mill
Black Smith & Tack Shop
Sneed's Feed & Grain Store
Dover Hardware
Reynold's Rope
Bun's Bakery
Nuthouse Restaurant
Kellogg's Clothiers, Men's Fine
  Clothing & Tailoring
Women's Fashions, Hats and Handbags
Big Bang Explosives
Arturo Caruso, Plumber/Electrician
Far East Apothecary, Tea and Herbs
Top's Soda Shop & Candy Store
Rosenbaum's Jewelry and Timepieces
Maxwell's Machine Shop
Vasco Bardelli, General Contractor
Boomtown Garbage Service & Recycle

BOOMTOWN

Written & Illustrated by

NOWEN N. PARTICULAR

THOMAS NELSON
Since 1798

NASHVILLE   DALLAS   MEXICO CITY   RIO DE JANEIRO   BEIJING

ʲ Nowen
PARTICULAR

BOOMTOWN

© 2008 Nowen N. Particular (a.k.a. Marty Longé)

Published in Nashville, Tennessee, by Thomas Nelson. Thomas Nelson is a registered trademark of Thomas Nelson, Inc.

Page design by Mandi Cofer.

Thomas Nelson, Inc., titles may be purchased in bulk for educational, business, fund-raising, or sales promotional use. For information, please e-mail SpecialMarkets@ThomasNelson.com.

This novel is a work of fiction. Any references to real events, businesses, organizations, and locales are intended only to give the fiction a sense of reality and authenticity. Any resemblance to actual persons, living or dead, is entirely coincidental.

Library of Congress Cataloging-in-Publication Data

Particular, Nowen N.
  Boomtown / Nowen N. Particular.
    p. cm.
  ISBN 978-1-4003-1345-7
  Summary: On the day of their arrival in Boomtown, Washington, Reverend Button and his family make a grand entrance into town by accidentally blowing up the firecracker factory, and as they settle into the community their escapades continue.
  [1. Family life—Washington (State)—Fiction. 2. Adventure and adventurers—Fiction. 3. Washington (State)—Fiction. 4. Humorous stories.] I. Title.
  PZ7.P25625Bo 2008
  [Fic]—dc22

                        2008019439

Printed in the United States of America

08 09 10 11 12 QW 8 7 6 5 4 3 2 1

For my dad, "Sparky,"
who burned down a chicken barn,
worked in a match factory,
and set a paint room on fire.
(Those are the only incidents we know about;
there were certainly others.)
You ignited an entire family of crazy inventors.
Thank you.

For my dad, "Sparky,"
who burned down a chicken barn,
worked in a match factory,
and set a paint room on fire.
(Those are the only incidents we know about;
there were certainly others.)
You ignited an entire family of crazy inventors.
Thank you.

Contents

Acknowledgments

If this book is worth reading, it's because better books have already been written by better authors. Will anyone ever write a children's book better than *The Lion, the Witch and the Wardrobe*, *The 21 Balloons*, or *Charlie and the Chocolate Factory*? Cheers to C. S. Lewis, William Pène Dubois, Roald Dahl, J. R. R. Tolkien, Lloyd Alexander, Madeleine L'Engle, Dr. Seuss, and so many other favorites. As a boy, these authors introduced me to the great adventure of reading. As a writer, they have shown me how to find Boomtown.

Neither could I have found Boomtown without the constant support of my wife, Jamie, and my four children, Brandy, Christian, Faith, and Brittany. They championed the project from the very first day, especially my youngest, who read each chapter as it was finished and laughed in all the right places (thanks, Bert!). My father, Bob, is the inspiration for many of the crazy inventions you'll find in Boomtown—we'll never forget the car he built out of spare parts and Elmer's Glue. Also thanks to my mom, Betty, who taught me to love life in general and books in particular. I'm grateful to my brother and sister and my extended family for their encouragement and humor.

I am deeply grateful to those who edited the early drafts of this book with brutal honesty and keen insight. A special thanks goes to Faith Longé and Rachelle Longé for technical expertise and guidance. My friends Seth Crofton, Julie McIntire, Shane Taylor, and especially Darin and Janell Jordan and their children, Tommy J. and Julie, and Chad and Lisa Larrabee and their children, Davis, Annabeth, and Mitch, have been cheerleaders since the very beginning. You have been voted honorary citizens of Boomtown.

Sam Barnhart, the music minister from Common Ground Church, introduced me to Jennifer Gingerich at Thomas Nelson Publishers. She and her editorial team have been especially kind, finally turning my dream into reality. They prove what the people of Boomtown have always said: *Nowen ever succeeds on his own.* Every victory is a shared triumph.

A final nod goes to all the English teachers and history teachers over the years who never quit on me, even though I gave them a thousand reasons to do so. You are the unseen heroes of any book that will ever be written or has ever been written. Keep on teaching! You're changing the world one dreamer at a time.

Introduction

If you are anything like most kids, you will *not* read this introduction. You want to skip past the boring parts and jump ahead to where the dragon is attacking the castle or the detective uncovers the most important clue. If you are like that, you are among the thousands of children who do not read introductions to books. Tedious paragraphs that explain why reading a particular book is going to be "good for you" is like having your parents make you eat lima beans before you can have dessert. How dreadful. It may be *good* for you, but it certainly isn't any *fun*.

I used to be like that, but then I grew up and got boring. Just ask my kids, Ruth, Jonny, and Sarah. They're the sort who love firecrackers and bottle rockets shooting every which way, bouncing out of control. I prefer candles sitting in a window, quiet and predictable. That's the *opposite* of what I found in Boomtown. It was a strong dose of medicine, and I had trouble swallowing it.

As you read this story, you'll see what I mean. This book tells all about the unusual things that happened to us in an odd place called Boomtown. After reading this account, you'll probably think I made the whole thing up. It certainly *sounds* like I did. But I promise you, it's all true.

It was 1949, and we'd had enough of the craziness of California. So I decided to move my family to upper eastern Washington to a town called Boomtown. We were looking forward to wide-open spaces, quiet streets, picket fences, rows of charming houses, and snow at Christmas. The plan was that I would be the pastor of a small-town church with quiet small-town ways. Janice would escape the pressures of being a minister's wife in a large urban congregation, while our three children would find friends their own ages. We pictured an idyllic postcard life surrounded by rolling hillside farms and simple, charming people. That's what we were looking for, and that's exactly what we found—along with a few hundred unexpected surprises.

Boomtown turned out to be a place where everybody's favorite thing to do was to blow stuff up. I was also surprised by the ethnic makeup of the town; in spite of their varied backgrounds, men and women and children worked together as a community of equals. They valued education more than money, worked hard, stayed married, loved their children, cared for the environment, and honored the heritage of other cultures.

You may ask, "How is that possible?"

I see your point. A place like that can't be real.

But it should be.

A Shaky Start

I almost died today. Not quite, but *almost*. Not by any of the most common methods—heart attack, car accident, drowning, old age—that sort of thing. My survival was measured in *inches*. If my truck driver hadn't tackled me; if he didn't have the foresight to jump on me and knock me into the water; if he had hesitated even for a moment, this book would be five sentences long and it would end with dot, dot, dot . . .

Obviously, I *didn't* die, or I wouldn't be sitting here writing this story and telling you exactly what happened. I'm not sure you'll believe it. I'm not sure that *I* do.

It all started early Friday morning on the last day of our journey from California to Washington. We had stayed overnight at the Travelodge in Wenatchee, where we'd arranged to catch up with our moving truck and driver. From there we followed in the shadow cast by the lumbering, bright orange vehicle as it made its way up Highway 97 toward our new home in Boomtown.

Ruth, our oldest at age sixteen, and her younger siblings, Jonny and Sarah, ages thirteen and ten respectively, kept their noses pressed against the windows of our old Chevy station wagon.

"Look, Mom, *apple trees!*"

"Look over there—pears and peaches and raspberries."

"Look at all the cows and horses and sheep. And what are *those*, Mom?"

Janice answered, "Those are llamas, dear."

Sarah said, "Really? A herd of llamas? Can I have one?"

"Of course not. They're only for looking at."

"Can I have a cow instead?"

"No dear, you can't have a cow."

"What about a sheep? They aren't very big. I could keep it in my room."

I interrupted the negotiations. "Be serious, Sarah, what would you do if you had a sheep for a pet?"

"They make *wool*, don't they? I could cut off the wool, and Mom could make yarn out of it. She could knit sweaters. That's what people do in small towns. They have sheep and they make sweaters."

"Your mother doesn't know how to knit."

"She could *learn*."

"Maybe she will, but you *still* can't have a sheep. They're very messy."

"That's okay!" Sarah answered. "So am I. You'd hardly notice."

"No!"

We drove past sparkling canyon streams, scrubby pine forests, and golden wheat fields. It was all so beautiful. The kids had lived their entire lives in the crowded city streets of California. Janice was from San Francisco, and I was from New York. The only place you could see animals in New York was at the zoo or in the subways during rush hour. With thirsty eyes, we drank it all in.

Janice sighed. "Wide-open spaces. Bright blue sky. Puffy white clouds as far as the eye can see. It's like paradise."

The moving truck continued its lurching trek north as we rolled through the small mining town of Ainogold. Our arrival included curious onlookers who stopped to stare at the strangers. New neighbors perhaps? Not this time. We halted at the single traffic light and continued on.

A few months later, someone in Boomtown told me the interesting history of how Ainogold got its name. "It happened nearly a huner't years ago during the days of the Yukon Gold Rush. A certain prospector named Coyote Jones came up from California to stake his claim. Spent all he had buying the land and securing the equipment he needed to dig his mine. Ah heard he was up in the hills almost a year and a half 'fore he came back down to the main camp without nary a nugget to show for all his trouble. He weren't the only one. Must have been two huner't other miners with the same bad luck. Coyote Jones said, 'There just ain't no gold!' Get it? *'Ain't no gold.'* Ainogold!' The name sorta stuck and they been callin' the place Ainogold ever since."

After leaving the little village, we traveled alongside a wide river with rugged cliffs rising to our left and open fields to the right with an occasional farmhouse dotting the landscape. Our map showed Boomtown only eight miles farther up the road. I made the announcement, "Only a few more minutes and we'll be there!"

We turned east onto Blasting Cap Avenue and Jonny cheered as the tires bumped across the Ifilami Bridge and over the Okanogan River. We were greeted by a brightly painted sign that said Welcome to Boomtown! Underneath were the words *Home of Chang's Famous Fireworks Factory*. There was also a round logo with the portrait of an Asian man painted in the center. I had to assume it was the face of the aforementioned Chang, founder of his Famous Fireworks Factory.

"Dad!" shouted Jonny. "Did you see that sign? They've got a *fireworks factory*! You never said nothin' about a fireworks factory!"

"I never said *anything* about fireworks," I replied, correcting his grammar. "It's because I didn't know. The search committee from the church didn't mention it."

"But where is it? I want to *see* it!"

"I don't know, Jon. Let's get settled in our new house first. We'll have time for fireworks later."

Actually, we didn't have to wait very long. Following the hand-drawn map the church secretary had mailed to us, we turned left onto Dynamite Drive and saw the huge factory looming in front of us. Just beyond it to the right we could see Chang's Black Powder Plant, with trails of smoke snaking upward from its twin cones, like two smoldering witches' hats. Even from inside the station wagon, we could smell the pungent odor of sulfur.

But it was the fireworks factory that commanded our attention. It was five stories tall and built entirely out of red brick, with what seemed like a hundred windows along each side and almost three hundred feet in length. On the roof were four towering smokestacks that had the name of the company painted in black. The stacked-up letters spelled out CHANG'S FAMOUS FIREWORKS FACTORY, big enough that you could see them for miles. Black wrought-iron stairs climbed the outer walls like spider webs, and we could see dozens of workers busily moving up and down carrying supplies and equipment like ants in an ant farm. Several railcars were parked alongside the building and were in the process of being loaded. Everywhere you looked, there was bustling activity.

I was so busy studying the building that I almost slammed into the back of the moving truck when it lurched to a sudden halt. From behind the truck, we couldn't see why. We sat for a minute wondering what was going on until I pulled over to the shoulder, shifted the gear into Park, and turned off the ignition. I opened my door and climbed out to investigate. Janice and the kids quickly unbuckled and opened their doors to follow me.

I turned back to them. "You can stay in the car. I'm just going to talk to the driver."

"Stay in the car, Mr. Button?" responded Janice. "You want me to keep three kids trapped in a hot station wagon while you go running around a fireworks factory?"

"I'm not going *into* the factory, Janice. I just want to find out why the moving truck stopped."

Jonny and Sarah ran up beside me. "We want to find out too!"

"And me," added Ruth.

Overruled, I shrugged my shoulders and walked around

the moving truck to the front, with my family right behind me. We found the driver talking to a Chinese man wearing a white lab coat and surrounded by three other men who were dressed similarly. The lab technician—that's what he appeared to be—held a clipboard and was gesturing to an object anchored in the center of a wide, shallow pond situated in front of the factory.

"Excuse me," I inquired, "is there a problem?"

The Chinese gentleman answered politely, "No, sir. But as you can see, we were about to conduct a test. Pardon us, but if you need to get past this point, you will have to go back to Blasting Cap Avenue and drive around through the town. Sorry about the inconvenience."

Jonny, his eyes alight with excitement, pushed past me and asked, "What are you doing? What *kind* of test?"

In the center of the road was a small console on a metal stand. Sprouting from the console was a nest of black and red wires connected to a black box and running across the ground. The wires led to the pond, and from there they disappeared underwater. I guessed they were connected to what appeared to be a small boat. The boat was heavily anchored—we could see the ropes—and inside the boat was a silver tube lying on its side, about the size of a small water heater, with a metal bell at one end and a cone on the other.

"Jonny," I said, ignoring his enthusiasm, "how many times have I told you not to interrupt when adults are talking?"

"But, Dad . . ."

"Don't argue. These people are busy, and we need to get out of their way."

The Chinese gentleman smiled. "It's quite all right. We're *never* too busy for curious children. My name is Han-wu," he said, extending a hand toward Jonny. "And who are you?"

"My name is Jonathan, but people call me Jonny. This is my big sister, Ruth, and my little sister, Sarah. I call her 'Sorry' though."

"Sorry?" Han-wu asked.

"Yeah, because she's always saying, 'I'm Sorry.' Like the time she broke open a pen to find out where the ink was coming from. It made such a mess, we had to replace our sofa and the carpet."

Sarah laughed and said, "I'm Sorry!"

Ruth added, "Then there was the time she tried to wash the cat—except she couldn't find the soap, so she used Vaseline instead."

"Vaseline?" exclaimed Han-wu.

"Yes, *Vaseline*, a whole jumbo-sized jar of it! By the time she finished, the cat was so slippery it took us a week to catch it. Then it took another month to wash out the Vaseline. You can't imagine how hard it is to wash a wet, oily cat."

"I'm Sorry!" Sarah giggled.

"Oh, sure, you're *Sorry*," said her mother. "Like the time you wanted to see what would happen if you put marshmallows in the clothes dryer."

"Or when you jumped out of the baptistery closet during Communion and Mr. Gray dumped an entire tray of grape juice cups all over Mrs. Larson's new white dress," Jonny said.

"I'm Sorry! I'm Sorry! *I'm Sorry!*" Sarah said, taking a bow.

Han-wu and his team laughed. "I guess we shouldn't turn our backs on you or maybe *we'll* be Sorry—you think so?"

Sarah nodded vigorously. "I'm trouble, that's for sure! Just ask my dad."

I agreed wholeheartedly. Sarah had gotten herself into all kinds of crazy situations in the ten short years since she was born. She was aptly named. I had named her Sarah after the wife of Abraham. The Old Testament Sarah was famous as the mother of Isaac and the grandmother of Israel, but she was also famous for laughing at God. There were times when I wondered if God wasn't laughing at *Sarah*. She could be hilariously funny—and impossibly infuriating—at the same time.

Then there was Jonathan, named after the son of King Saul, also from the Old Testament. As a king, Saul was a disappointment; but his son Jonathan was a hero. Since Jonathan was my first and only son, I dreamed that maybe someday *he'd* do something heroic. I had no great ambitions for myself except to be the pastor of a small congregation. That was enough for me.

But Jonny—who had just turned thirteen—was so incredibly *smart*. He had a natural aptitude for math and science and engineering. I thought he might grow up to build skyscrapers or bridges or rockets to the stars. But he tended to be lazy in school; he had some trouble paying attention; he was always dreaming of imaginary worlds and fantasy adventures. Instead of finishing his homework, he'd doodle dragons and knights in the margins.

So who could say? Prince Jonathan of the Bible ended up taking matters into his own hands—to the chagrin of his father, but to the ultimate salvation of his people. Maybe my Jonathan would end up doing the same thing. I'd have to wait and see.

Ruth was everything the other two were not. She was sixteen, in high school, beautiful like her mother, and exceptionally responsible. As the oldest sibling, she too had been aptly named. Ruth, from the book of the same name, was gentle and quiet and faithful, a servant to everyone. When I looked at my older daughter, I saw a young grown-up. I could always count on Ruth to watch over her younger—and less predictable—siblings.

I shook the hand Han-wu offered and continued the introductions. "This is our driver, Lars, from the moving company. This is my wife, Janice, and our three children, whom you've already met. And I'm the father of this group, Arthur Button. The *Reverend* Arthur Button. Perhaps you've heard—the new pastor over at Boomtown Church?"

Han-wu gave me a warm smile. "Reverend Button! Of course! We heard you were coming. It's an honor to welcome you to Boomtown."

He introduced the others who were standing with him, each of whom bowed respectfully as their names were called. "These are three of the members of my research team, Lu-shan, Tong, and Wei. We all work together in that building over there." He pointed across the pond at a smaller outbuilding near the driveway entrance.

After the introductions, Han-wu turned his attention back to Jonny. "You were wondering what we're testing this morning? You like gadgets? Machines? Rockets? That sort of thing?"

"I *love* all that stuff!" Jonny answered excitedly. "My favorite thing is my Erector Set. I make cars and Ferris wheels and trains and weird machines. I like the motors and all the gears. And *rockets*! I always wanted a rocket, but my dad won't let me have one," he frowned, glancing at me. "Is that what you got out there on the boat? A rocket?"

"Exactly so. Except it's not a boat, not precisely. Why don't you follow me so we can get a better look at it?"

We followed Han-wu across the road and down a small slope where we could stand next to the water. "This is Popgun Pond, and the small stream you see flowing in and out of it is the canal we dug to form the pond. It also supplies water for the factory and for the fire hydrants—in case of emergency." We could see brightly painted red fire hydrants scattered over the factory yard. "We try our best to avoid using those. Safety First, that's our motto!"

He pointed at the boat with the rocket mounted inside. "The boat-shaped object you see out there is actually one of our testing platforms. Whenever we want to test something new—and potentially dangerous—we put it on one of those boats, float it out into the middle of the pond, and anchor it down with ropes and weights. This morning we're testing a new rocket motor, something with a little more power than anything we've tried in the past."

"A rocket motor?" I asked. "Exactly what are you planning to shoot off with that thing?"

"Fie-tann, he's the current manager of the fireworks factory, has been wanting to build this rocket for a while now.

So far, we've had to build all our fireworks displays on the *ground* and shoot individual rockets up into the air. You're familiar with how that works?"

"Sure," I answered, "I've been to the big fireworks show in Pasadena, the one they have at the Rose Bowl every year. They build a large launching platform with hundreds of launch tubes for all the rockets. I've seen that."

Han-wu explained, "Fie-tann was wondering if we could lift the fireworks display *off* the ground. Instead of shooting all the rockets from down *here*, we'd lift them up and set them off from up *there*," he said, pointing upward. "For that we need to build a powerful rocket engine. If it works, then we'll build four of them and mount them to a larger rocket tube. Together, they'll have the lifting strength we need to get our fireworks display airborne."

"Are you serious?"

"Why not? Can you imagine if we get this to work? We'll be able to ship an entire fireworks display in *one* container— anywhere in the world. San Francisco, Denver, Dallas, Tallahassee, New York, Paris, London, and so on. Set it up on its end, unpack the crate, light the fuse, launch the rockets, and once it's airborne it will go off all by itself —automatic."

I stared at him incredulously. "But what if something goes wrong? What if the rocket takes off in the wrong direction? What if the whole thing just blows up on the ground? People could get hurt. You could knock down a building. You've got to *think* about those sorts of things!"

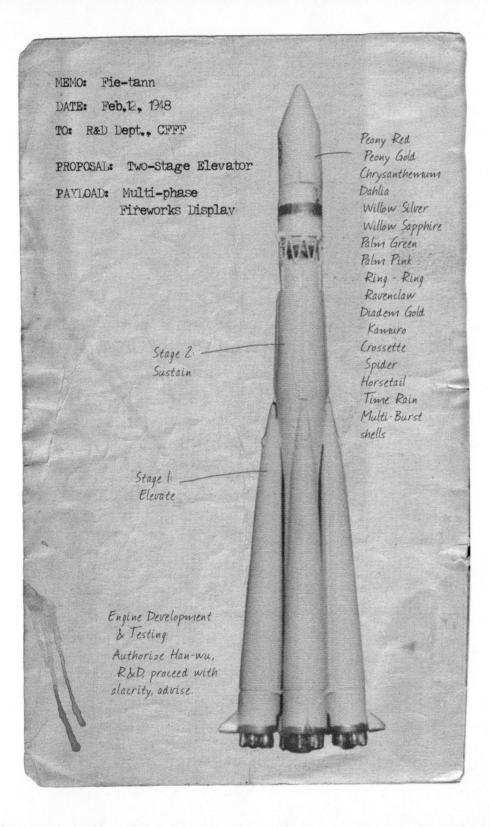

MEMO: Fie-tann

DATE: Feb.12, 1948

TO: R&D Dept., CFFF

PROPOSAL: Two-Stage Elevator

PAYLOAD: Multi-phase
Fireworks Display

Peony Red
Peony Gold
Chrysanthemum
Dahlia
Willow Silver
Willow Sapphire
Palm Green
Palm Pink
Ring - Ring
Ravenclaw
Diadem Gold
Kamuro
Crossette
Spider
Horsetail
Time Rain
Multi-Burst
shells

Stage 2:
Sustain

Stage 1:
Elevate

Engine Development
& Testing:
Authorize Han-wu,
R&D proceed with
alacrity, advise.

"That's what *testing* is for," smiled Han-wu, dismissing my concerns with a wave of his hand. "We shoot off a test rocket and correct for any problems. And besides that, it's a lot of *fun*! Isn't that right, Jonny?"

When Jonny didn't answer, I turned to look for him, but he wasn't anywhere to be found.

"Jonny? Sarah? *Now* what are they up to? They were standing here a minute ago."

We started looking around, thinking Jonny and Sarah had gone over to the fireworks factory to get a closer look. Maybe they were heading around to the other side of the pond. Ruth hadn't seen them go. Neither had Janice. Suddenly, Han-wu spotted them back up on the road.

"There they are!" he pointed.

I wasn't there to witness it, but after it was all over, I managed to weed the whole story out of my two wayward children. Apparently after Jonny heard about the rocket test he whispered in Sarah's ear, "Let's go take a look at the launcher!" They scampered back up the slope and stood next to the metal stand while Jonny explained to Sarah how he thought it might work.

"Look here," he said, indicating the black box on the ground. "I think that's the battery. These wires run up to the panel here and hook into the switches. That red switch, the one with the yellow square around it, that's probably the trigger button. When you flip it, the battery power runs through the wires and goes out to the rocket boat. That's how I *think* it works, anyway."

Sarah said, "Then what?"

"Then the electricity sets off an ignition pack and that lights the rocket fuel and then it blasts off!" Jonny said knowingly. " I read all about it in a copy of *Popular Science*."

Sarah stood on her tiptoes to get a better look at the control panel. You mean *this* switch right here?" she asked.

"Don't *touch* it!" Jonny hissed, grabbing for his sister.

By then it was too late. By the time we started yelling at them to get back, Sarah had already flipped the switch and ignited the rocket motor. Gouts of flame and smoke flared out of the nozzle. The deafening roar of the engine split the air. We cringed at the noise, covering our ears with our hands and spinning around to see what was happening. Workers from the fireworks factory heard the noise, and in a few moments fire crews came running out of the buildings carrying coils of hoses and wrenches so they could hook up to the fire hydrants and turn on the water. The noise got louder and louder as men and women scattered in every direction shouting and waving their arms.

At first I couldn't figure what all the commotion was about. True, the rocket wasn't supposed to be set off by my *children*, but it *was* supposed to go off—that was the plan—so at first I didn't know why everyone was panicking. But I soon saw what everyone else had already seen. The ropes and the anchors weren't strong enough. The boat was heading across the pond and picking up speed.

"Run!" shouted Han-wu. "Run for your lives!"

I couldn't hear what he said over the ear-shattering blast of the rocket boat that had turned into a projectile. It was all I could do to stumble over to Janice and Ruth and grab their hands and pull them around the far end of the pond, opposite from the direction of where the rocket was pointing. At least, that's where it *used* to be pointing until the ropes finally tore loose and the rocket boat broke free. Now it was a boat *missile* as it gained speed, hit the edge of the pond, and launched into the air. The weight of the boat caused it to spin wildly, first turning toward the fireworks factory where it chased a group of workers across the asphalt, and then it spun around and headed straight back in the direction from where it had come. Now it was on a trajectory straight to where Jonny and Sarah stood gaping wide-eyed and frozen on the road. It probably would have flattened them if it hadn't spun sideways and headed directly toward the moving truck and our car. It bounced off the roof of the truck and was deflected, this time in the direction of where the girls and I were trying to escape.

"Get down!" shrieked Janice, throwing her body on top of Ruth. They fell in a tangled heap at my feet, while I continued to stumble forward. I watched the rocket loop left and then right, barely missing our station wagon, bouncing off a tree, through some nearby bushes, scraping along the ground, skipping down the driveway and making a beeline for my head.

At the very last second, Lars the truck driver, a former pro football linebacker, grabbed me in a running tackle and drove me head over heels into the pond. *Splash!* Down I went with a three-hundred-pound man on my chest and the air knocked out of my lungs—just in the nick of time!

As I went under the water and sank in the mud, I saw the rocket streak over our heads. What I *didn't* see was the moment it smashed into the research building in a shower of shattering glass and flying furniture. Under the water, I felt the explosion when the rocket detonated, igniting all the flammable materials stored in the lab. I surfaced sputtering and gasping for air in time to see the building as a raging inferno, surrounded by teams of firefighters from the factory as they tried to extinguish the flames.

The conflagration was fueled by bursts of silver and gold and red and green sparks as various chemicals and compounds ignited in the blaze. We could hear the whistle of Piccolo Petes and the staccato bursts of firecrackers and the flash of sparklers and Roman candles as they exploded from the heat. In fact, if it weren't for the absolute devastation of the building, you could have almost described it as "pretty." But it *wasn't* pretty. Not in the least.

While Janice and the others helped Lars and me out of the pond, Ruth ran to our car to fetch some towels. I thanked Lars for saving my life, even though it felt like I'd been hit by a freight train. Han-wu ran around making sure that no one was hurt in the accident, while Fie-tann, manager of the factory, made sure the fire didn't spread to the rest of the complex. The workers fought to get the blaze under control. There were hoses and bucket brigades everywhere you looked.

During all of the chaos, Jonny and Sarah had slipped behind the moving truck, where they took a few moments to decide which country they should run away to. They found a hiding spot behind the front tire where they waited for the next explosion, the one that would happen once I got my hands on them. I came around the corner and found the two of them crouched down in a huddle, shivering like two rabbits caught in a trap. I stood over them, hair and clothes dripping from the pond, a thunderstorm painted on my face. The two children could guess what was coming next.

Sarah whimpered, "I'm *Sorry*?"

"*Sorry*?! You're *Sorry*?! You're *gonna* be Sorry!"

I gathered what was left of my raveled nerves and prepared to unleash a barrage of angry words upon my two children just as I heard the sound of the research building collapsing. The ground shook as the roof and walls caved in, raising a cloud of ash and smoke, until all that was left was a pile of smoldering rubble. I watched it through the windows of the truck.

As it tumbled down, so did my out-of-control anger. Yelling wasn't going to fix anything. *Nothing* could fix this. Instead, I pictured the crumbling building taking my career as a pastor down with it. How was I ever going to face the people of Boomtown after something like this? This wasn't a dryer full of melted marshmallows or a cat covered in Vaseline. This was the disaster to beat all disasters!

Deflated? Absolutely. *Mortified?* Certainly. *Embarrassed?* No doubt about it. But there simply isn't a single word to describe how I was feeling. I don't think the dictionary has *invented* the word for it yet.

Fireworks Factory in Flames
Research Bldg. at Chang's Burns to the Ground

Workers at Chang's Famous Fireworks Factory attempt to douse the blaze allegedly sparked by Jonathan and Sarah Button (age 13 and 10 respectively).

BOOMTOWN — Early Friday morning the Reverend Arthur Button and family arrived in Boomtown and interrupted a scheduled rocket test, leading to the destruction of Chang's Famous Fireworks Factory research building.

Witnesses place Jonathan (13) and Sarah Button (10) near the controls when the rocket was accidently launched, resulting in a catastrophic conflagration involving the entire research ts.

Employees from the factory, organized by Han-wu, senior researcher, and Fie-tann, factory manager, limited the blaze to the single building.

Han-wu said, "I don't recall the last time we've enjoyed this much excitement. We had a lot of fireworks stored in the lab. It was a spectacular show! I only wish more people could have seen it."

Damage was estimated to be in the tens of thousands of dollars. No injuries were reported.

CHAPTER 2

The Big Bang Boom Box

As it turned out, I completely miscalculated the reaction of the people of Boomtown. We weren't outcasts; we were *celebrities!* Word of the explosion spread quickly, so by the time we finally pulled up in front of our rental house, we were surrounded by people wanting to know the gritty details.

One of those people was a man who showed up with his wife and several children. He slapped me on my sore back and spoke in a very loud voice, "My name is Matthieu LaPierre, and this is

my wife, Pauline. We're your neighbors, five (

right. I just had to come on over and shake y(

"You did?"

"Sure, sure! You really know how to mak(

down the research lab at the fireworks fac

first day! How about *that!*"

"It was an accident. Really, we didn't d(

"'Course you didn't, I know that. But t

anything. You done it! Wow! What a story

there to do it myself!"

"You do?"

"Absolutely. I've never been lucky enoug

down. My only real claim to fame is our twe

"Twelve?"

"Yep, with lucky thirteen on the way. Th

dozen!"

I tried to be polite. "That's . . . um .

to feed."

"We manage. I got my farm—and with a

we get quite a lot of work done."

"You have a farm? Just down the stree

"Nah. That's just the house. The farm i

Highway, south of here."

"Oh, I see. So what do you grow out th(

"All sorts of things. Radishes, potatoes,

the usual stuff. And I got a petting zoo. Th

"Petting zoo?"

"Sure, people stop by and pay a little to ƒ

a cobra, a yak, a coupla' skunks and a porcupine (I wouldn't
those if I were you), two buffalo, a gorilla, three ostriches, and
lligator. Just got me that one. Shipped it in from Florida."

"An alligator? In a petting zoo?"

"Well, he's not really for *petting*. I got him because of the
. I got a huge rat problem in my barns."

"Why didn't you get a cat?"

"A cat! The alligator would *eat* a cat if it ever had the chance!"

"I meant why didn't you get a cat *instead* of an alligator."

"Oh, that would be boring. *Everybody's* got a cat. Cats is
rywhere. But I'm the only one who's got an *alligator*."

Matthieu LaPierre wasn't the only one who surprised me
afternoon. Han-wu and Fie-tann stopped by at the house
r the fire was under control to make sure I was okay.

"I don't know what to say," I told them. "I am *so* sorry. Jonny
Sarah should not have gone near that control panel. I don't
w what they were thinking. And now your lab is burned to the
und. I'll try to pay for it somehow—if you'll give me a chance."

"*Pay* for it?" chuckled Fie-tann. "Why would we make you
for it? It wasn't your fault. The ropes broke. The rocket was
powerful. It would have happened with or without you. All
day's work, that's what I say. Don't worry about it."

"But what about the damage? I feel responsible."

"Nonsense," replied Han-wu. "If *I* had been the one to
the switch, then *I* would have been the one responsible.
t's really the only thing I'm upset about. Now I won't get
rag about it to my friends."

"You're *glad* this happened?"

"Well, no, because now we have to rebuild the research lab. But we sure do love a good show here in Boomtown! This was one of the best ever! We'll be talking about it for years, thanks to you."

It wasn't any use. No matter how hard I tried to apologize, they just wouldn't accept it. They were too excited about the spectacular fireworks show—and they were especially pleased about how powerfully the rocket had performed—never mind that it destroyed part of their factory. Fie-tann said, "We'll just have to cut back on some of the rocket propellant and get some thicker rope. Then we'll fire it up again!"

After greeting several more neighbors, we finally were able to get to the front porch. I wasn't looking forward to the daunting task of moving all our furniture into the rooms and up the stairs—and my back was killing me after being tackled by Lars. There were all those boxes and chairs and tables and books to lug across the lawn—a lot of work for Lars and me. After the disaster at the fireworks factory, I wasn't looking forward to all the stress—but I needn't have worried. We were surrounded by an army of volunteers, all of them insisting on helping the new minister and his family of firebugs move in.

It was *perfect* by the way—the rental house, I mean. With the help of the church secretary, we'd found a cozy three-bedroom house that was walking distance from the church. It had a large backyard with a picket fence, a small garage, and a front porch bordered by flowers. There was a large bay window in the family room, a small kitchen, a pantry, one bathroom, and three bedrooms upstairs. There was an extra room downstairs where I could put a desk and my books for a study.

I talked to Lars about a plan for unloading. Fortunately, he had clean overalls in his cab to replace the muddy ones he was still wearing. And I found a fresh pair of jeans and shirt in one of our suitcases. In the meantime, the kids were excitedly jumping up and down on the porch and chanting, "Let us in! Let us in!" Janice saved Sarah from having a heart attack by unlocking the front door. The kids ran from room to room, out the back, around the side, back inside, up the stairs, and began to fight for bedroom territory.

"Sarah and I will take this room at the end of the hallway," Ruth announced.

Jonny answered, "You can *have* it! This one's mine!"

He wanted the bedroom with the window that opened into the branches of the backyard tree. He wasted no time climbing out the window—to the absolute terror of my wife and the delight of Sarah, who insisted on trying it immediately. (That particular tree was the same tree Jonny later used to sneak out of the house for his nocturnal raids—something that turned out for the best in the long run—but I didn't know about it until much later. We'll get to that soon enough.)

After the brief exploration, Ruth released our cat, Effeneff, from his carrier. This was the cat Sarah had "greased" a few years before. It stretched its long gray body, shook out its fur, licked each of its paws carefully, then scampered across the lawn and began to patrol the perimeter of the front steps and porch, looking for mice and shrews. Sarah had given the cat its name; she insisted he was descended from the great lions of Egypt.

"He's Fierce *and* Friendly," Sarah had said.

We soon shortened that to "F and F," and the name stuck. After only a minute or two, Effeneff pounced and captured a shrew and went to find a shady spot where he could play with it in private.

Janice said, "That's a good sign. If a cat likes a house, then it's probably a good place for people too."

With help from all of our neighbors, the job of unloading was finished quickly, leaving the more time-consuming job of unpacking and putting everything in its place. As the sun crawled higher in the sky, Edna Kreuger, the widow who lived next door, brought us a huge lunch of ham and cheese on wheat bread, homemade potato salad, bright red apples, and a delicious blackberry pie with vanilla ice cream. The lettuce, potatoes, apples, and berries had been grown in her very own garden, she proudly declared.

"There's lots more where *that* came from!" she said. "You'll never go hungry with Gramma Edna next door!"

She turned out to be a faithful member of Boomtown Church, where I'd be preaching that Sunday. Sarah fell in love with her immediately and adopted her as her own grandmother. We've called her "Gramma" ever since.

Matthieu LaPierre volunteered to fix the front screen door while others went from room to room unpacking boxes, hanging pictures, setting up beds, and organizing the kitchen. The ladies from Gramma Edna's sewing circle showed up with ironing boards and irons; they smoothed out the wrinkles from our clothes and linens while they got to know Janice better and helped her fill up the dressers and closets.

Ed Gamelli, the mailman, stopped by at around three o'clock and added our names to his route list. Then at four o'clock we met Leona Peasley, hostess of the Boomtown Welcome Wagon and lead soprano at St. Bernard's Lutheran Church. She presented us with a straw basket decorated with green and yellow ribbons and filled to the brim with apples, pears, peaches, and several jars of homemade marionberry jam. She handed us an envelope filled with all sorts of things: a welcome letter from the Wagoneers, a note of greeting from the mayor, and coupons from local businesses.

Leona said, "There's a coupon in there for a free Family Gutbuster Sundae from Top's Soda Shop. A free hairdo for Janice when she visits Gertrude's Beauty Parlor for the first time. There are special offers from the Boomtown Bookstore, the Hobby Center, Bun's Bakery, Martin's Mercantile, the Red Bird, and of course, Big Bang Explosives. And speaking of that . . ."

Behind her she had a large gold-colored box, trimmed in red and green, with the Chang's Fireworks logo emblazoned on the side. It was about the size of a small steamer trunk with wheels at the four corners and a handle for pulling it along. On the lid and on each of the four panels, in bright red letters, were printed the words *Big Bang Boom Box*.

Leona presented it to us with a wink. "Every family who moves to Boomtown receives the deluxe one-hundred-and-fifty-pound box of Chang's Famous Fireworks as a welcome gift from the factory. You've got sparklers, firecrackers, smoke bombs, Roman candles, fountains, spinners, flaming whistles, aerial repeaters, rockets, and mortars. There's enough firepower in there to relocate your house if you're not careful!"

Jonny was the first one to react. "This is for *us*? All of it? For *free*?"

I put my hand on his shoulder. "Hang on a minute, buster, before you start lighting any matches. We've had *enough* fireworks for one day, don't you think? Probably enough for a lifetime."

"Ah, c'mon, Dad. Just look at it. A hundred and fifty *pounds*!"

Leona cut in. "Now, Reverend, don't look so worried. On every fourth Friday, from May through September, everyone gathers down by the river in Chang Park and shoots off fireworks. It's all carefully supervised and a real *blast*, if you know what I mean. My husband will be there—quite a number of adults, actually—and the fire chief with his truck."

"And an ambulance? And maybe a few stretchers? You heard what happened at the fireworks factory?"

Leona laughed. "Sure, I heard about it. You really know how to make an entrance!"

"Well, I'm not looking for a repeat performance, not tonight anyway. It's totally out of the question." My back started to hurt again just thinking about it.

"Dad!" Jonny complained. Sarah joined in. "It's not fair!" Even Ruth was pouting.

Janice came to the rescue. "Listen here, Mr. Button. We're new in this town and you know what they say: 'When in Rome, do as the Romans do.' We should *join in*. We'll meet more of the neighbors and let the kids have their fun. We'll be there to watch. It'll be fun for us too. Please?"

"That's right, Reverend," Leona added. "It's a great way for the kids to make friends. Just think about it—after this morning Jonny and Sarah are *famous*! The park will be swarming with kids from the town. I'll be down there with my family. The whole Welcome Wagon committee will be there. Please say you'll come."

I was almost convinced, but not quite. *When in Rome, do as the Romans do?* I thought about what the Romans were famous for—it usually involved mass destruction and quite a bit of slashing and burning. After the episode that morning, I wasn't game for any more of it. But I looked into the eyes of my wife, then the faces of Jonny and Sarah and even Ruth, and figured I didn't have any choice. That was happening a lot lately.

"Okay," I said, "we'll go, but only on *two* conditions."

Once the cheering subsided, they asked me what they were.

"Number one, we aren't going anywhere until we've finished moving in. That goes for *all* of you—*especially* you, Sarah—all your things put away, your room cleaned up, your bed made."

"I will! I promise!"

"And number two, you will *not* under *any* circumstances push *any* buttons or flip *any* switches without complete and total adult supervision, and *not* until I am hiding behind a rock—is that understood?"

"Thanks, Dad!" Jonny said, pumping my hand. "It's a deal!"

"All right, now that's settled. Let's get back to work."

Unpacking continued without further interruption. By the time it started to get dark, all the furniture was in position, all the boxes were unpacked, all the beds were set up, and we still had time before the fireworks show to eat another delicious meal. Gramma Edna and her sewing ladies insisted on feeding us until our stomachs were ready to burst. I could already tell that in Boomtown we'd never starve.

By eight o'clock I was so tired and sore that I tried to get out of going to the park, but Jonny and Sarah wouldn't leave me alone.

"C'mon kids, I have to get some sleep. Tomorrow is Saturday. I have to get ready for my first Sunday. I'm going to stay home. Ruth and your mother can take you."

"But you *gotta* come, Dad! Have you even *looked* inside the box?"

I had, actually. The Big Bang Boom Box consisted of two parts. There was a latch that held the lid closed. Once it was opened, the lid contained all the loose fireworks: strings of firecrackers, Roman candles, sparklers, fountains, bottle rockets, and that sort of thing. There were smoke bombs and squirmy snakes and smoke worms and spinning flowers and buzzing fire bees, but there was also something I'd never seen before. It was an army of little tin soldiers (made out of cardboard, of course) that when you lit the fuse, they would go marching across the ground until the fuse hit the main charge, after which their heads would go shooting off and explode with a bang. There were also about twenty fire frogs; light the fuse and they went jumping all over the place, flipping upside down, spewing fire and smoke, and finally disappearing in a blast of green flame and sparks. Those were really something to see.

But that was nothing compared to the second part. The main box contained a preset fireworks display, complete with launcher tubes and a timed fuse mechanism. All you had to do was set the box an appropriate distance away from spectators, light the extra-long fuse, duck for cover, and watch as the rockets' red glare filled the air. Pink ones, blue ones, green ones, gold and silver bursts, loud explosions, balls of fire, shooting and crackling and whistling fireworks for almost ten solid minutes. I was forced to admit I was suitably impressed by the display. I marveled at the clever inventors at the fireworks factory who had designed it.

However, as enjoyable as the fireworks turned out to be, the best part of the evening had to do with the people we met, especially the children of Boomtown who took to our kids like mice to a hunk of cheese. Ruth met some other high school girls who invited her to try out for the cheerleading squad. Sarah and Jonny were that night's celebrities and they both went home with a dozen new friends. It was everything Janice and I had been hoping for.

It started with a boy about the same age as Jonny who

came over and introduced himself. "Howdy! The name's Busy. What's yours?"

"Jonathan. But people call me Jonny—or sometimes Jon for short. *Your* name is kinda weird, though."

"What, *Busy*? Nah, that's not my *real* name."

"What is it then?"

"My *real* name is Bartholomew Zed Gunderson—that's a mouthful, ain't it? My initials are B. Z., so my friends just call me 'Busy.' Get it?"

"Sure, I get it now."

"My *dad's* nickname is the weird one. It's 'Lazy.' Lazy Gunderson—sorta the opposite of mine."

"Why do they call him that?"

"'Cause he flattened our house with a tractor."

"He did?"

"That's right!" Busy grinned proudly, hitching his thumbs in his pants. "Flattened the house! Flat as a pancake!"

"You're making that up," Jonny said.

"It's true! He was out in the cornfield one day. It was hot and he fell asleep—which is no big deal usually; he's always taking a nap it seems like—'cept this time he was still on the tractor."

"What happened then?" Sarah interrupted, getting caught up in the story.

"Who's this?" Busy asked.

"That's my little sister. She's Sorry."

"Sorry 'bout what?"

"Sorry about everything, usually. Just wait a few minutes. I'm sure she'll come up with something."

Sarah punched Jonny in the shoulder. "I'm not *that* little. I'm ten years old. I'm big enough to keep up with any of you farmer kids."

"You think so?" Busy replied, sizing her up. "Well, I'm the leader of my gang, and I say we don't have any *girls* to go in it. We'll take Jonny. 'Course we want *him*, after he blew up the fireworks factory and all. He's my new captain; that's what *I* say."

"I am?"

"Sure 'nough. I need a guy who knows his way around rockets and stuff."

Sarah cut in. "That's not *fair*! I burned down the fireworks factory too!"

Busy thought about it for a moment before he answered, "That's true. I heard you was the one who threw the switch. I'll have to talk to the other guys about it, but I won't make any promises. We don't want to catch no girl germs."

Sarah crossed her arms and pouted. "Don't bother, cootie breath. I'll start my *own* gang! You'll see." She stomped off into the night looking for any girls she could recruit.

"She's a real firecracker," Busy decided. "She always goin' off like that?"

"Yeah, pretty much every five seconds. Anyway, you were talking about your dad?"

"Right, I was," Busy nodded. "So my dad, he falls asleep on the tractor with his foot jammed on the accelerator and the engine still in gear. The tractor starts to turn in this big circle, you see, right through the rows of corn he'd already planted, right across the field, right through the fence!"

"He didn't wake up?"

"Nah, he was really tired on account of the fact that he missed his morning nap and it was so hot and all. So he just slept right on through, even when the tractor drove through the barn. The doors were wide open—he went in one side and out the other!"

"Boy, I wish I was there to see that!"

"Same here. I was in school so I missed the whole thing; so did my brother and sister. My mom was there, though, outside in the front yard hanging the laundry. That's where she was when he went rolling on by—right through her clean sheets—right over the top of her laundry basket! She started screaming and chasing him across the yard, but still he didn't wake up till he was halfway through the living room—'course by then it was too late."

"You're joshin' me!"

"Nope. There he went, right on across the porch, through the front door, across the living room, into the kitchen, and right out the back!"

"What'd he do when he woke up?"

"About the time he was smashing through the kitchen, he opened his eyes and saw what was going on, but before he could get the tractor out of gear, he was in the back yard. There was nothing he could do about it, with this big ol' gaping hole right through the middle of our house! My mom ran around to make sure he was okay, just as the house tipped over and fell down flat as a penny on a railroad track! *Whomp!* Just like that!"

"Wow!"

"Yep. Ever since then people 'round here call him Lazy. Lazy Gunderson, that's my dad!"

Jonny said, "You're so lucky. Your dad is *famous*."

"Hey, your dad was almost killed by a *rocket!*" Busy answered back. "What could be better'n that?"

After the boys got to know each other, Busy introduced him to the rest of his friends, and from that moment on Jonny was never to be seen alone. It was always Jonny and Busy and Frank and Rocky and Bobby and Lonnie and all his other buddies as they went fishing or camping or tree climbing or exploring or who knows what else. In fact, I credit those boys for some of what ended up happening, although I share a large portion of the blame. If I hadn't been so *hard* on Jonny, maybe he could have trusted me.

What none of us knew was that there was another new-comer in town that night. We wouldn't find out until much later, but he was there watching the whole fireworks display from his hiding place in the trees. None of us heard him gasp when he laid eyes on the Big Bang Boom Box—when he saw the picture of Chang for the first time. None of us knew who the mysterious visitor was or what he was doing there.

But we would find out soon enough.

CHAPTER 3

Walt's Barbershop

In spite of the late night, Janice and I were up early the next morning. She had a few more things to put away, and I wanted to review my sermon notes before Sunday. We let the children sleep in. They were exhausted after all the excitement of the day before.

Gramma Edna popped in with some freshly baked muffins for breakfast. We sat and had some coffee while she talked about where to find things in Boomtown. Janice wanted to visit some of the shops, especially Gertrude's Beauty Parlor, and I needed to get a haircut. I was determined to make a good first impression on my new flock. My hair would be freshly trimmed, and I'd wear my best preaching suit and my favorite tie.

Gramma Edna provided directions to the local barbershop. She chuckled and said, "We aren't the biggest town in the world. For the gentlemen, there's Walt's Barber Shop on Bang Street and for you, Janice, you're already planning to go to Gertrude's Beauty Parlor on Boom Boulevard. Those are your only choices."

Just as she was telling us this, Sarah came barreling down the stairs and jumped into Gramma Edna's lap. *"Oof!"* Edna said, almost spilling her coffee. With Sarah on the scene and the other two close behind, Edna could only squeeze in a final word of advice: "Whatever you do, Reverend, if you stop in for a haircut—*don't upset Walter!*" I never got the chance to ask her what she meant.

Gramma Edna left shortly after breakfast, and we spent the next hour straightening up, getting dressed, and taking turns in the only household bathroom. Following her directions, we strolled down our street past Chang Park on our left and the river beyond. The road gently curved around Boomtown Church on the right, where I'd be preaching the next day, and past the La Pierres' house, until it crossed Bang Street. We didn't see Matthieu, but Jonny and Sarah stopped to talk to eight or nine of his children.

"Where you goin'?"

"Into town."

"Watcha gonna do?"

"Get haircuts."

"That's boring."

"Yeah, I know. Maybe we'll get ice cream."

"Really?"

"Yeah, we got a coupon for Top's Soda Shop."

"You gonna have the Family Gutbuster?"

"Yeah, I hope so. What's that?"

"It's an ice cream sundae with twenty scoops of ice cream, any flavor you want, with bananas and pineapple and nuts and chocolate sauce and whipped cream. Alonzo—that's Mr. Top, the man who owns the soda shop—he puts it in this big silver bucket as big as your head and you eat it and eat it and eat it until your tummy wants to explode! We went in there once, me and my mom and dad and my brothers and sisters, and we tried to eat the whole thing but we couldn't and we got sick and couldn't eat anything else for a whole week!"

Sarah's eyes got as big as two dinner plates. She grabbed my hand and started yanking on it. "Can we go, Dad? Can we have a Gutbuster? I'll bet I can eat it all by myself. Can we?"

I rolled my eyes and answered, "Twenty scoops of ice cream and our stomachs explode and we get sick for a week— sounds like fun."

"You mean it?"

"We'll see. I've got to get my hair cut first. You and Ruth and your mother are heading to Gertrude's. Jonny and I wanted to pop in at the bookstore."

Janice said, "We could split up and meet back at the soda

shop. It's eleven o'clock now. We could meet there at two thirty. That should give us enough time."

I shrugged and answered, "Bring a spoon—and some Bromo-Seltzer."

After that was settled, we turned right on Bang Street and walked down one of the busiest streets in town. We passed the offices of Dr. Goldberg, family physician, and Dr. Xu, the town dentist. We peeked in the windows of the Red Bird General Store on the right. We saw the music store, the bookstore, and a butcher shop on the left. As we walked along, we were greeted by all kinds of folks who were out shopping on a Saturday—ladies in their hats, men in their best overalls, and children running in and out of Top's Soda Shop, the bell ringing merrily every time the door opened and closed. We stopped long enough to look inside where we would meet up later that afternoon.

Janice and the girls went on ahead to the beauty parlor, while Jonny and I stood at the intersection of Cave In Road with Town Square another block in front of us.

"I think we've gone too far, Jon," I said, scratching my head and trying to remember what Edna had told us. "Pretty sure Gramma Edna said the barbershop was on the left-hand side near the bookstore, but I didn't see it."

"Why don't we go in here? Maybe they know where it is."

Jonny was talking about the store directly in front of us. The canvas awning had the name printed boldly on its fringe: Guenther's Gun Corral. We pushed open the door and stuck our heads inside.

"Hello? Anybody here?"

We looked around at the racks of hunting rifles and boots and coats and gloves and rain gear and didn't see a soul.

"That's strange. I wonder if someone's in the back room."

Just then a tall figure stepped out from a display of camouflaged hunter's suits. He was dressed head to toe in sandcolored fabric. He had a large hump on his back and a hood over his head. He blended perfectly into the background.

"Hello, dere," he said in his thick Swedish accent. "Sorry to startle you. Der name's Guenther. Dis here is my shop. Who vould you be?"

"We're new here in town," I answered, trying not to stare. "Just moved in. I'm the new pastor at Boomtown Church, Arthur Button, and this is my son, Jonny."

"Pleased to meet you, I'm sure. Is dere some vay I can help you?"

"We're looking for the barbershop. We seem to have missed it."

"Yah, sure, you betcha. It right over dere. You see it, next to bookstore?"

"Where?"

He took us to the door. "You see sign over dere? The vun dat says Butcher? Vith the chicken leg and pork chop painted on der vindow? That's Valt's, for sure."

"But that's a *butcher* shop."

"Yah, you betcha."

"That's where we get *haircuts*?"

"For sure, yah."

We opened the door, but on the way out I just had to stop and ask, "What do you call your suit? I've never seen anything like it—with the hump and all."

"Yeah," added Jonny, "it makes you look like a camel."

"Oh, dis vun here? Dis is vat I call 'Camel-flage.' Great for hunting in dry grass. It verks vonderful, yah?"

"Yah."

We waved good-bye to Guenther and crossed the street until we were standing underneath the wooden chicken leg and the pork chop. Peering through the window, we could see that it was the barbershop after all. Along its length was a white counter with a glass case and a weighing scale and meat hooks and refrigerators, but instead of beef and poultry in the glass case, it was full of hair tonics and combs and scissors.

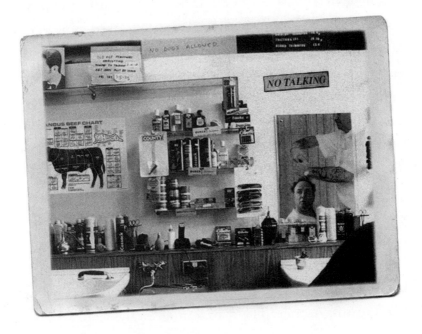

Jonny pointed. "Look, Dad, there's a poster showing how to butcher a cow right next to the prices for shaves and haircuts. That's weird."

Near the door were some men reading magazines waiting for their turn in the barber chair. They looked up and nodded to us as we came in. There were two empty spots at the end. We slipped into our seats and took a closer look around the room. That's when we saw Walter for the very first time.

He had to be more than seven feet tall. His head almost brushed the ceiling when he stood up straight. His arms were like tree branches, covered in a forest of hair and tattoos. Each of his legs was as big around as Jonny, and his shoulders were as wide as a bale of hay. His shaved head was bumpy, like the bark of a walnut tree. His nose was a lumpy potato, and he had tiny black eyes and a crooked mouth full of broken teeth that looked like splintered glass. His hands and fingers were as big as two bunches of bananas. They were fiercely clutching a comb and a giant pair of scissors half as long as my arm. Walter loomed over the poor man in the chair who squirmed nervously as he heard the scissors *clip, clip, clip* right next to his ears.

Walter shouted and the windows rattled. "Hold still, you little runt! One slip and you'll lose an ear! *Then you'll look like me!*"

Walter thought it was a pretty good joke and started to laugh. It sounded like a thousand marbles being sucked up by a vacuum cleaner. The man fainted in the chair.

"Looks like you lost another one, Walt!" observed one of the waiting men.

Walter propped the man's head with a towel and quickly finished the haircut. He growled. "Easier that way. They don't squirm so much."

He whipped off the apron, lifted the unconscious man with one hand, and plopped him in a chair off to the side.

"*Next!* Who's next? I haven't got all day!" He glared at the shivering group of men and then pointed a huge finger at one of them. "*You!* You're next. Get in the chair!"

His next victim stumbled across the room. I heard him whispering a prayer as he went by. Ed Gamelli, our mailman, was sitting next to us. He nudged me and whispered, "More people find religion at Walt's than they ever will in church, eh, Preacher?"

I didn't know what to say other than to whisper, "So what's the story about the butcher shop? How did *he* ever get to be the barber?"

The mailman just smiled and answered, "Ol' Walt? He's not as bad as he looks—though his bite *is* worse than his bark, if you know what I mean." While we waited for our turn in the chair, he told us all about Walter the Butcher.

"You see, Walter's ancestors, the Kravchukniaks, hail from old Russia. You can trace his lineage all the way back to the Siberian wasteland. His forefathers crossed the frozen tundra on foot and then crossed the Bering Sea by canoe. His great-great-grandfather, Vladik Kravchukniak, settled on Kodiak Island near Chiniak Bay, married a Shoonaq

Eskimo, and joined a whole bunch of other Russians who were fishermen and fur trappers like him."

Jonny whispered, "He's part *Eskimo*? He doesn't look Eskimo."

"Oh, he's Eskimo, all right—and part Russian—and part Kodiak bear, I imagine."

"So you were saying," I urged, interested in the story.

"Right. Among other talents natural to men of their size and strength, Walt's family had a reputation for cold weather endurance. I heard tell about a snowstorm in the dead of winter—forty degrees below zero and snow blowing sideways. Vladik and his son got out to get firewood and they got lost in the blizzard. Three months go by and everybody figured they're long dead until the spring thaw when they came marching back into camp without so much as a how-do-you-do, like nothing ever happened."

Another man leaned over and chimed in. "I heard it was more like *four* months."

"*Four?* I heard it was *five*," said a third man.

The mailman huffed. "It was *three*."

The second man said, "And it was *twenty* below, not forty."

"Listen here, George, this is *my* story. Let me tell it *my* way."

"That's fine. You go ahead. Just get it right, that's all I'm saying."

Jonny listened to their good-natured arguing for a minute or two and then pulled on the mailman's sleeve. "S'cuse me, Mr. Gamelli, what happened? How did they make it through the blizzard?"

"Well, son, I was trying to tell you that before these old codgers butted in. Here's the way it was. They wander around in the pitch dark and the blinding snow for about three days until they fall into this cave, you see? Vladik has his flint, so they dig around in the dark and find some dry wood. They build this fire and dry out all their clothes. 'Course, there's no going back by then, with the snow drifting twenty feet high and forty feet deep, besides having no idea of where they are. So they decide to hunker down and ride out the winter in the cave. They survived by catching sea otters and eating seaweed and oysters."

"I heard it was beavers and pine cones."

"I heard it was moose meat and tree bark."

"Don't start that again!"

"I'm just saying what I heard."

"What difference does it make?"

"It makes a *huge* difference. Ever eat a sea otter?"

"No, I haven't, not that it matters a hill of beans. *I'm* saying it was seaweed and oysters. That's what they ate until the weather cleared up. As soon as it did, they got up out of that cave, climbed a hill, and headed for home. That's how it happened."

Jonny was enthralled by the story and wanted to hear more. "But how did Walter end up here in Boomtown?"

"Good question, son. Soon after that long winter, the Kravchukniaks decided to work their way down the coast of Alaska and find a more hospitable climate. They kept moving until they arrived here in the Northwest. At the time, it was an untamed place quite suitable for folks of their wild and giantish nature. They've been here ever since."

"So that's when he became a barber?"

"No. Not right away. Just look at him. Seven and a half feet tall, three hundred pounds of pure muscle, as ugly as a flowered couch and as angry as a bee up your sleeve. Nah, he followed in his pappy's footsteps and took up logging, just like his grandpappy 'fore that. I figure Walt's spent his whole life cutting things up or cutting 'em down, one way or another. He has what you'd call a natural talent when it comes to sharp objects."

Jonny glanced over as Walt used the giant scissors to snip away at his cringing customer's hair. "I don't think I *want* a haircut, not from him."

"Oh, don't you worry none," the mailman grinned. "He's been cuttin' my hair for years. I still got both my ears and my nose. You just got to keep your mouth shut while you're in the chair."

Ed continued. "As I was saying, Walt was a whiz when it came to cutting down trees. You see other men wrestling with one of them two-handed saws, but not old Walt. He'd pick up an ax about as big as your head and chop down a tree with a single swipe! I seen him do it! Trees falling one after another like dominoes. I seen him clear an entire hillside in a single afternoon.

"But then we started running out of trees on account of the fact that he'd already cut most of them down. That's when Walt got himself a job working at the mill. He'd strip the bark off the logs with his bare teeth, then wrap his big old arms around the logs and put them into the saw all by himself. After the wood was cut, he'd stack up the boards and haul them out to the yard for sorting, 'bout forty boards at a time. Didn't even break a sweat."

"Really?"

"Sure thing. But when the logs started to run out, the mill shut down and Walt was out of a job. That's when he decided to open up the butcher shop."

The other fellow piped in. "You forgot about the bear."

"I didn't *forget* about the bear. I was about to say something about the bear until you stuck your big fat nose in. Who's telling this story, anyway?"

"You are. Just not very well."

The mailman shook his head and continued. "After he lost his job, Walt went way up into the hills to try and figure out what to do next, when all of a sudden a bear as big as a house fell down out of a tree right in front of him. Walt looked at the bear. The bear looked at Walt. They were the same size and had almost the same amount of hair. They circled each other—round and round—until all of a sudden the bear charged old Walt, and they got each other in a bear hug! Can you imagine?"

"What happened?" Jonny asked, perched on the edge of his seat.

"It was pretty much an even match, that bear and Walt being similar in size and strength and generally of the same peevish disposition. They wrestled day and night until finally that old bear up and died from sheer disappointment. Soon as it was dead, Walt took his hunting knife and had the bear-skin off in five minutes flat! Chopped him up and had enough bear steaks to feed half of Boomtown. He figured it was a sign from heaven, so the next day he opened up a butcher shop right here in this very spot."

The mailman leaned back and crossed his arms over his chest, proud of the effect his story was having on Jonny.

Jonny's brow furrowed with a next question. "So when the trees started running out, Walt worked in the mill. And when the logs ran out, he opened the butcher shop. I get all of that. But where did the barbershop come from?"

Ed smiled. "You are quite the clever boy—you noticed, huh? Let me tell you what happened next. After Walt had his butcher shop for a while, a new supermarket opened over in Stickville. Up until then we got all our groceries here in town, including our meat from Walt's Butcher Shop. But when they put up the supermarket only ten miles away, some of the folks here in Boomtown started shopping over there. It wasn't a problem at first, but after a while, enough folks stopped coming into Walt's. That didn't make him a bit happy, no sir.

"After losing two careers already, Walt was madder'n that old bear. He ran the whole ten miles over to Stickville and busted into the supermarket. He was still wearing his red-stained apron and he had two butcher knives—one in each hand. He charged up and down the aisles until he found the owner of the store and cornered him back by the milk and eggs. By the time Walt got done yellin', all the hair on that poor young feller's head had fallen out.

"Walt figured it was another sign from heaven. He closed up the butcher shop and put in a barber chair. He's been cutting hair ever since."

"Wow! Isn't that something?" Jonny exclaimed.

I had listened quietly to the tall tale, not believing most of it. But I was concerned about Walt's temper. "That's a very interesting story—rather hard to believe, if you ask me—but here's what *I'm* wondering about."

"What's that, preacher?"

"Walt's *temper*. The man's a hothead; he might even be dangerous."

"*Dangerous?* Walt? Nah, he'd never hurt a fly."

"He killed a bear!"

"Not on purpose. It was mostly the bear's fault."

"But what about all of you? *You* haven't done anything wrong. Why do you all put up with him? I don't understand."

The three men stared at me like I had two heads. "What are you talking about?"

"I mean, why keep getting haircuts from a man who's so hard to deal with? Why not go someplace else?"

The mailman answered, "We can't turn our backs on Walter. *He's one of us!* He's part of the town—like the fireworks factory. You think we should get rid of the fireworks? Just because they're loud and every now and then something burns down? Is that what you think—get *rid* of anything that's difficult? We can't live without fireworks! Why would we want to live without Walt?"

Before I could answer, we suddenly had something more

urgent to deal with. We overheard the man in the barber chair make some sort of offhanded comment about the haircut he was getting.

"Oh no!" hissed the mailman.

Everyone in the room stopped breathing. Walt's face turned white and then bright red. His beady eyes swelled up as big as two silver dollars and change. His hands began to shake. The tiger tattooed on his arm started pacing back and forth. The top button of Walt's shirt popped off and put a hole in the wall. His body began to shake like a train coming into the station. I could almost see steam coming out of his ears.

Ed jumped up and shouted, "It's quittin' time! Everybody out! Right now! *Walt's about to blow!*"

We all made a mad dash for the door. The man from the barber chair pushed past us and ran down the street with the cape flapping from his neck like a flag in a storm. Jonny and I dashed across the street and watched the rest of the men scatter left and right and duck behind telephone poles and mailboxes. Everyone else who was outside realized what was happening. They ran inside and slammed the doors and pulled down the shades. It only took another few seconds before we heard the explosion.

An earth-shattering scream split the air, followed by the unique sound of a two-hundred-and-fifty-pound barber chair flying through the roof of the butcher shop. It sailed up and up and up—at least forty feet in the air—high enough to clear the entire street. Not something you see every day, a

barber chair passing over the sun like an eclipse, the chrome handles of the arm rests glinting in the afternoon light, the soft brown leather seat and headrest casting a shadow onto the ground. I couldn't seem to take my eyes off the flying chair as it reached its peak and headed back down. I could hear someone yelling something—it was hard to say who it was. My ears were still ringing from Walter's scream.

"Dad! Dad! *Look out!*"

At the very last second, Jonny pushed me to the side and then jumped out of the way. The chair buried itself two feet deep in the sidewalk—exactly in front of the entrance to the Red Bird General Store. It landed in the precise spot where I had been standing only a second before. If it weren't for Jonny, I wouldn't have needed a haircut. I would have needed an ambulance.

The Sunday edition of three different newspapers in neighboring towns reported hearing Walt's yell as far away as Stickville. Lazy Gunderson claimed that his prize cow was so upset that it stopped giving milk. All the dogs stopped barking for a week, and some people noticed that there weren't as many birds in Boomtown as before, but that may have just been a coincidence.

Myself, I lay there on the sidewalk with a bruised backside and a splitting headache, finally remembering what Gramma Edna had tried to warn me about.

"Whatever you do," she had said, "*don't upset Walter!*"

CHAPTER 4

The Spirit Has Whiskers

It was my first Sunday to preach at Boomtown Church, and I was more anxious than usual. I didn't connect the dots until much later, but in retrospect that morning happened to be the same morning our lawn mower mysteriously disappeared from the front lawn. It was the first of what would become dozens of unexplained robberies that began to happen all over town.

Of course, I didn't notice it was missing because I was too

busy trying to get everyone showered and brushed and break-fasted and out the door on time. It didn't help that one of the buttons from my suit jacket popped off and I had to sew it back on. Janice was busy getting herself ready while fixing Ruth's hair and helping Sarah change her dress for the second time after spilling milk on the first one and getting jelly on the second, while Jonny dawdled in the bathroom.

I refused to preach that morning with a missing button, and besides, it was my favorite brown suit, with the matching brown vest and the brown pants and my brown tie and freshly pressed white cotton shirt and the brown shoes I had so carefully polished the night before. This was my *uniform*; I felt safe and confident whenever I put it on. Can you imagine the Reverend Button standing in front of his new flock with only two buttons? People would notice. They would talk. They would gossip about their new pastor, the one who was one button short of a full set. I was *not* going to leave the house until it was fixed!

My obsession about the missing button was the last thing I should have been worried about. I wanted to make the perfect first impression on my congregation. But years later, when people told the story about my first Sunday morning at Boomtown Church, no one ever mentioned what I was wearing.

We walked down the street on a beautiful late summer morning to arrive at the church about twenty minutes early. (After all my fussing, we were still on time!) The building was situated on a two-acre plot, north of the center of town and across from the park. Trees and bushes lined the sidewalks, and flowers ringed the small parking lot. The main building on the property was a picturesque white chapel where worship services had been held for more than seventy-five years. Ever since its foundation, the church had been lovingly preserved, including its lofty bell tower and the large, cast-iron bell that still rung every Sunday morning promptly at 9:05 a.m. It had beautiful stained-glass windows along each side, wooden pews with soft cushions, an old pipe organ and a loft up above, where most of the kids sat during the worship services. It was charming and pleasant and smelled of oiled wood and tradition.

BOOMTOWN CHURCH 1889

The first person we met as we walked through the main double doors was the "hall monitor," Gertrude Feeny, the owner of Gertrude's Beauty Parlor. She was fifty-four years old and built like a drill instructor—broad shoulders, short, muscled legs, gnarled fingers, and a stern, puckered face that looked like she was sucking a lemon. Even though she had met Janice and the girls the previous day, she acted like she'd never seen them before. She barked at us the instant we walked through the door.

"Good morning! Here's a bulletin. Are you visiting? Put this visitor's ribbon on your lapel. Have you signed the guest book yet?"

Before we could answer, she was pinning a bright, silk ribbon on each of us with the word *Visitor* printed in large, black letters. She pushed bulletins and flyers into our hands. She shoved a pen at me, grabbed my arm, pulled me over to the guest book, and hovered over me like a hungry vulture. I didn't have the courage to tell her I was the new minister. I signed the book and let each one in the family do the same.

When we were finished, she checked our entries for spelling and penmanship and waved permission for us to move along.

Another woman standing nearby saw the whole thing. "Don't mind Gertrude," she said. "She's really quite harmless. She lost her husband a few years ago when he tried to dig their new sewer using dynamite. Should have used a shovel, I suppose. After that . . . oh well, just do what she says and you'll be okay."

She smiled and continued. "You must be our new minister. I'm the church secretary, Ingrid Hofler. We're so glad to have you here."

After meeting the Widow Feeny, it was a relief to see a friendly face. "Of course, Ingrid. We spoke several times on the phone. It's nice to finally meet you in person."

I introduced Janice and the kids, and then Ingrid took us into the sanctuary to meet some of the other members. We saw a number of people we'd already met. Gramma Edna was there; Guenther from the Gun Corral, Ed. Gamelli and his wife, and Matthieu and Pauline LaPierre. While we shook hands, Sarah caught sight of two LaPierre girls and ran off to play. We were introduced to the town sheriff, Burton Ernie, and his charming wife, Laverne. We met Vera DeFazio, the song leader for that morning, and Manfred Heinzmann, the presiding elder.

The introductions continued until Ingrid pulled us to the side. "We have a few more minutes before the service starts. Do you want to come and see where your office is?"

The four of us followed Ingrid down a hallway that led past several classrooms. "The bathrooms are here. The storage closet and office supplies, right there. My office and your office are down here."

As we investigated, I noticed a series of photos hanging on the long wall of the hallway. Jonny noticed them too. "Look at all these pictures, Dad. They got names and dates under each one of them. See?"

Each photo seemed to be of a former minister with his name engraved on a gold plaque underneath. I made a quick count as we walked along: Five. Six. Fifteen. Sixteen. Twenty-three. Twenty-four—until I finally came to an empty frame—number twenty-five. I assumed it must be for me.

"Ingrid," I asked, "you've had *twenty-four pastors* since the church was founded? That's about one pastor every three years."

She smiled proudly. "And you're the twenty-fifth!"

"But twenty-four? No one mentioned anything about that in our letters or when we talked on the phone. Twenty-four pastors in about seventy years?"

"Is that a lot? I've never really thought about it, although, now that I do, I suppose you're right. First Presbyterian has had only three pastors since it started. St. Bernard's has had only four."

"What *happened* to all of them? What about him?" I pointed at the man who preceded my empty frame. "It says 'Pastor Sergeant Gibson, In Loving Memory, 1947–1949.' In *loving memory*? What happened to him?"

"Oh, the dear man. I simply adored him. Tragic story."

"Tragic?"

"We were having several baptisms over at Canyon Creek just below Lookout Falls when all of a sudden the weather changed. Pastor Gibson *insisted* on finishing even though it started raining something fierce. 'It'll pass!' he said, bless his heart. He was *so* dedicated. Then we heard this roar from upstream. Mabel was getting baptized that day. She was just coming up out of the water, so she managed to escape—but poor Pastor Gibson—he didn't."

"Didn't what? Escape what?"

"Flash flood. A real gully washer! Pretty rare 'round here. Washed him downstream, and he was gone. Just like that."

"A flash flood? Honestly? He was never found?"

"No. At least, we don't think so. There's been a rumor that he turned up in Chelan County and he's been preaching at the Baptist church in Gorton, but that's never been confirmed."

"What about *this* one? Pastor George Stomopolis? He lasted only a year."

"It was just terrible. Train accident. It jumped the tracks just as he was coming home from performing a funeral. Ironic, when you think about it."

"And *this* one? Pastor Albert Vanderpool?"

"Sink hole."

"And him?"

"Lightning strike."

"And him?"

"Snake bite."

"And this one?"

"We're not exactly sure."

We worked our way back down the hallway until we reached Phineas Cullpepper "Beloved Founding Pastor," who had somehow survived a miraculous five years in the pulpit.

"And what about *this* guy? Five years. That's a record for this group."

Ingrid shook her head. "The saddest story of all. I wasn't here at the time, of course. He was pastor long before I was ever born. But a few of the older members like Werner Holz—he's ninety-four this year—he could tell you all about it."

"So what happened?" I asked anxiously.

"Pastor Cullpepper was down south ministering to the railroad men as they put in a spur from the main line. He was always doing that, visiting the miners up in the hills or the farmers out on their farms or the railroaders down at the tracks. He was a true evangelist. On that particular day, just as he was finishing up a prayer meeting, he caught his foot on the handle of a pickax and fell backward onto an open case of nitroglycerin. They say he almost reached heaven before he came back down. Such a shame too. Everybody *loved* Pastor Cullpepper, or so they say."

Phineas Cullpepper c.1896

By the time she finished, my eyes were red and my head was pounding. "So what you're telling me is that you've had twenty-four pastors in seventy-five years, *all* of whom have either died tragically or disappeared under mysterious circumstances—and now I'm the twenty-fifth?"

"That's right."

Jonny exclaimed, "This is *great*, Dad!"

"Great? How can this be great?"

"It's like a *curse*! Wait till I tell the other guys! Busy isn't going to believe this!"

"But I don't want to be part of a curse!" Turning back to Ingrid, I asked, "What about these twenty-four other ministers? Have any of them ever been killed by a rocket boat?"

"Not so far."

"Any been crushed by a flying barber chair?"

"Nope. You would have been the first."

"You're right I could have been the first! My picture would be at the end of the hall with a plaque under it! It would say, 'Here today, *gone* today.' I don't like the sound of that."

"The important thing is that you *weren't* hit by the rocket or the chair."

"But I could have been! What's next, a falling meteor or maybe a cattle stampede?"

"Oh, don't worry, Reverend! We've got you covered. All the women on the Ladies Guild are praying for you."

Sure, I thought. *Just like you prayed for the other twenty-four pastors.* Just then we heard the piano. I grabbed Janice's hand and tried to smile as we weaved our way back to the sanctuary and down to the front. As if I didn't have enough to worry about, Sarah came running up the aisle and shoved a white gerbil in my face. "Look, Dad! Isn't he *cute*? Can I have one?"

"Sarah! What *is* that? Get it out of my face! Whose is it anyway?"

"It's a *gerbil*, Dad. It's Katrina's. She's got a whole mess of them. Can I have one?"

"What? No. Sarah, the service is about to start! Janice, can you do something about this? Ruth?"

Ruth took Sarah's hand. "I'll take care of it, Dad. C'mon, Sarah."

I heard Sarah chattering nonstop as Ruth dragged her back up the stairs and to the balcony. "His name is Whiskers. See how long they are? Do you think Dad will let me have one? I wonder what it eats? I want a black one. Or maybe a white one like this, what do you think? I can make a nest in a shoebox. I got one in my closet. What do they eat? Do gerbils smell?"

Janice squeezed my hand. "I don't think you'll have to worry about rock slides or stampedes."

"No?"

"You'll probably die from a nervous breakdown before Sarah gets to be eleven."

"I think you're probably right."

After the piano overture, the service started with announcements from Vera DeFazio. But before I continue, I should like to explain something about what I was *expecting*. After fourteen years with my previous congregation, I had gotten used to a rather somber environment. Quiet hymns played slowly on an ancient organ by a woman who was twice as old as the hymns. Long prayers and long sermons attended by silent congregants sitting on hard pews; that was the custom.

I'm not complaining, you understand. Most of my members were elderly, having attended the same church and sat in the same seat since they were children, probably prepared to die sitting in the same spot. Most objects in the building had one of their names on a plaque indicating the date of when they or their parents or their parents' parents had donated the pulpit or the altar or a stained-glass window or one of the hymnals. That's the way it was. The members were like part of the furniture.

It was my job to be their minister—to care for the sick, visit the lonely, and preach on Sundays. I had faithfully done so from the first day until the last, each day as similar to the one before as the one that followed. In the entire fourteen years I was a pastor of that church, I was never once *surprised*. We followed the liturgy to the letter. People stood up and sat down on cue. I preached my sermons. That's the way it was.

So perhaps that will help to explain why I was so amazed by what I saw on my first Sunday at Boomtown Church. I was used to a high level of formality and decorum, but the people of this church seemed to possess none of it. Vera leaped up from her seat and ran down the aisle smiling and waving at her friends as she came to the stage.

"Don't forget," she announced, "October is just around the corner. We're hosting a booth in Farmers' Park from the last week in September until Halloween. We'll be selling cakes and pies to raise money for our missionaries. Also, this coming weekend, the youth are having a campout on Left Foot Island. The theme this time is 'Antarctic Adventure,' so remember to wear your penguin costumes and your mukluks!"

Announcements were followed by fifteen minutes of the most enthusiastic singing I'd ever heard in church. If it was loud and they could clap to it, that's what we sang. Ingrid, the church secretary, was also the pianist and she banged away on the keys like she was pounding out flour. The members of the choir clapped their hands and stomped their feet in time with the music. Every now and then someone called out the name of a favorite hymn, and we'd sing that too. The worship could only be described as *exuberant*; I'd never seen people have so much fun in church before.

After the music, it was time for the offering meditation and then the morning prayer. Manfred Heinzmann—he must have been a hundred years old if he was a day—stood up to deliver the prayer in a steady and confident voice, belying his advanced age. It was a surprise to hear someone of his generation talking to God as though they were *friends*. Manfred was genuinely thankful for the church's new minister, and he prayed with such sincerity and concern that I was ashamed of my earlier fears. He asked for protection and long service for me. On behalf of the members, he committed them to the same. Then he closed with a simple thank you for the blessings God had granted. It was really quite out of the ordinary and wonderful.

Then Manfred introduced me to the congregation for the first time. "Friends! As you know, in the absence of our former minister—who may or may not have drowned, may he rest in peace whatever the case should be—it is my pleasure to introduce his replacement, the honorable Reverend Arthur Button. We hope he will endure far longer than his beloved, yet unfortunate, predecessors."

The announcement was met with a loud round of applause and a room full of hopeful smiles. I wasn't sure how to take it. All this *clapping* in church was a new experience for me.

"As you well know, our minister has already distinguished himself as the father of the two children who nearly burned down the entire fireworks factory. The young man, Jonathan, is sitting here in the front pew with his mother, Janice, and his older sister, Ruth. And I believe his younger sister, Sarah, is up in the balcony?"

"That's me!" she shouted. "I'm Sorry!"

"Yes," said Manfred, "we know you are, but *we* aren't! We are thrilled to welcome you this morning! Welcome to Boomtown!"

This was followed by sustained applause that lasted nearly three solid minutes. I was so embarrassed I didn't know what to say. I prided myself in always being prepared for anything unplanned in church—which, of course, never happened with my former congregation. But in Boomtown, I was constantly being knocked off balance. It was one surprise after another from sunup to sundown ever since we drove over the Ifilami Bridge. Rocket boats, giant bear-wrestling lumberjack butchers, flying barber chairs, Big Bang Boom Boxes overflowing with fireworks, and now this morning—an assault by Gertrude Feeny, a hallway full of pictures of dead ministers, loud music, stomping, applause, and what next? Confused by all the attention, I counted all my buttons to make sure they were still there. Three on my vest, four on the coat. Thank goodness. I counted them again.

The applause faded, but I couldn't remember what I was supposed to do. Jonny saved me by waving and saying, "C'mon, Dad. Preach for us."

That's all I needed. I thanked everyone for their kindness and hospitality, especially those who had helped move us in. I nodded to Gramma Edna, Ingrid, Matthieu and Pauline La Pierre, Ed Gamelli, and all the other people we'd met that morning. All of them sat quietly, eagerly anticipating the message. I have to admit that in spite of the distinct possibility that I would die in some tragic accident, I could still taste the flavor of excitement that I only felt when standing in the pulpit. There wasn't anything I enjoyed more than preaching to an eager audience.

I commented briefly on the hopes and aspirations I had for the congregation over the next few years (the more the better), and then I opened to the passage for that morning. All over town, similar gatherings were taking place. In Boomtown, Sunday worship was a mainstay and the pews were always filled. There were three congregations from which to choose. Those of Scandinavian descent tended to gravitate toward First Presbyterian. Germans were most comfortable at St. Bernard's Lutheran. That left Boomtown Church for the denominationally unaffiliated.

I soon learned that in Boomtown one's religious affiliation never interfered with the more important duty of working closely with fellow citizens. Every person regarded himself as an essential part of Boomtown community life. There were no outsiders in Boomtown.

Time flew by as I preached. It seemed like I'd only started when just as quickly I'd reached the conclusion of my message—*and that's when it happened.* All of a sudden, an older woman who was sitting near the back jumped up from her seat. She'd shuffled down the aisle using a walker to steady herself. Her back was bent and her legs were thin and shaky, but now they seemed to be on fire. She launched from her seat like one of Han-wu's rockets.

"Ahhhhhh!" she squealed, leaping over the pew. "Ahhhhhhhhh!"

All eyes swung around to see what was happening. Everyone there, of course, knew Mrs. Beedle, a woman who for the last ten years had been unable to stand on her own without help. Now for some odd reason she was leaping and jumping and praising God, at least, that's the way it appeared.

"Ooooh," she squirmed. "Eeeee!" she squeaked. "Woooohoo!" she squawked.

Corine Beedle was a woman who had visited every doctor in town (there was only one) and every other doctor in the county (there were only three). They all told her exactly the same thing. She was perfectly fine. Nothing was wrong with her at all. It was completely in her imagination. But she knew better.

"They're all *quacks*!" she'd insist. "Charlatans, counterfeits, con men, cheats, swindlers, phonies, humbugs, flimflam artists!"

No matter what they told her, she was absolutely convinced that she suffered from an unidentified disorder. She had contracted some sort of exotic tropical disease. She was dying from a mysterious ailment. Her joints ached, her muscles hurt, her back was out, her feet were swollen, her eyes were blurry—even her hair was sore.

"No, no, no!" she persisted. "Something is *wrong* with me! Something is terribly, dreadfully, incurably wrong!"

But now, for some inexplicable reason, she was standing. She wasn't just standing; she was wiggling around. She wasn't just wiggling around; she was turning, gyrating, hopping, jerking, jumping, leaping, twisting, and twitching. She spun to the left. She spun to the right. She grabbed her legs and back and sides. She hooted and howled and yelped and yammered.

"It's a miracle!" someone shouted. "Mrs. Beedle has been cured!"

Everyone started talking and pointing all at once, but Mrs. Beedle was too busy to notice. She ran up and down the aisle squeaking and squawking and squirming. She jumped up and down like popcorn on a hot plate. She spun like a windmill in a tornado. She screamed like a boiling teapot on a hot stove.

Manfred Heinzmann stared. Vera sang. The Widow Feeny blocked the door. Matthieu and Pauline LaPierre chased their laughing children. Everyone else just stood there wondering what it all meant until someone finally shouted, "I know what it is! I know what's happened! *She's got the Spirit!* Old Mrs. Beedle has *finally* got the Spirit!"

Everyone gasped and fell silent, gaping in awe at the miracle happening in their very midst. Then they turned and looked at me, their new minister, the instrument of the Almighty, the one who had drawn Mrs. Beedle up out of the pit of disease and turned her into a shooting star. Somehow *I* had done it; I was responsible; it was the only possible explanation.

In the silence that followed, other than Mrs. Beedle swinging from the chandelier, I heard the distinct sound of Sarah, up in the balcony, laughing her silly head off. *Oh no*, I thought. *Tell me it isn't true! Tell me that Sarah didn't have anything to do with this!*

"Sarah!" I shouted. "This *isn't* funny! This is *serious!*"

Janice agreed with me for once. "Sarah, honey, Mrs. Beedle has got the *Spirit*. That's not something to laugh about."

Sarah leaned over the railing and tried to catch her breath. In between giggles, she finally managed to say, "Mrs. Beedle hasn't got the *Spirit!* She's got *Whiskers!*"

Whiskers? What? Mrs. Beedle had a dark shadow over her lip. I guess it sort of looked like a mustache; but you could hardly call it "whiskers." A waxing would help, a little concealer perhaps, maybe a light shave. That didn't explain why she was twitching so much.

Sarah banged on the railing and laughed and laughed. "Not whiskers on her *face!* Whiskers up her *dress!* Katrina's gerbil! He got away, and Mrs. Beedle found him!"

Just then, Mrs. Beedle jumped down from the chandelier. When she landed, Whiskers the gerbil finally popped loose. He must have climbed down the stairs and made his way under the pews until he found a warm, dark spot where he could hide. Unfortunately, it happened to be under the folds of Mrs. Beedle's skirt.

Now that she was free from the furry little rodent, Corine Beedle made a hasty exit. She grabbed her purse and straight-armed her way past the Widow Feeny at the door. She left in such a hurry that she even forgot her walker.

"Wait!" I called after her. "We're so sorry! Don't leave!"

But she was gone, and it felt like she took the Spirit with her. At least, that's what I thought. All I could think was that in the seventy-five years that Boomtown Church had been going, with twenty-four ministers who had been crushed and burned and drowned and blown up, every last one of them died with their boots on. To be buried in an avalanche—*that's* something I could accept! To be carried off by a pack of ravenous wolves—okay, fair enough. To be trampled by a herd of angry goats, stung by killer bees, drowned in my own bathtub, or choke on a peanut! *Fine!* I could deal with any of that! But to have my ministry come to a bitter end after only one day because of a *gerbil*? It was humiliating!

But this was Boomtown, I kept forgetting. Never in my wildest dreams could I have predicted the reaction of the members. I was suddenly surrounded by people who pounded me on the back, slapped me on the shoulders, and insisted on shaking my hand.

"Good job, preacher!"

"Excellent!"

"Outstanding!"

"Inspirational!"

"How you gonna top it next week?"

In the middle of it all was Sarah, like a shining star, carrying Whiskers (who seemed to be none the worse for wear). She was the perfect center of attention, being treated like the queen of the Nile. All the other little girls wanted to stand next to her. Most of them wanted to *be* her.

"Wow!" they said. "You burned down a building *and* you healed an old lady. What else can you do?"

I don't think I wanted to find out. For my part, I stood at the door of the church sheepishly shaking everyone's hand as they exited. Without exception, they each said it was the best church service they'd ever attended. I thought it was the worst disaster I'd ever seen—worse even than the whole burning-down-the-research-lab disaster from two days before. But the members of Boomtown Church thought it was the greatest thing since the day they put fire into firecrackers. *What had I gotten myself into?*

When the sanctuary was nearly empty, a fellow stopped at the door to make his acquaintance. The man's name was Terence Krebbs. He told me it was the very first time his family had visited the church.

"We haven't been to church in more than fifteen years. But when we heard that the new preacher in town had blown up the fireworks factory, we wanted to come by and check things out. I just want to say that we have never had so much fun in church in our entire lives! We're coming back next Sunday—and we're gonna bring some friends. We can't wait to see what happens next."

They went out the double doors, chatting happily as they went. Janice stood next to me, patting my hand. Ruth and Jonny grinned from ear to ear. And then there was Sarah, holding Whiskers up to her face, kissing his head and whispering in his tiny ear.

"You see that, Dad? It's just like you always say."

"What do I always say?"

"'The Lord works in mysterious ways.' I hear you say it all the time."

I looked down at my younger daughter and tried to be upset with her, but I couldn't seem to manage it. I laughed and reached out my hand and ruffled her hair.

"There's no mystery here. You're my lucky penny, that's what you are. You somehow manage to land heads-up every time."

"Yep!" she agreed, beaming with pride. "I'll *never* be Sorry about that!"

CHAPTER 5

The Stickville Slugs

Two weeks passed following that fateful first Sunday, as we settled into our new home and ministry. The leaves began to change as September arrived, signaling the single most important event in our little corner of the world—the start of football season.

In Boomtown, high school football was the first and foremost obsession (other than fireworks). Everyone—and I mean *everyone*, including the mayor's three-legged dog—was fanatically, fantastically, firmly, and forever committed to the Stickville Slugs. As far as anyone was concerned, they were the only game in town. Whenever the team played an away game, a huge caravan of fans would faithfully follow them wherever they went. You *knew* when it was game night. Boomtown turned into a ghost town.

Everywhere you looked there were signs: *Go Slugs! Slime Time! Stick with the Slugs!* My personal favorite: *We May Be Slow, but That's because We're Slugs!* Local chapters of the Hug-a-Slug Booster Clubs held regular meetings and printed flyers with the team schedule so no one would miss a game. The local radio station, KSLG, interviewed the coach of Stickville High School. He promised another exciting season for all the faithful fans.

Jonny came home one day from school wearing his new Slugs sweatshirt bearing the team colors: muddy brown and slime green with a silver slime trail running down both sleeves. He told me what the hullabaloo was all about.

"The Slugs are *famous*, Dad; did you know that?"

"Famous for what?"

"For *losing*! Busy was telling me about a game last year against the East Wallop Hogs—62 to nothing—the Slugs got squished flat!"

"They lost?"

"*Sure* they lost! They *always* lose! They played nine games last year and lost every single one. They didn't even score a field goal."

"In nine solid games, they didn't even score *one* point? Not even by accident?"

"Nope. That's why they're so famous. The Stickville Slugs haven't won a single game in over forty years!"

So you can imagine my surprise when Ruth registered for high school in Stickville and immediately went out for the cheerleading squad. She was very excited about it. She came home after the first week of school wearing her new uniform, a solid brown skirt with green stockings, a silver stripe down the middle of her back, the letter "S" sewn in green felt on the front of her sweater, and bright silver pom-poms.

She gathered the family in the living room and showed us one of her cheers:

"Give me an S! *S!*

Give me an L! *L!*

Give me a U–G–S! *U–G–S!*

What does that spell? *SLUGS!*

What does it spell? *SLUGS!*

What does it mean?

Slime time! Yeeeeaaah!"

At the end of the cheer, Ruth threw her pom-poms into the air, fell on the floor, and wiggled around. She said, "It's supposed to look like a slug with salt on its back. You know—a slug dying a horrible death. That's what the Slugs do every time they play."

It was gross. It was strange. It was tradition.

The day of the big opening game approached, and excitement around town continued to build. I decided to use the occasion as an illustration for a sermon I was preparing for the Sunday after the game. The sermon was called "Playing for a Winning Team," and it was about working for the church. God is our coach; he calls the plays from the sidelines; we go out into the field and fight the good fight. It sounded like a good idea at the time, but I found out later that every other preacher in Boomtown preached the same exact sermon every single year. Nonetheless, in preparation for the sermon, Jonny filled me in on the history of the Stickville Slugs.

"The school has lost every single game it's played since 1909. They don't just lose; they get *smashed!*"

"For example?"

"Busy told me about the worst game ever played—it was about fifteen years ago, I think he said. Slugs lost by a score of 138 to 3! They only got the three points by accident when the quarterback passed the ball and it bounced off someone's helmet and went through the goalpost."

"That's not really a field goal, is it?"

"Nah. But the referees felt so sorry for the Slugs they gave it to 'em anyway. Then there was this other game where the quarterback came down with the flu, and since they didn't have a backup quarterback, the placekicker had to take his place. He didn't know how to throw the ball, so he spent the whole game *kicking* it around the field. The Slugs lost *that* game 97 to 0."

"I can't believe it. That's awful!"

"You think that's bad? There was this one game where the Slugs scored three touchdowns for the *opposite team* 'cause they kept running the wrong way."

Fumbles, broken plays, penalties, bad calls, bad passes—you name it, in some inexplicable manner, the Slugs figured out new ways to mess up on the field. But that didn't keep the entire town of Boomtown from showing up the night before the big game for a huge rally on the Stickville High School football field. They danced around the bonfire and shot off firecrackers and rockets. They shouted and laughed and told stories about the games they'd seen over the years. They were absolutely convinced that *this* year was the year the Slugs would finally win a game.

As the new minister in town, I was asked to say a prayer

for the Stickville Slugs. This is what I prayed: "Dear Lord, I don't know if you're a Slug fan—I don't know if you're a *football* fan—but these people most certainly are. Lord, for their sakes I'm praying for a *miracle*. That's what it's going to take for this team to win. So I'm asking that if it lies within the scope of your infinite mercy that you would intervene on behalf of this team and for once—just *once*—let them win! Or maybe score a touchdown. Or lose by less than fifty points. Whatever you can manage, that would be fine. Amen."

Afterward, everyone said it was a very nice prayer. Nothing could dampen their spirits. Not even the tremendous rainstorm that blew through town during the night, one of the worst in Boomtown history. I'd never *seen* such rain! We'd spent the last fourteen years in Southern California, where it rained maybe ten or twenty times a year and even then, not so much. But in Washington, they had more than one hundred words just to *describe* all the different ways it rained. Jonny showed me his spelling homework one night just to prove it.

"See this? 'Blowing, blustery, cloudy, damp, dark, drenching, droplets, drizzly, gusty, humid, hurricane, misting, moist, overcast, pattering, pouring, precipitous, raging, rainy, roaring, showery, spitting, spattering, sprinkling, squally, steamy, stormy, tempestuous, tornado, watery, wet, wild, windy.' That isn't even *half* of 'em!"

That night before the game, it came down in *buckets*. It rained cats and dogs. It rained cows and horses. It was Noah's ark weather. The gutters on the street filled up, and once those were full the roads turned into streams. Yards turned into ponds, and fields turned into lakes. We stood on the porch and watched as Gramma Edna's lawn furniture floated by, followed by Matthieu's flock of plastic pink flamingos, a watering trough, a picnic table, and a family of plastic lawn gnomes. Last, we saw Fred Cotton's pickup truck as it sailed past our front door and disappeared down the road.

Sunday's paper reported that it was probably washed into the river, but later on it was blamed on the person (or persons) who had stolen my lawn mower. It turned out to be the same person who took advantage of the storm by removing one hundred feet of Lazy Gunderson's fence and grabbing the blades off of Tom O'Grady's thresher. None of this was known at the time because we were too busy to notice. We were bailing out our basements and trying to keep our cars from floating away. Ed Gamelli came around in a rowboat, faithfully delivering the mail and giving reports as he rowed from door to door. Just as night was falling, I saw a chicken coop sail by with its owner standing on the roof waving to everyone as he went. And still it continued to rain.

By morning, Boomtown looked like a dripping wet sponge left overnight in a sink full of dirty water. Everyone came out of hiding to start cleaning up the mess, picking up the garbage, rounding up cows and sheep and horses that had gotten loose, propping up fences and signs that had fallen over. They worked and worked without stopping all the way up until 3:00 p.m. At that very second, everyone dropped what they were doing, jumped in their tractors and trucks and horse carts, and headed for Stickville. It was *game time*! A local flood, forest fire, earthquake, or Armageddon wouldn't stop the fans from supporting their team.

We hopped in the car and drove out to the field. The highway was washed away in several places and road crews had built makeshift detours, but like everyone else they had abandoned their shovels in order to make the game on time. In spite of the bad road conditions, we found enough dry back roads and made it to the stadium early enough for Ruth to join her cheerleading squad for warm-up. We made our way through the gates to the bleachers and got our first glimpse of the football field.

PHOTO BY DON WATERS

1949 Boomtown

It was a *swamp*. There were large, standing pools of water on the grass, and one of the end zones was completely under water. A flock of ducks swam around the field, and there were frogs croaking among the fallen leaves and branches. The Stickville Slugs and the Ainogold Giants were already on the field making matters worse, churning the grass into a muddy, mucky, slimy mess.

"Look, Dad," Sarah said pointing. "The mud is *moving*."

Jonny added, "There's a *head*! With antennas! Eew, gross!"

I stared at a blob of mud and watched as it crawled across the ground. Mixed in with the mud were hundreds and thousands of *slugs*. They were in the grass. They were on the benches. They were all over the bleachers. Everywhere you looked, there were slugs—big ones, small ones, long ones—leaving a trace work of silver slime trails everywhere they went. The heavy rains had driven them out of their hiding places. It looked like every last slug in Okanogan County had showed up for the game. What a sticky, icky mess!

In spite of the conditions, the stands were soon filled to capacity with supporters for both teams. The Giants were decked out in bright red and green and gold; it looked like Christmas on the other side of the field. Our side looked like yesterday's lunch. We were dressed in the school colors: muddy brown and slimy green. Even the school mascot wore the colors, a teenage kid dressed in a slug costume. He looked like a rotten hotdog with antennas and legs.

Of course, we had the weather to go along with it. The sky was overcast and dark; it was miserable and cold and windy and the slugs kept crawling over our shoes. The playing field got muddier and sloppier and nastier. The fans couldn't have been happier. One man sitting next to us shouted with excitement, "This is *perfect* Slug-playing weather! We got a fighting chance—*Go Slugs!*"

We watched as the referees gathered both teams and their captains in the middle of the field. They flipped a coin and promptly lost it in the mud. After three more tries, it finally came up heads. The Slugs would be first to receive the kickoff.

The advantage hardly seemed to matter. The Giants were easily twice as big and strong as the poor Slugs. They had better equipment, better players, more practice, smarter coaches, faster runners, better blockers, fancier plays. It promised to be yet another humiliating defeat.

It didn't take long to see what the Slugs were up against. When the Giants lined up for the kickoff, they kicked the ball and it bounced and skidded through the water. The Slugs slipped and slid and crawled through the mud until they finally reached the ball. Four of them fell on it and got all tangled together. When they finally sorted out their arms and legs, they couldn't decide who should carry the ball, which really didn't matter because by then the Giants descended on them like a gold and white cloud. The Slugs got squished under their massive bodies.

It went from bad to worse. The Slugs ran three plays and lost fifteen yards. Then the kicker slipped on the mud and kicked the ball into the bleachers. It was worse than I ever imagined, but the man sitting next to me said, "This is *fantastic*! This has to be the best they've ever played!" The Slug fans were going wild.

It was time for the Giants to carry the ball. As they lined up for the first play, a hush fell over the crowd. You could hear the cheerleaders chanting, "Slugs. Slugs. *Slugs!*"

We saw it happen from the bleachers, like a slow-motion ballet. The center hiked the ball. The Giant quarterback took the ball in his hands. He stepped back to throw. The slippery mud-covered ball squirted through his fingers and flopped on the ground. A Slug player tripped over his shoes and fell on it.

"Did you see that, Dad? Fumble recovery! The Slugs got the ball! That's probably the first fumble recovery in Slug football history!"

The Slug fans were going nuts. The bleachers rumbled with their stomping feet and their flag waving kicked up a small breeze. The cheerleaders led them in a group cheer. Everyone stood up and did the Slug Wave. They shouted, "EEEEEEEW! EEEEEEEW! It's the *Slugs!*"

Ruth led the crowd in a cheer: "It's better to be *gross* than to be good! Go *SLUGS!*"

And go they did. By some miracle, as the first half continued, the Slugs rose to the occasion. Somehow, they fell down at just the right moment and tripped the Giants. If that didn't happen, the Giants slipped on the mud or dropped the slimy ball or stumbled over each other. Instead of blocking, players were picking slugs off their uniforms.

As the game continued, the football field was transformed into a grimy, slimy, gooey, sloppy, disgusting mess. By half-time, neither team had scored a point. By the final whistle, it hadn't changed. The game was tied: 0 to 0!

Slug fans shouted and screamed and ran around in circles and waved their flags and did the Slug Dance. Slime Dogs (hotdogs dripping in relish) and Slug Slush (shaved ice with lime flavoring) sold like crazy. Everyone was talking and laughing and cheering and giving each other high fives. As far as the Slug fans were concerned, their team had already *won* simply because they hadn't *lost*.

Then both teams returned to the field, and tension began to mount. Was it possible? Could the Slugs actually *win* in sudden-death overtime? Would the Giants lose to the worst football team in the history of high school sports? Maybe so. It seemed that no matter what they tried, the first overtime ended with the score still tied. Same with the second. Then the third.

By the time the whistle for the fourth overtime blew, a light rain had begun to fall. Darkness descended over the field and the lights winked on, glistening on the puddles of water and off the backs of the slugs as they crawled through the mud. It was dreamlike as the teams took the field for the fourth and final time.

The Giants had the ball on their own twenty-yard line, eighty yards from the end zone and victory. The quarterback took the snap and handed off to his running back. Four more Giants immediately surrounded the running back;

together they formed a five-man wedge. The wedge was able to keep the running back on his feet as they bullied their way through the mud and the Slug defenders. They covered more than thirty yards before the stunned Slugs managed to drag the five players to the ground.

Jonny said, "They've come up with a new strategy. If *one* guy can't run down the field, maybe *five* can do it."

We watched as the Giants tried it again. Twenty more yards. Then a third time. Fifteen more. The coach of the Slugs called an emergency time-out, yelling at his players and waving his arms.

"I got an idea, Dad!" Jonny said, jumping up from the bleachers and running down to the sidelines.

"Jonny! *Get back here!*" I tried to grab his sleeve, but he was already gone.

He squeezed his way between the quarterback and the coach. There was some animated discussion and then the referee's whistle. The squad broke up and headed back onto the field. The coach slapped Jonny on the shoulder, and he ran back to his seat.

"What did you say to him?" I asked.

"You'll see."

On the very next play, the Giants pulled the same trick. They surrounded the ball carrier with a wedge and pushed forward, but as soon as they did, the entire defensive line of the Slugs fell flat on the ground. When the Giants trampled over the top of them, the Slugs reached up and grabbed their legs. The wedge collapsed in a Giants heap with the ball carrier in the middle, like a Slug sandwich drenched in mud sauce. They stopped them once. Twice. Three times.

"You see, Dad? It's the one thing the Slugs are good at— *falling down*."

The Giants found themselves stranded on the ten-yard line, down to their very last play. At that distance they couldn't possibly miss the kick. They broke from the huddle, lined up for the field goal, and hiked the ball.

"Ten! Fourteen! Six! Hut, hut, *hut!*" The center hiked the ball to the holder, slugs flying in every direction. The holder threw up his hands to guard himself from the sticky missiles. The football squirted past him out onto the open field. Loose ball!

The Slugs scrambled forward, sliding and stumbling and squirming toward the ball. This would be their only chance. Out in front of them lay a wide-open field. All they had to do was get to the ball, hold on to it, slog their way through the mud, and reach the end zone. Unfortunately, the Giants' placekicker reached the ball first.

He scooped it up, turned around, and looked for someone—anyone—to whom he could throw the ball. Near the goal line, he caught a glimpse of one of his teammates jumping and waving his arms. *There!* He released the ball just as he disappeared under a pile of muddy Slugs.

The football wobbled up into the air like a rubber chicken with a broken wing; it had just enough strength to reach the receiver. At the very same moment, Ruth and her cheerleading squad were completing their favorite cheer. They threw their pom-poms in the air and flopped on the ground in a squirming pile. Ruth's pom-pom sailed into the air, over the heads of the other cheerleaders, over the sideline, and right on top of the Giants player's head! The slippery pom-pom landed on his helmet and covered his eyes at the same exact second the football was reaching his outstretched hands.

The player was instantly blinded. The football bounced off the top of his helmet and plopped right into the arms of one of the Slug players. He stood there staring at it. He'd played in twenty games, but in all that time he'd never even *touched* the ball. He didn't know what to do with it.

The coach yelled, "*Run!*" He just stood there. The players on the bench yelled, "*Run!*" He looked down at the ball.

The cheerleaders yelled, "*Run!*" He turned toward the end zone. The crowd yelled, "*Run!*" His legs began to move.

The boy's name was Waldo Wainwright, number 35, a name and number that would go down in the annals of Slug football history. It was the day a Slug slipped and tripped and squirmed ninety-seven yards *untouched* into his own team's end zone. It was the day the Giants lost to the worst high school football team in history. It was the day the wind and the rain and the earth and the slugs came together and helped lead our team to victory! We cried for joy when we saw that big, clumsy teenager trip and slip and squish and slide his way down the field and collapse under the goalpost. We cheered when the referee blew the final whistle. The game was over. The Slugs had won *6–0!*

The next day we held a parade down Main Street in Stickville. Waldo Wainwright and our two conquering heroes, Ruth and Jonny Button, rode in the lead car, hailed by thousands of loyal Slug fans. They waved brown and silver flags. They ate Slime Dogs and Slug Slush. They released a thousand brown balloons into the air. Mayor Touissaint of Stickville made a speech. They even proposed making the day an annual holiday in honor of the amazing victory.

Everyone gathered together in the streets and sang Stickville High School's fight song:

In a state, in a valley, in a town so very small,
Is a place you will find the oddest school of all.
A place where the slimiest of all God's creatures crawl.
The home of the Slugs; we're the Slug capital!

They make their presence known with a bright
  and silver trail.
Silently they move, over hump and hill and dale.
Nothing ever stops them; their progress cannot fail.
That's why we love Slugs! The Slug is what we hail!

Finally, around ten o'clock that night, the crowds began to disperse and we made our way home. The next morning, Waldo, Ruth, and Jonny's picture appeared on the front page of the *Stickville Times* under the caption: "Three Local Teenagers Make History." The headline read: SLUGS SLIME THE GIANTS.

As I drank my morning coffee and gazed at their smiling

faces in the picture, I was never so proud of my clever son and my wonderful daughter, who gained notoriety in such an unusual and unexpected way. It was the proudest day of my life.

Except maybe at the Homecoming Dance a few weeks later, when Ruth was named the Slug Queen. That was pretty special too.

CHAPTER 6

The Amazing Chang

The weather soon turned to crisp autumn air and falling leaves. As the weather changed, so did the fortunes of the Slugs. They lost their next three consecutive games by scores of 97-0 and 76-0 and then the rematch against the Giants, 112-0. Not that it mattered. The conversation in every store in Boomtown was about the Slugs' "winning season," with friendly wagers on how long the next losing streak would last. The odds pointed toward another forty years, but serious optimists were betting the Slugs would win another game sometime in the next decade.

Janice and I had other concerns. Jonny wasn't his normal rambunctious self. It was shortly after Halloween when Janice came to me and said, "Does Jonny seem *tired* to you lately? I don't think he's been sleeping well."

"I noticed. He seems to be *eating* a lot more too. Have you noticed that? Like we can't keep anything in the refrigerator these days."

Janice had Jonny come into the kitchen. She put her hand on his forehead and looked down his throat. "Are you feeling all right? You've got bags under your eyes."

"I'm okay, Mom. I've had a lot of extra homework. I'll go to bed early tonight, okay?"

Now Janice was convinced something was wrong. *Early to bed?* Not Jonny! She got out the thermometer, checked his temperature, looked in his ears, and made him cough a few times.

"I'm *fine*, really!"

Considering all the food that was missing from the pantry, we figured he had to be eating enough. It was probably just a growth spurt. Since he didn't have any other symptoms, we decided he was okay and turned our minds to other things—like the situation at church.

People were still talking about the day when Whiskers got loose. They wondered if Corine Beedle would ever come back. Two of our elders went out to see her, but she wouldn't answer the door. I called on the phone a few times without success. I even sent three letters of apology. The mailman brought them back unopened. I finally decided to go on out to the Beedles' farm to see if there was some way I could make amends.

"You're going with me," I told Sarah.

"Why?"

"You know why. You're going to apologize. You're going to beg Mrs. Beedle for forgiveness."

"She oughta be *thankin'* me. She doesn't need that ol' walker anymore."

"That isn't the point, and you know it."

"Can we bring some brownies? Maybe that'd help."

"That would be very thoughtful."

"And I'll make her a card. I'll draw a picture of Whiskers on it."

"*No Whiskers!* But the card would be a good idea."

Sarah made a very nice card with a pink ribbon on it, and she promised to be good. We drove to the Beedles' farm, parked the car, pushed open the gate, and walked up to the front door of the farmhouse. As we approached, Sarah pointed and whispered, "I saw Mrs. Beedle in the window, right over there."

"Don't point, Sarah." The curtains swung shut, and no one opened the door when I knocked. I kept at it for a few more minutes, but still no answer. Just as I stepped off the porch and was heading back to the car, a man came around the corner from behind the house.

"Howdy, there! Can I he'p you?"

"Please. Are you Mr. Beedle? I'm the Reverend Button, from Boomtown Church."

"Sure, Reverend. I know who you are. 'Course, I didn't recognize you at first, not without your three heads and the horns."

"What? Oh, is that what Corine told you? I don't blame her, I guess. She's still pretty upset?"

"No more'n usual." He put out his wrinkled hand, and I shook it. He looked to be about sixty-five or seventy years old, with a friendly smile, black horn-rimmed glasses, a wisp of graying hair, blue overalls, red flannel shirt, and cowboy boots. You could see he was a commodious sort of person, especially when he smiled. He had a pipe in his left hand that he used as a pointer when he talked.

"And this here," he asked, gesturing to Sarah, "would this be the little miracle worker? Sarah, ain't it?"

"That's me!" she announced proudly.

"Of course it is," he said. "I heard all about you."

"You have?"

"Sure 'nough. Healed my old lady, how 'bout that! What else can you do—raise the dead?"

"I don't think so. But I *did* bring some brownies."

"Well, that's very neighborly of you, Miss Sarah. My name's Paul. Beedle. Is that a card for Mrs. Beedle?"

"Yes. I made it myself."

"It's very pretty," he said, accepting the card. "I'll have to take it in to her, though. Don't think she'll be coming out. That ol' woman is as stubborn as spinach stuck in your dentures. Never been able to get her to do nothin' she don't want to."

"Same as me," Sarah admitted. "I *rarely* do what I'm told."

Mr. Beedle chuckled. "Well, I sure am grateful to you, young lady. Her mood ain't improved any, but she shore is gettin' around a whole lot better. I don't trip over her walker no more. No more silly doctors neither."

"You sure she won't talk to us?" I insisted. "I'd really like to apologize to her. What I mean is that *Sarah* would like to apologize. Isn't that right, dear?"

Mr. Beedle pointed a thumb over his shoulder. "Tell you what. Why don't we sit for a spell on the porch? When she sees you ain't leaving anytime soon, maybe she'll come out and say somethin'. But I wouldn't bet on it."

It sounded good to me. I didn't have any pressing engagements and, besides, it would give me a chance to get to know Paul. We pulled our coats a little tighter and took chairs on the porch. He had a small outdoor stove going, so we leaned in to warm our hands and he started to brew some coffee in a dented blue coffeepot on the cooktop. He broke open the brownies and offered one to Sarah, who was more than happy to eat it. Then he carefully loaded his pipe, lit it, leaned back in his rocker, took a deep draw, and blew a tight little smoke ring into the cool, autumn afternoon.

"Do it again!" Sarah exclaimed.

He sat quiet for a while, puffing on his pipe and blowing smoke rings. Then he turned an eye to me and said, "Preacher, you're new to small-town life, sure as I'm sitting here. Has anyone told you about Boomtown's history?"

"No, I don't know much about it. My wife and I wanted to move the kids out of California, so we applied to several small churches here in Washington. When Boomtown Church called, it was just what we were looking for—a small town, rural area, down-to-earth people—a way for us to stay in the ministry but get away from the big city. So here we are. I probably should have done more homework; then maybe I wouldn't have been so surprised."

"Oh? Surprised by what?"

"Everything! Like the name Boomtown. I thought it was like one of those towns that spring up all of a sudden; you know, a town that grows really fast. I never took it *literally*—a town that's always blowing stuff up. BOOMtown? Who'd have guessed it?"

Mr. Beedle smiled as he leaned over to pour two mugs of coffee from the freshly brewed pot and handed one of them to me. "Well, son, you really shoulda done your research, 'cause how Boomtown got its name is an interestin' tale if there ever was one. If you've got some time on yer hands, I'll tell it to you. Maybe by then Corine will poke her head out and say boo."

I sat back to nurse my coffee and listen to Paul's account of Boomtown history. What follows is my recollection of his story, as best I can remember:

"Boomtown wasn't always called by that name. It used to be a spot situated between nowhere and someplace else. It was a hodgepodge of tents and shacks thrown up way back in the days of the railroad. There was the main stretch of railroad that reached from coast to coast, but with more folks coming out West, they started adding branch lines north and south. This was back when the northwestern United States was still mostly Indians, buffalo, and a few brave pioneers.

"One day, a Chinese man named Chang showed up in the area. Like his countrymen, he worked his way across the United States as an explosives expert for the railroad. He had learned how to work gunpowder from his father, Bang, and his grandfather, Zang. His talent was in great demand by the railroad companies. He could take the smallest pinch of his homemade gunpowder and blow the spots off a ladybug without killing it, that's what they say. He was the best in the business.

"The building of the transcontinental railroad was sparked by the California Gold Rush in 1848. By 1850, the gold started to peter out, but there were still plenty of prospectors infected with gold fever, and they weren't ready to give up so easily. So they abandoned California and disappeared into the wilderness, seeking their fortune in the hills and mountains of Nevada, Oregon, Montana, Washington, and the Yukon. Once Chang reached the West Coast, he quit the railroad and followed the fortune hunters north and supplied them with gunpowder.

"'Round here, there was a certain prospector who

struck a mighty vein of gold—right up yonder over there on Rocket Ridge—you can see it from here. Word spread quickly until every hillside was covered with mining operations. Chang was right in the thick of it. He was the main supplier of high-grade black powder for opening mines and blasting tunnels. The Washington gold rush turned Chang into a very popular and wealthy man.

"A small town sprung up—shops, grocers, a blacksmith, a school, a church. People came and stayed. Soon there was the prettiest little town you ever saw, nestled on the top of a hill with Chang as one of its richest citizens. To celebrate his good fortune, Chang threw a huge party every Fourth of July and invited everyone from miles around. They would come to see his magnificent fireworks and rockets and firecrackers. The future was looking bright for everybody.

"But Chang wasn't satisfied. He was always itching for new ways to use his gunpowder. He was the one who invented the exploding welcome mat—maybe you've heard of it—Chang's Ding-Dong-So-Long, available from Martin's Mercantile in the main square. Only $4.95 plus tax. An elegant way to scare off those pesky traveling salesmen.

"Chang was also the one who came up with the handy, easy-to-use Chang's Drain Gun. No more clogged drains. Just put the rubber flange against the sink opening and pull the trigger.

"Then he came up with the Tree Magician, a combination drill and plug kit. 'Removes Trees Like Magic,' or so the package claims. Drill a few holes, stuff four to five bomb packets into the root mass, light the fuse, and stand back. Guaranteed to relocate the tree or your money back.

"Next came Chang's TNT Tea Bags, in convenient two-ounce packets. Steep one teabag in a gallon of rubbing alcohol for one hour, pour, and light. Useful for starting campfires (or burning down barns if you aren't careful).

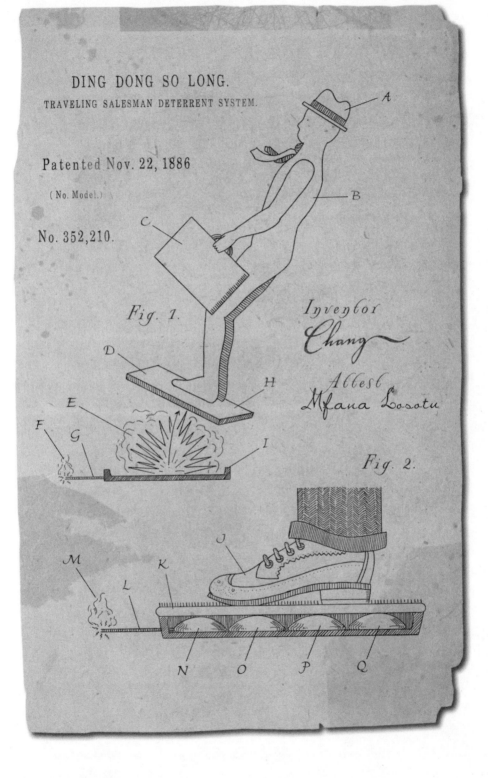

DING DONG SO LONG.

TRAVELING SALESMAN DETERRENT SYSTEM.

Patented Nov. 22, 1886

(No. Model.)

No. 352,210.

A

B

C

Fig. 1.

D

H

E

F

G

I

Inventor
Chang

Attest
Mfana Losotu

Fig. 2.

J

M

K

L

N   O   P   Q

"Chang also experimented with mixing gunpowder with fertilizer to put in his garden. From the beginning, he met with mixed results: zucchinis that exploded on impact, pumpkins that popped, apples that blew holes in the ground when they fell off the tree. But through trial and error, Chang managed to work out a stable formula that eventually produced remarkable results.

"Soon he was selling Chang's POPcorn (every kernel guaranteed to pop), Chang's Firecrackers (gunpowder-laced wheat crackers that'll cure the most stubborn case of constipation), and Chang's Hotcakes (pancakes that explode when stepped on). It's a great way for getting gophers to relocate—and they taste pretty good with maple syrup (the *pancakes*, I mean, not the gophers).

"But probably his most *famous* invention happened entirely by accident. Some of his POPcorn got mixed in with the regular feed he gave to his chickens. One afternoon, one of the chickens tripped in the hen house and *boom!* Scrambled eggs and fried chicken.

"Chang was absolutely mortified. He *loved* that chicken. But it gave him a crazy idea. Nobody knows how he did it—it's still a carefully guarded Fireworks Factory secret—but somehow he came up with a way to turn regular chicken eggs into *exploding* chicken eggs.

"It took some trial and error. At one point, he must have used too much gunpowder because he blew the roof off his lab and knocked over his neighbor's fence. Scared the fur off his dog too. But after some more tinkering, Chang got the mixture just right. The eggs were golden yellow with gray speckles and had an extra thick shell. If you were careful and handled them correctly, they were more or less safe. He decided to call them Hen Grenades.

"He contacted the U.S. Army and was soon doing a brisk business supplying the military with the little egg bombs. Very few people know this, but them eggs were an important secret weapon during the first World War. The Allies in France were able to sneak ammunition through enemy lines disguised as breakfast, a dozen Hen Grenades at a time.

"'Course, not all of Chang's ideas were successful. There was Chang's Dandruff Destroyer. It was supposed to get rid of dandruff—that it *did*. It also removed a person's hair. Very bad.

"There was the Chang BOOMerang. Throw it at crows to scare 'em out of your fields, and then it comes back to you. Unfortunately, there was a slight problem with the timing mechanism. Very, very bad.

"Then there was Chang's Bee Blaster Kit. It included a ten-foot pole and a long fuse so you could insert a blast pack into a bee's nest to scare 'em off. Chang had to give out quite a few refunds for that one. It was very, *very* bad.

"In spite of a few setbacks, most of Chang's inventions worked. Of course, in order to support all of his operations, he needed a steady supply of raw materials. Chang stumbled onto a rich deposit of sulfur, leftover from volcano explosions in the area. The second ingredient—charcoal—he got by burning oak and hickory trees, which were all over the place, and Chang's neighbors were more than happy to donate ashes from their stoves and fireplaces. For the final ingredient, Chang demanded the highest-grade saltpeter. Chang got permission from the miners to gather bat guano from inside the mining caves that dotted these hills like rabbit warrens.

"Soon he was producing his own black powder out of a small barn on his property. It had two vats for distilling and a big grinding stone. But the more his inventions caught on, the more he needed to expand his operations. In a few years, his powder factory was the biggest business in the area, with demand for Chang's Super Rich Black Powder coming from the railroads, the military, and mining companies all over the country. An entire cottage industry sprung up around it: a dynamite-making business, a gunsmith and bullet-making company, and, of course, Chang's Famous Fireworks Factory, where some of the best fireworks in the world are still being made.

"It was at that point, in 1878, when the citizens, under the leadership of Councilman Alden Purdy, drew up the town charter and filed papers with the state applying for recognition as a duly formed township. In gratitude for the important contributions Chang had made, they wanted the new city to be named after him: Changville, Changton, or Chang City.

"But Chang refused. He was a shy man and didn't want the credit focused in his direction. He said, 'We built this town together—not just one person, but *all* of us. Many thanks, but I don't want the town named after me.'

"That's when Councilman Purdy, soon to be Mayor Purdy, made a brilliant suggestion: 'Let's add an "e" to the end of Chang's name and call the town *Change*.' Everyone agreed, and Change, Washington, was born on May 18, 1878.

"The town adopted the motto 'Change Is for the Better' and the chicken as its official mascot. That's why you'll find a chicken on the egg-shaped town seal, encircled by the motto and holding two crossed sticks of dynamite in its claws. And in spite of his objections, you'll also find a statue of Chang erected in the middle of Town Square. It's out in front of the courthouse, with two chickens in his lap and one at his feet. And right there on the monument, you'll find these words carved in stone: 'Chang, Founding Father of Change, Washington. September 8, 1830 – April 12, 1892.'"

Mr. Beedle fell silent and leaned back in his rocking chair and sipped his coffee. He noticed the look of confusion on my face. He was just waiting for me to ask the question he knew I was going to ask.

"This isn't Change, Washington. It's *Boomtown*. And it isn't on a hill. It's mostly flat. It doesn't fit your story."

Paul smiled and said, "Well, young feller, that's a mystery, of course, since the only one who really knows what happened is Chang himself. He died on the same day the town of Change changed forever, so of course we can't ask *him*. You could ask Olaf Stevenson or maybe Klaus Kanderhoffen if you get the chance. They lived here back in those days."

Sarah persisted. "But what happened? Why'd they change the name of the town?"

"Well, young lady, there's a couple of theories floating around, but here's what I think. It was way too dangerous to be storing the gunpowder and dynamite and fireworks and Hen Grenades and everything else Chang was making right out in the open. All you needed was a spark, and this whole town'd go up like a tinderbox!

"So Chang started stockpiling the inventory down in the caves and tunnels that were dug all over the place, like holes in Swiss cheese. It was a pretty good idea, seeing that there were miles and miles of tunnels down there, what with the mining for gold and then the digging for sulfur. Besides, it was as dry as a cigar box down under the ground."

"That *was* a good idea!" Sarah said.

"Maybe so, maybe not. Some think another one of Chang's chickens got loose and went down into the tunnels. It got into a stockpile of POPcorn, and you remember what happened the first time! Chang went chasing after it as it flew from one cave into the next. The story goes that the chicken flew up onto a shelf and it started to cluck like crazy. When the bird got finished, there was a fresh new Hen Grenade. 'Course, it was *round*, so it started to roll down the shelf—Chang dove in there and almost caught it. And then . . ."

"What? What happened?"

"Nothin'. The egg was a dud. It just bounced."

"It didn't blow up?"

"Nope. But that's not the end of the story. Chang was so happy that he started jumping up and down and cheering. Scared the chicken half to death, and it laid another egg—BOOM! Up went the chicken. Up went the gunpowder. No more Chang."

I looked out over the fields in front of us, as flat as the eye could see with hills rising up in the distance. "But you said this town was on top of a *hill*. We're in a valley."

"That's what I said. It *used* to be on a hill, until that egg went kablooey. It set off a chain reaction. First the Hen Grenade, then the fireworks, then the dynamite, then the black powder, and all the sulfur and so on and so on—you get the picture. With all the explosives stored in the mining caves, it pretty much turned the hill inside out. Went up like a Roman candle—*whoosh!* Musta really been something to see."

"You're pulling my leg, right?"

"Scouts' honor, Reverend! It was a real mess. Fortunately, no one else died in the blast, but it took more'n five years to rebuild everything. After that, they changed the name to Boomtown. You really should stop by the Boomtown

Museum and take a look. And you oughta take a closer look at that purty statue of Chang in Town Square. There's a plaque beside it that tells some of the story."

I glanced at my watch and saw that it was getting late. But there was still no sign of Mrs. Beedle. "I was hoping to talk to Corine today. You sure we can't smooth things over before we leave?"

Mr. Beedle squinted at me and said, "Well, Reverend, I'm sure you know your business better than *I* do, but some things don't *ever* get fixed. Try as hard as you want, Mrs. Beedle may never come around. She's pretty stubborn."

"I don't believe that. I like to think that you can fix anything if you try hard enough."

Mr. Beedle shook his head. "You think so? I'm not so sure. But I'll tell you what. I haven't been to church in years, but I like you. I'll tell Corine that if she'll go back to church, I'll go with her. That oughta do it. She's been trying to save my sorry soul since before we was hitched. I'll see you this Sunday, Reverend, how's that sound?"

"Okay, sure. I guess so. Thank you, Paul," I said, accepting his offer.

Sarah and I shook his hand and then waved good-bye from the car window as I drove away thinking about what he'd said. How was I any different than Corine? I could be as stubborn as a mule. I wanted everything to run smoothly. I wanted everything to be calm and predictable. I thought if everyone would just follow the rules and behave properly, then we'd all be at peace.

Was that fair? What if people couldn't
be the way I wanted them to be? What if
Paul was right? What if some things *couldn't*
be worked out? Was there enough mercy
in my world to make room for people
who didn't fit?

As promised, Paul was in
church that Sunday, and so was
Corine (without a cane or walker,
I might add). After church, we went
out to lunch and then Paul took
me into Town Square to take a
closer look at the statue. There
was Chang sitting on a chair,
surrounded by chickens, with
his name carved on the pedestal
just like he'd told me. I hadn't
noticed it before, but the town
motto was inscribed underneath:
CHANGE IS FOR THE BETTER.

I thought, *Maybe it is. Maybe I*
ought to try it sometime.

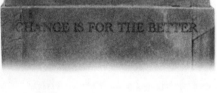

CHANG
Founding Father of
Change, Washington

SEPT. 8, 1830
APR. 12, 1892

CHANGE IS FOR THE BETTER

CHAPTER 7

A Boomtown Christmas

On Mondays, I always try to get a slow start: Sleep in until 8:00 a.m. Kiss the kids good-bye on their way to school. Eat a light breakfast. Drink coffee. Read the paper. Walk to the church office. I love Mondays.

Janice was out the door ahead of me on her way to help some of the ladies decorate the sanctuary for Christmas. "Some of the decorations are in bad shape, so I suggested we get together and make some new ones. Wait until you see how they look!"

"It sounds like you and the ladies are getting along swim-mingly," I said with my nose in the paper.

"Yes!" she answered cheerfully. "I missed that at our last church. I've got more friends now than I can count. I love it."

"Mm-hm. That's nice, dear. Have fun."

My attention was consumed by what I was reading in the *Stickville Times*. The main headline read: RASH OF ROBBERIES CONTINUES. The article listed the items reportedly missing:

Fred Cotton's truck (disappeared during the storm)

Lazy Gunderson's fence (likewise)

Tom O'Grady's thresher (just the blades)

8 trees from the north end of André Soisson's
 property

2 bicycles from in front of Martin's Mercantile
 (gone in broad daylight)

42 railroad ties from the train yard, 300 feet of track

Farmer Higgins's posthole digger

600 feet of Christmas lights (off the trees in front
 of the courthouse)

Miscellaneous pickaxes, shovels, and pry bars

Not to mention that my lawn mower was still missing!

No explanation was given in the article. No eyewitnesses. No clues. No suspects. Mayor Tanaka of Boomtown and Mayor Touissaint of Stickville formed a joint task force and autho-rized Sheriff Burton Ernie to deputize as many men as he needed in order to bring the crime spree to an end. Everyone was encouraged to be on the lookout for the "criminal or gang of thieves who may or may not be armed and dangerous."

Sheriff Ernie attended our church, and in public he was shocked and dismayed over these seemingly random robberies. In private, he was as thrilled as a man could possibly be. After all, the worst thing that ever happened in Boomtown was mailboxes being blown up by teenagers, which, quite frankly, was encouraged. There was an occasional speeding ticket, a few jaywalkers, and the random fire caused by errant fireworks. Other than that, Boomtown was as quiet as a church (not *our* church, of course) as far as crime was concerned.

As I turned to the sports section to read about the Slugs' latest drubbing, a small announcement caught my eye. It listed the date of Boomtown's upcoming Living Nativity and the names of the ministers who were hosting. My name was listed in the ad.

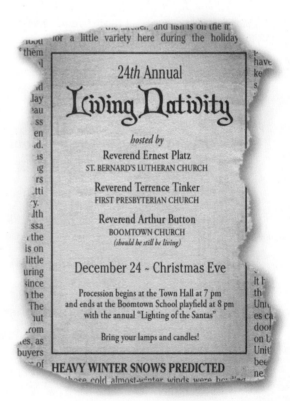

for a little variety here during the holiday

24th Annual
Living Nativity

hosted by

Reverend Ernest Platz
ST. BERNARD'S LUTHERAN CHURCH

Reverend Terrence Tinker
FIRST PRESBYTERIAN CHURCH

Reverend Arthur Button
BOOMTOWN CHURCH
(should he still be living)

December 24 ~ Christmas Eve

Procession begins at the Town Hall at 7 pm
and ends at the Boomtown School playfield at 8 pm
with the annual "Lighting of the Santas"

Bring your lamps and candles!

HEAVY WINTER SNOWS PREDICTED

As usual, I was the last to know. I'd been thinking about a lovely candlelight service, the choir singing, and a simple sermon about the true meaning of Christmas, that sort of thing. Now, apparently, I was expected to participate in a Nativity pageant, involving lots and lots of fireworks, no doubt. Not something I'd signed up for.

I got dressed, grabbed my Bible, picked up an umbrella, went to put on my coat—and found it missing. It was always hanging on the hall tree by the front door—it was there just yesterday—but now it was *gone.*

What was going on around here? First my lawn mower. Now my coat? Then I noticed something else—what was that? Leading from the back door, through the kitchen and up the stairs—muddy footprints. I followed them into Jonny's room and found a pile of filthy, muddy clothes thrown in the corner along with a pair of muddy boots. I'd have to talk to that boy when he got home.

I was in too much of a hurry to hunt for my coat. I pulled on a thick sweater, hunched outside into the misty drizzle, and walked as fast as I could down to the church. As I came up the sidewalk, I saw two men talking to Ingrid at the main door.

"Reverend Button!" she said, waving to me. "You're just in time!"

"Here he is now," she said to the men. Then to me she said, "Let me introduce you to Reverend Platz from St. Bernard's and Reverend Tinker from First Presbyterian."

I regarded the two gentlemen for a moment, one dressed

all in black and the other dressed all in gray, as different from one another as wet is from dry. Reverend Platz was as wide as he was tall, round and red like a ripe tomato, with a circle of white hair crowning his head. He reminded me of Santa Claus, with his red nose, jolly laugh, and firm, happy handshake. His companion, the Reverend Tinker, was the polar opposite: seven feet tall and thin as a beanpole. He had a thin face, gray eyes, black hair, and long bony fingers and arms. He was as white as a snowman and about as talkative. He shivered in the cold and managed a quiet hello before Reverend Platz took charge.

"Hello! We finally meet at last, Reverend Button. We should have come by the minute you arrived, but we like to see if the new minister at Boomtown Church lasts a month or two before we make our acquaintance." He chuckled. "Nothing personal, you understand, but Reverend Tinker has buried so many of your pastors over the years it's almost a full-time sideline, isn't that right, Terrence?" He giggled and elbowed Reverend Tinker good-naturedly, but his stoic companion pulled his overcoat tighter and didn't crack a smile.

"Not that we're expecting anything like that from you at all," the jolly Reverend Platz continued, "since you seem so virile and healthy and certainly forewarned, I should say. Keep your eyes open and your head down, that's good advice! I'm sure you'll be just fine."

"Yes, thank you . . . I think."

"Of course, of course. We're all friends here. All together in the Lord's work. All playing for the same team. Time to put our heads together and get this Living Nativity off the ground."

"Yes, the Living Nativity," I said. "I came down here as fast as I could when I saw the notice in the paper. I was going to ask Ingrid about it and then contact you."

"Wonderful! We're all on the same track. Running the same race. Reading from the same script! Couldn't be better. That's why we're here. Come along, come along."

Before I could say another word, Reverend Platz had me by the arm and was dragging me back down the sidewalk. "Let's head on down to Mabel's Diner where we can make our plans. Worst coffee you ever tasted, terrible service, but it's close by. Hop to it, Terrence! Follow along and keep up. No dawdling. We'll talk on the way. Get to know one another. Get the lay of the land, so to speak."

And speak he did, incessantly, nonstop, as he chugged down the street, right on Bang, left on Cave In, right on

Nitro, acting as tour guide as we rushed along with the Reverend Tinker bringing up the rear.

"My compatriot here has been with First Presbyterian for more than forty years now. They say he came with the building. Been marrying and burying folks as long as anyone can remember. And myself, I started at St. Bernard's nine years ago. Attended all the funerals of your predecessors since I've been here, and I've been part of the Living Nativity every year. It's a town favorite, that's the truth; I wouldn't miss it."

He paused every now and then to point out the holiday decorations that hung from every light post, fence, window, and tree. "The Christmas chickens look especially festive this year. Red and green bows, very nice. Which reminds me, will you be helping with the Hen Grenade and Hotcake Breakfast this year? December 22 at St. Bernard's. Annual tradition. We can count on you? Wonderful. Oh, my, look at the beautiful frozen cow. Old Boyd has outdone himself this year!"

There it was. Staring at us over a fence, its sad eyes gazing through a solid block of ice, six feet high, four feet thick—a frozen cow.

I couldn't believe my eyes. "It's a frozen cow!"

"Well, yes, it most certainly is. Another one of those fantastic Boomtown holiday traditions! Old Boyd's been doing it ever since the winter of '39. You remember that, don't you, Terrence? You were here then, of course."

Reverend Tinker had caught up to us by then and opened his mouth to answer, but Reverend Platz cut him off. "Worst winter on record. Started to rain on a Tuesday. Didn't stop until Thursday; it was Christmas morning, I think. Three days of sleet and freezing temperatures and blizzard winds. Terrible. Just terrible! People trapped inside their homes. Doors frozen shut. Snow piled high as your head. Ice everywhere. Old Boyd, there, got his entire herd caught out in the storm; it was too late to bring 'em in from the fields. They froze solid like cow popsicles without the stick. Stayed that way for a month. Then, we had a warm spell in January like you've never seen. Those cows thawed out quick as you please. Every last cow survived. To celebrate, Boyd invited everyone over for the biggest barbecue the town has ever seen.

"He's been doing it every year since as a way of commemorating the event. He makes a great homemade barbecue sauce, baked potatoes, cole slaw, the works. You'll love it. Lots of fun. Late January. Sunday afternoon. Bring the whole church."

We kept walking and soon reached Mabel's Diner, pushed open the door, and found a booth by the window. Mabel swooped in from out of nowhere, poured a coffee-like substance into our mugs, and disappeared. Reverend Platz was right. It was the worst coffee I'd ever smelled or tasted. It was blackish, burnt goo. I watched Reverend Tinker, moving as slow as a glacier, carefully pour ten teaspoons of sugar and two packs of creamer into his cup and stir, stir, stir.

He looked across the table and pushed the cream and sugar at me. I decided to drink water instead.

Reverend Platz gulped his coffee straight, too busy talking to notice. "So, let's discuss the Living Nativity. Twenty-seven years and counting. Wonderful tradition. Lovely. Moving. Half the town gathers at Town Square carrying kerosene lamps and candles. We all sing Christmas carols as we march through the snow-covered streets, following Joseph and Mary as they make their way through town. Tebs Olsen and Gerty Capshaw did it last year, and maybe they'll do it again. The Bouchard brothers—Louis, Maurice, and Jean-Claude—will be the three wise men. Busy Gunderson has promised to be the shepherd. He can get a couple of sheep from Lazy's farm. Sam Sloan will provide the horse. We'll fix up a hump and make a camel out of him. Then, of course, the children from all our churches will dress up like angels and sing around the manger. And we'll finish the festivities with the Lighting of the Santas. It will be fabulous, as always."

I interrupted. "Right. I read that in the newspaper. It mentioned the 'Lighting of the Santas.' What's that?"

"The Lighting of the Santas? The best part! The highlight! The crescendo! People wait all year for the big moment. You'll see! It's spectacular! Marvelous! Explosive! Jim Dougherty's boy, Rocky, took the big prize last time. One hundred and seventy-five feet, who'd have believed it? He's looking good again this year. My money's on him. Or maybe Guenther's boy—he came in a close second. Too top heavy, I think."

"What are you talking about?"

"Santa Shooters, old boy! Reindeer Rockets. Exploding Elves. We're talking fireworks, son. Fireworks!"

"Fireworks on *Christmas*?"

"Of course, of course! Got to have fireworks. This whole town was built around fireworks and gunpowder. That's how it got its name. Every holiday. Christmas, New Year's, Groundhog Day, St. Patrick's, Easter, May Day, the Fourth of July. The bigger, the better."

"But Reindeer Rockets? And Santa Shooters?"

"And don't forget the Exploding Elves. Those are some of my favorites."

I looked at Reverend Tinker. He just shrugged.

"Right now, as we speak, the older school kids are working on their end-of-the-year project. You've got a son at the Boomtown School, don't you? Hasn't he mentioned it? He better get busy if he wants a chance at the prize."

"What prize?"

"The team that wins first place gets to ride in the lead float in the Fourth of July parade. Then they get to light off the first rocket, the one that sets off all the others during the big fireworks extravaganza in the park. Big fun. A great honor."

"You mean to tell me that right now, my son is building a *rocket*? In class, during school time?"

"Oh, most certainly. Absolutely. It's a big part of their science grade. Don't worry, it's all perfectly safe and supervised. No problem. There is the occasional mishap, of course, but nothing serious. No deaths. Some damage. The reports are exaggerated, I'm sure."

"Nothing serious?" I couldn't believe it. There was *no way* I was going to let Jonny build a *rocket*. It just wasn't safe!

I jumped up from my seat, threw fifty cents on the table, grabbed my umbrella, and headed for the door.

"No need to panic! Everything will be fine. What about the Nativity? Reverend? Come back!"

I made it back to the church at a run, found Janice hanging evergreen swags in the foyer, and told her what I'd found out. Then we both jumped in the car and drove to the Boomtown School. We pounded through the front door and charged past the principal's office. Janice turned left to go check on Sarah. I shot straight down the hall and burst into Mr. O'Malley's eighth-grade science class. It was right in the middle of his demonstration of how to add ammonium to black powder as a binding agent.

"Mr. O'Malley! What in heaven's name is going on here?"

"Excuse me? Oh, you must be Reverend Button! Welcome!" He walked over and shook my hand. "Pleased to meet you. I'd love to stop and talk, but now isn't a good time. We're right in the middle of a lesson."

"Yes. I know. I just found out that you're building *rockets* in here!"

"Oh, I see. You're new in town. Someone should have told you sooner. Entirely my fault. Would you like to stay and observe?"

"Observe? I don't think so! I came to take Jonny out of here!"

"Dad! No! What are you doing?"

I turned to see Jonny at the back table with a group of boys, a mixing bowl in front of him, and a spoon in his hand. He was humiliated by my intrusion, I could tell, but I was too upset to back down.

"Look, son, this is *dangerous*."

"No, it isn't. Mr. O'Malley has taught us all about it. The ingredients are stable. You have to put a match to it—and there aren't any matches allowed in here."

I walked over to him and lowered my voice. "But Jonny, these are *explosives*. You're learning how to blow things up in eighth grade!"

"That's nothing, Dad. Most of my friends here learned how to do that in kindergarten. This is Boomtown, Dad. *Boomtown*. This is what people *do* here."

"But . . ."

"Dad, look at what we made. We're going to enter the contest, and we could win! This is Rocky. His team took first place last year. He's our team leader. Just look at our rocket! Isn't it great?"

In the corner stood a paper maché Santa Claus, arms stretched over its head like Superman, painted bright red, with black boots, glued-on paper strips for a beard, and a pointy hat. He had on a pair of airmen's goggles over his eyes and a yellow comet painted on his hat and the words *You Better Watch Out* painted on his chest.

"You see, Dad, his hat comes off like this, so you can pack rocket propellant down this tube inside the body. The fuse comes out here at the bottom. It's a really long fuse. You light it and run away. You got lots of time before he takes off. And when the fuel burns up to his head—BOOM!

A big ol' ball of fire. Our burst is going to have red and green trailers with gold sparklers in it. Isn't it super?"

I just stood there with my mouth open. What could I say? Jonny had never been this excited about school. He did well enough, but nothing ever sparked his interest like this. I was impressed—but I didn't want to let on. Should I be encouraging this?

"Dad, we're learning about chemistry, propulsion, physics, flight patterns, wind dynamics, all the math and stuff that goes along with it. It's the best thing I've ever done in school. I'm learning a lot! Please, *please* don't make me go home."

Mr. O'Malley came up behind me and put his hand on my shoulder. "Trust me, Reverend. I haven't lost a single student yet. And besides, when you see fifteen paper mâché Santas exploding into brilliant colors in the sky, you'll change your mind forever. It's a sight you're not going to want to miss."

So I didn't. Two weeks later at the Living Nativity, Janice and I marched along with all the other townfolk as we sang carols and sipped hot cider, following Mary and Joseph and the wise men and the shepherd and the sheep and the horse dressed like a camel. We marched past the frozen cow and the festive Christmas chickens out to the playfield at the Boomtown School. I stood shoulder to shoulder with Reverend Platz and Reverend Tinker as we prayed with our people, thanking God for another blessed year, remembering the heroes who fought in the war, and asking the Lord for another safe launch.

Did I mention that Tebs and Gerty were not Joseph and Mary that year? Nope. It was my own Ruth and Waldo Wainwright, dressed in robes, riding on the "camel" and leading the parade. And who was it marching in front of the choir of angels? It was none other than my very own Sarah.

"Sarah, as an *angel*?" I whispered to Janice as she went by. "That's quite a stretch, don't you think?"

"Don't be an old poop, Mr. Button," Janice replied. "Just look at her! She's having the time of her life!"

Sarah was definitely making the most of it. She marched along in front as the other angel girls sang "O Little Town of Bethlehem" and "Hark! the Herald Angels Sing." In one hand, she carried a huge sparkler on a pole, representing the Christmas Star. With her other hand, she waved to the crowd as she passed by, clearly enjoying all the attention.

Once we got to the school playfield it was time for fireworks. First came the Exploding Elves, with long fuses sticking up out of their pointy hats. *Boom!* Off with their heads! Then eight tiny Reindeer Rockets with Rudolph leading the way. *Woosh!* Then the climax of the evening—all the science classes lit their Santa Shooters. Sheriff Burton Ernie was the official judge.

"We want to thank Mr. O'Malley for his fine work with our kids again this year. We also want to thank the folks from Big Bang Explosives for donating the rocket fuel.

"We're also excited to be able to welcome Jonny Button to a team this year, led by last year's winner, Rocky Dougherty. We're expecting big things from that team—isn't that right, Reverend?"

"I certainly hope not!" I shouted back. Everyone laughed and applauded.

Once the laughter subsided, Burton said, "Okay, then, if everybody's ready to go, without any further ado, let's fire 'em up!"

The teams took turns shooting off their Santas. A few of them did pretty well; estimates ranged from fifty feet to as much as one hundred twenty-five feet. Each of the Santas exploded as expected, in lovely blooms of brilliant color, except for one that crash-landed on the roof of the school. Too bad it was a dud. It had actually traveled the farthest distance.

Then it was Jonny's turn. His team lined up their rocket while I watched the shining eyes of my son. I listened to his excited chatter as he lit the fuse, ran for cover, and yelled in triumph as their Santa rocket soared fifty, one hundred, one hundred fifty, two hundred feet and more into the air—right into the record books! Then I watched as his wonderful Santa rocket, caught in a winter gust of wind, made a graceful one-hundred-eighty-degree U-turn and plunged straight back toward earth, straight into the ground in the exact spot where I was standing—just before it blew me over the fence.

I woke up about twenty minutes later surrounded by a circle of concerned faces. Janice was feeling my forehead. Doctor Goldberg was checking my pulse. Jonny was accepting congratulations from his team members. Reverend Tinker was working on a rough draft for my eulogy. He gave a huge sigh of relief when he saw my eyes open. He tore up his notes and declared, "He'll live!"

The announcement was greeted with cheers from a worried crowd. I think they were mostly happy because now the rest of the Santas could be launched without further interruption. My church members were happy since they wouldn't have to start searching for a new pastor. I was happy just to be *alive*.

Janice helped me to my feet and led me over to the car, where we sat and watched the remainder of the launches from relative safety. We could see Ruth with her high school friends leading Christmas carols for the children. Sarah was in the front row with a bent halo, dressed as an angel and trying her best to act like one. Jonny was helping his buddies light off the last of the Exploding Elves and the Rocket Reindeer. It was strange and fun and disturbing and wonderful all at the same time.

"Merry Christmas, Mr. Button," Janice said, giving me a kiss on the cheek.

"And a Merry Christmas to you, Mrs. Button," I answered, kissing her back.

Then she smiled mischievously. "I suppose I better wish you a Happy New Year *now*. You know, just in case you don't live long enough to see it."

"Oh! Very funny!" I groaned, handing her the car keys. "And since you are so funny . . . *you* can drive us home."

CHAPTER 8

A Gift from the Hopontops

Christmas morning at the Button house meant getting up early, eating toast, sipping coffee and cocoa, and checking our Christmas stockings to see what Santa brought us that year. We found the usual things: a hairbrush and hairclips for Ruth, a yoyo and some new gears and wheels for Jonny's Erector Set, and a whistle and some doll clothes for Sarah. Then Janice and I got the biggest surprise of all.

While we sat in the living room opening our presents,

Janice heard the sound of crying coming from the front porch. Sarah was the first one out the door.

"It's a baby!" she shrieked.

"No, it's not," Jonny argued.

"You don't think I know what a baby looks like?" Sarah replied, holding up the bundle so all could see. We saw a tiny brown and blue face peek out from inside an Indian blanket and heard the sound of whimpering.

"Sarah," Janice implored, "please hand the baby to me."

"*I* found it!"

"I know that, dear, but it's a *baby*, not a toy. It's probably freezing—and hungry too."

Jonny grabbed the handmade basket where the baby had been lying, and we all came inside to take a closer look. Peeling aside the striped blanket, we saw dark hair over a small narrow face, ruddy cheeks, brown skin, and bright blue eyes. The baby was probably no more than a few weeks old, dressed in cotton pajamas and a pair of cotton socks. Janice rewrapped the baby tightly in the blanket and we shuffled into the living room to stand by the heater. In a few moments, the crying subsided and Janice took command.

"Ruth, run down to the LaPierres'. They have their new baby and all. Ask them if we can borrow a bottle, some infant formula, and diapers. Jonny, fetch me a few more blankets. Sarah—stop dancing around—in the bathroom are some cotton cloths that will work for diapers for now; bring those to me, will you please? Arthur, get that note pinned to the corner of the blanket. Can you read it?"

I reached over and undid the safety pin that was holding a note written in crooked scrawl and spattered with tears. I flipped it over and looked at both sides. Not much there.

"It says, 'Please take her as your own.' That's it. Nothing more. No signature."

"A girl," Janice hummed, rocking the baby gently. "That's what the note says."

"A baby on a doorstep; a mysterious note; no explanation. I've read about this sort of thing happening," I murmured. "I just didn't think it was going to happen to *us*."

Sarah came barreling into the room waving the cloths. "I heard you! A *girl* baby! And *I* was the one who found her! Can I keep her, Mom? Dad? Can I?"

I grabbed her by the shoulders to keep her from lifting off into outer space. "Really, Sarah, please. Of course you can't keep her. She's not a pet; she's a *baby*. A baby with a mother and a father. We have to find out who they are."

"You never let me have nothin'!" Sarah pouted.

"I never let you have *anything*," I corrected. "Which isn't true. I let you have all sorts of things, but this is different."

"C'mon, Dad, please? I'll give back all my presents. I'll keep my room clean. I'll never get in trouble ever again. Can we keep her? Please, please, *pleeeeease!*"

"Janice. Help me out here?"

But Janice wasn't any help at all. She was too preoccupied with cooing and cradling the infant—and once Ruth came back from the LaPierres', feeding the hungry child a bottle of warmed-up formula. Ruth sat on the left and

Sarah on the right, and the three of them ignored the two males in the room.

"Another *girl*," sniffed Jonny. "Why couldn't it be a *boy*? It just isn't fair."

"No, it isn't," I agreed, grumbling to myself. "None of this is. But, I suppose, *someone* has to be the bad guy. It looks like *I'm* the one who has to do something about this."

It was Christmas morning, so I didn't really want to bother anyone at home. It had to wait until the next day. Until then, I had a lot to think about. Where had the baby come from? How would we find out? How would we get her back to her family? *What if we couldn't?*

Janice snuggled with the baby all that day and all through the night sleeping by her side on the couch. No baby had ever been loved and cherished as much as that little thing. The next morning, while the kids were still asleep, she and I talked about it.

"Janice, we *can't* keep the baby. You know that."

"I was thinking I should call the sheriff. He might know where to start."

"And Doctor Goldberg. We can have him come over and make sure the baby is healthy." She clutched the infant more tightly in her arms.

"Thank you, Janice," I said, standing up. "I know this is hard for you, but we've got to do the right thing—for the baby's sake."

I called Sheriff Ernie and Doctor Goldberg. They arrived in less than an hour. By then, the kids were up and having breakfast in the kitchen. Sarah had some pretty strong opinions about "giving away her sister," and Ruth insisted on standing nearby while the doctor checked the baby. His opinion was frank and to the point.

"I'm not telling you anything you haven't already figured out. The baby has thick black hair and bright blue eyes. She has ruddy skin and a broad nose, but otherwise very fine and delicate features. One of the parents is probably white. The other parent is certainly Indian.

"But she's healthy," he pronounced, "and a pretty little thing, too, in spite of the circumstances. You know what we're dealing with here, don't you, Reverend?"

"I'm pretty sure I do," I answered warily. "The only question is what tribe. Who's the father? Who's the mother?"

"Probably the Hopontops," Sheriff Burton Ernie suggested.

"The who?"

"The Hopontops. Our Indian neighbors just over the river. We can go talk to them, but I'm not sure they'll talk to us. They pretty much keep their business to themselves."

"Still, we've got to *try*. You'll go on over with me, won't you, Burton?"

"'Course I will. But the Hopontops . . . as I said, this isn't going to be easy."

"No. It won't be easy for *anyone*," I agreed, glancing at Janice.

Just then the phone rang, and I went to answer it. "Janice, come over here." I spent a furtive five minutes on the phone, after which Janice and I huddled for a few more minutes in anxious discussion. The kids wanted to know what it was all about—they could tell it had something to do with the baby—but I didn't want to talk about it, not right at the moment.

After I hung up the phone, I said, "Burton, can we go see the Hopontops *now*? I don't want to wait, especially after what I just found out."

"Sure 'nough, Arthur. Let's go."

Janice and I thanked and said good-bye to Dr. Goldberg, and then Burton and I prepared to leave. Jonny insisted on coming with us, but I put my hand on his shoulder to stop him. "Not this time, Jon. This is pretty serious. You stay here."

He frowned. "I'm *thirteen*, Dad. I'm not a little kid anymore."

"I didn't say you were. It's just, I don't have the time . . . I mean, I've got to take care of this right away, without . . ."

"What? Without me getting in the way? My teachers don't think that—other grownups don't say that! There's this one man I know . . . *he* doesn't think I'm in the way . . . *he* trusts me . . . he—"

I interrupted him. "What do you mean, 'this one man I know'? Exactly *who* are we talking about? What man?"

Jonny clammed up and stared at me bitterly. "Doesn't matter who he is. I guess I'll just stay home and *baby-sit*." He stomped off into the other room.

Janice came over to me, cradling the baby in one arm and holding out my new coat (I never found the missing one). She leaned in and whispered in my ear, "Arthur, take your son."

"But Janice . . ."

"*Now.* Call him over. Please. This is too important to leave him out."

"Okay, okay," I agreed reluctantly. Who was running this house, anyway? "Jon! Put on your boots and a heavy coat. Get your gloves too. It's freezing outside."

Once Jonny was dressed, the two of us headed out the door and followed Burton down the snowy sidewalk. His police cruiser was parked out front. I climbed into the passenger seat, and Jonny bundled into the back. Burton pulled away from the curb and headed east out of town and across the Hoponover Bridge.

"We'll go talk to Chief Knife Thrower," Burton said. "If anyone knows who the father of the baby is, it'll probably be him." As we drove out to the reservation, Burton filled us in on the Hopontop Indians.

"About a hundred fifty years ago, there weren't many white men; this was strictly Indian territory. You had the Salish, Chinookan, Klikitat, Cayuse, Nez Perce, Umatilla, and the Hopontops. Their villages and camps covered the hills and the plains like they had for hundreds of years. They raised crops; they hunted buffalo; they fished the rivers; they raised their families. This was their home.

"It wasn't all peace and harmony, though. The tribes fought sometimes. They wanted control over the best hunting grounds, the most abundant rivers, and the most fertile fields. Mostly they kept to themselves, but every now and then a skirmish would break out. They'd hold a war council, beat the drums, and shoot some arrows. Sooner or later they'd work out a compromise."

"What kind of compromise?" Jonny asked, fascinated by Burton's story.

"Well, you see, the tribes 'round here could be pretty fierce if they had to be—except for the Hopontops. They didn't want no part of it. Year'd go by all peaceful and quiet, and then all of a sudden something would flare up and the Hopontops would find themselves smack-dab in the middle of it. They just wanted to trade with the other tribes and otherwise keep to themselves. So they came up with an idea.

"Turns out a lot of 'em had an amazing talent for acrobatics. They were also pretty good with horse tricks, things like that. The other tribes around here heard about it, and pretty soon, groups would show up just to watch them do flips and handstands. Word spread, and pretty soon they started scheduling performances every full moon. Worked like a charm. It kept the other tribes settled down, and it kept the Hopontops out of the fighting, since nobody wanted to hurt the performers."

I looked at Burton. "You're making this up, right? You're telling me that the Hopontops are circus Indians? *Circus* Indians? Are you serious?"

"No fooling, Reverend Button. *Everybody* knows about the Hopontops! I'm surprised you never heard of 'em."

"Apparently I haven't heard about a lot of things," I muttered.

"Well, listen to this. The Hopontops have a two-hour show including bronco riding, tricks on horseback, tomahawk throwing, blindfolded archery, tumblers, rope tricks, and that whole death-defying trapeze lake-of-fire thing they do. It's really something."

Jonny piped up when he heard that. "Lake of fire? What's that?"

"They call it the Flaming Dive of Death. One of the braves climbs up on a rope, flies into the air, does a triple somersault, and lands in a flaming pit of water. Most amazing thing you've ever seen."

"Wow! You ever see it?"

"Yep. I've been watching 'em since I was knee-high to a grasshopper. Everybody loves 'em! In fact, back in 1911, the president of the United States himself made a detour just to come by and see their show."

"The president?"

"Sure 'nough! Stopped right here in Boomtown! President William H. Taft rode the Great Northern Railway over from Seattle. It was in May, right before the Hopontops went on tour. They put on a command performance just for him and his cabinet. That was just about the time they were perfecting the Flaming Dive of Death trick. President Taft's photographer took pictures with Chief Back Flip. They're on display at the Boomtown Museum. Hey, speaking of that, Arthur, you been over there yet?"

"Where?"

"The Boomtown Museum! You gotta take a tour. It's open every Saturday and every afternoon and evening during the week."

"Sure thing, Burton," I answered. "It's right on the top of my list, first thing after I take care of this baby business. No problem."

We turned left off the main highway and went down a dirt road heading west. We drove for another couple of minutes while Sheriff Ernie talked nonstop about the Hopontops, some of the shows he'd seen, their newest tricks, the mountain lion taming act, and so on. He was hoping we could see them practice while we were there.

As we bounced along the unpaved road, I tried to reconcile what Burton was telling me about the Hopontops with my preconceived ideas about Indians. I couldn't stop thinking about what I'd seen in books and pictures and movies. You know what I mean—shirtless braves on horse-back shooting arrows at buffalo, doing rain dances around bonfires, wearing feathers and war paint, raising their right hand and saying "How" all the time. Like most kids, I grew up playing Cowboys and Indians. Like most adults, I'd never met a real one.

So I didn't know what to expect when we crested a hill, passed a stand of cottonwoods, and looked down upon a snow-laced valley. What I saw was a huge circus tent surrounded by smaller tents and a staging area with brightly painted trucks and wagons. Beyond that was a neat encampment of teepees, each with a curl of smoke climbing into the clear, frosty sky. In the center was a longhouse built out of logs and roofed with bark shingles. I could see corrals with horses and sheep and cattle and sturdy barns filled with hay and oats. Behind that were rectangles of farmland sleeping under a carpet of snow. Down to my left were Hopontop children building a snow fort and having a snowball fight in one of the fields.

"Pretty as a picture, isn't it?" Burton said as I nodded in agreement. We drove down the hill and into the center of the village, past the main tent on our left, and parked in front of the longhouse.

Burton hopped out and whispered, "Hey, Jonny, before we hunt down the chief, why don't we take a peek inside the Big Top?"

Before I could object, Burton was jogging across the road and poking his head through a flap in the tent. Jonny was at his shoulder. They waved me over.

"Looky here. We can slip in and watch for a few minutes. Some of the Hopontops are practicing right now."

"Burton, that's not why we're here," I reminded him.

"Come on, Arthur; have some *fun!*" Burton said, his eager expression looking very much like my own thirteen-year-old son's. Jonny and Burton disappeared inside. What now? I pulled open the flap, climbed the wooden bleachers, and took a seat next to them.

The main tent must have been more than a hundred feet tall, with three sections supported by massive poles. Each pole was carved with intricate Indian pictures. Up above were ropes and rigging and nets for the high-wire acts and small platforms at the tops of each pole. These had rope ladders hanging down for climbing. The canvas walls were painted with elaborate scenes in traditional native colors depicting Hopontops performing some of their more famous acts. There was a painting of Dark Cloud the Magician and another showing the Flaming Dive of Death.

Around the edges were wooden bleachers, ten rows high, lining both sides of the long tent that was open at both ends so circus acts could enter and exit and where equipment could be moved in and out. The dirt floor and the three rings were covered in fresh sawdust. Its pungent pine scent made my nose itch.

"Look at that, Dad! In the center ring!"

Jonny was pointing at the trick-rider/sharpshooter going through his routine. His horse was tethered to a *longe* (a guide rope) that was held firmly by an assistant who guided the beautifully colored and costumed palomino round and round in a circle. The sharpshooter stood straight up on the horse while he shot stationary targets set up inside the center of each outer ring. *Bang! Bang! Bang!* He broke dinner plates and apples and clay birds and balloons without missing a single shot.

"That's amazing!" I exclaimed to Burton.

"That's Eye of the Eagle, their most famous sharpshooter," he answered. "But you ain't seen nothin' yet."

Eye of the Eagle did a backflip off his horse while shooting his final target. Then four assistants ran into the ring and started throwing Hen Grenades high into the air. *Bang! BOOM! Bang! BOOM!* One right after another, without missing one; the air was filled with the resounding echo of exploding Hen Grenades while fluffy, white scrambled eggs rained down on the floor.

The three of us applauded. "That was super!" Jonny yelled. "We saw the Ringling Circus once, but they didn't have anybody as good as him! What's next?"

As an answer, the tent flap swung open and in galloped ten horses and their whooping riders. They were dressed in full Indian regalia, traditional feather headdresses of eagles and hawks and mountain lions, fringed buckskin pants, beaded moccasins, and leather necklaces and wristbands with bells on their belts and reins of the horses. Next came four more horses pulling a heavy platform. It had eight wheels to support the weight of a large metal tub, three feet deep and eight feet across, filled to the brim with water. The horses strained against the heavy load as they pulled it to the center ring.

"We're in luck. They're going to practice the Flaming Dive of Death!" Burton announced.

"Woohoo!" Jonny couldn't contain his excitement.

The riders dismounted and seized two large ropes that hung from the poles supporting the canopy overhead. The ropes passed through a series of pulleys that were connected to another rope that stretched from pole to pole over the center ring high in the air above our heads. Suspended from the center was a third rope to hold the Fire Diver when he appeared.

"There he is!"

The diver entered to the sound of pounding drums, standing astride a black mustang galloping full speed. He had feathers along his arms and down his back and was wearing an eagle headdress with a curved wooden beak and glass eyes. He thundered into the ring, leaped from his horse, and grabbed the hanging rope. He soared up and out in a high arching circle, arms spread and feathers flapping. By taking turns pulling on the ropes, the assistants made the feathered Indian fly higher and higher, faster and farther, while the circle got wider with every pass.

An archer at the far end shot a burning arrow into the pool and the surface of the water burst into flame. With a final yank on the ropes, the soaring Indian swung directly over the pool of burning water, back and forth until the third pass. The drums silenced; the yelling stopped; the flying Indian released the rope from his harness. Arms outstretched in a swan dive, followed by one, two, three, four somersaults, the diver plunged headfirst into the tub and disappeared in a flash of smoke, water, and flames. The splash extinguished the fire, and a masking cloud of steam rose up from the dark pool. He was gone!

"What happened? Sheriff Burton? Where'd he go?"

Burton didn't answer. Instead, the black mustang suddenly reappeared and trotted across the tent and into the center ring with the Fire Diver sitting on its back! Neat trick! How did he get from the pool onto a horse? How did he get from inside the tent to the outside? How did he dry off so fast? We clapped our hands, whistled loudly, and stomped our feet in appreciation.

"That was absolutely amazing," I said. "How'd they do that?"

Burton just smiled and shrugged. "You got me. I've seen it twenty times, and I still can't figure it out."

We noticed a man break from the performing group and walk across the sawdust until he stood at the foot of the bleachers where we were sitting.

"Hello, Sheriff Ernie. It's been a while since you visited."

"I came out with the family for your end-of-the-season show in August. You were fantastic as always, Flaming Arrow."

"Thank you," the man said, bowing his head slightly. "What brings you out today?"

"We need to talk to the chief," Burton said. "You probably know why."

Flaming Arrow nodded. "I do. Chief Knife Thrower is across the road at the longhouse. He's holding tribal council today with the other tribal elders. You actually chose a good time to come. I don't know if he'll talk to you, though—not in public, in any case. Good luck." He turned and left the tent.

"Tribal council?" I asked after he was gone.

"Sure. Chief Knife Thrower and his leaders sit down twice a month and deal with Hopontop business. It's an ancient system, as old as the tribe itself. Anyone who wants can come and present a grievance, argue a case, announce a marriage, that sort of thing. The council hears them out, offers advice, passes judgment. After council is over, they have a community dinner, dancing, story-telling, and some friendly competitions—archery, wrestling, horse races, that sort of thing."

"Sounds interesting. Like Flaming Arrow."

"What do you mean?"

"His English was flawless. I don't mean to sound stupid, but I wasn't expecting that. I wasn't expecting *any* of this."

"Oh, I see what you mean. You thought they were ignorant savages?"

I didn't have a good answer.

"Let me help you out. Take Flaming Arrow, for example. He graduated from the University of Washington with a degree in civil engineering. He is in charge of the design and construction of the tents and staging; he directs the transportation, safety, and security; he's also pretty good with a bow and arrow. When he's not busy with the circus, he teaches math and science in the Hopontop school. But that's nothing unusual. Everyone around here knows what's up."

"Except maybe for me," I admitted.

Burton smiled. "Maybe. But you're starting to catch on."

We were out of the tent and crossing the muddy road on our way to the longhouse. Burton explained as we walked, "Over the years, a lot of tribes were almost wiped out, but not the Hopontops. They held on to their language, told their stories, and danced their dances. Sure, they've learned the knowledge of the new world, but they also held on to their traditions. What you see here is the result of hard work and determination. This is *their* land and *their* life on *their* terms."

"I'm impressed. I really am."

The three of us crossed the road and ducked our heads to enter the center door of the longhouse. We joined a short line of people waiting to see the council. Two older gentlemen stared, but mostly everyone ignored us. A few others slipped in behind us and waited patiently for their hearing. The dim building was lit by a low fire that burned in the center of the enclosure and three slits for windows along the south wall. The smoke drifted up and out through a hole in the ceiling. Blankets covered the floor and hung from the walls, muffling the voices of the council as they deliberated.

When it was our turn, the tribal scribe recorded our names in his register and presented us to the council. No one spoke. No one moved. Not until the chief nodded to the other men. Without a word they stood up, walked to the door, and took everyone else with them. Soon the room was entirely empty except for the chief. He pointed, inviting Burton, Jonny, and me to take a seat on the floor opposite from him. We did and waited for him to speak.

Chief Knife Thrower was nearly eighty years old, at my best guess. His face was lined with a dry riverbed of wrinkles. He had dark, intelligent eyes that glittered with insight. He wore a brightly decorated blanket around his shoulders, an intricately beaded breastplate on his chest, and he held a feathered arrow in his right hand, the symbol of his office. His wise face was a stoic mask until he finally broke the silence.

"I know why you are here," he said in a clear, deep voice. "You have seen the baby."

"Yes," I answered. "On my doorstep yesterday morning."

"She is well?"

"Yes. Quite well. The doctor has been to see her. My wife is caring for her."

"That is good."

"Of course, we were wondering about the *parents*." I hesitated, waiting for a sign from the chief. "You seem to know about it."

"I do."

"I'm assuming one of the parents was Indian? Hopontop, perhaps?"

"Yes. The father is Hopontop, one of our tribe. The mother is white."

"So I've learned," I explained, telling the chief and Burton and Jonny about the phone call I'd received. It was from Reverend Platz; it seemed that the parents of the mother were members of his congregation, but they wanted to remain anonymous.

"And what were you told?" the chief asked.

"The mother of the baby was heartbroken. She talked it over with her parents, and they decided it would be best for the baby to be placed for adoption. But leaving the baby on my doorstep, that wasn't exactly part of the plan; and the mother suddenly leaving town to stay with family in another state—that was a surprise too. Still, Reverend Platz wanted me to know that the grandparents were happy to have the baby end up with us. Except I don't know what to do next."

"Do? What is there to do?" the chief asked.

"There's the father to think about. You said he was a Hopontop. Can I speak to him?"

"No."

I wasn't expecting such an abrupt response. "No? What about the baby? The father probably has something to say about it."

"The father has left. He is gone and will not return."

"What? Why?"

"Like the mother of the baby, he thought it was best—and I agreed. Both of them were sorry for what happened; they knew they were not ready to be parents. And they thought that leaving would give the baby the best chance at being in a new family."

The two teenage parents were willing to make a difficult sacrifice in order to correct a serious mistake. I've always believed that people who give their children up for adoption are heroes. It was noble of them; they were to be commended. But it still wasn't exactly what I was hoping to hear. What was I supposed to do with a baby?

"Don't you think we should try and *do* something?" I persisted.

Chief Knife Thrower frowned. "Why must you *do* something? The white man *always* wants to do something. Always anxious. Has to *fix* everything."

"What are you suggesting? Do *nothing*?"

Chief Knife Thrower didn't answer, not right away. He thought for a moment and when he answered, it seemed like he was changing the subject. "You are the new minister in Boomtown."

"Yes. I've been here for about four months."

"You have been told about the history of our people?"

"A little. Sheriff Burton filled me in on the way here."

"That is all? You do not know enough. How could you possibly understand after a ten-minute car ride?"

"Explain it to me so I *can* understand."

The chief frowned and closed his eyes. We waited.

"We could adopt the baby ourselves, but that is not as easy as it sounds. I have a duty to preserve the heritage of my people—we have had to fight for it for hundreds of years—mostly against our white neighbors. So, it would be difficult for her, I think, if she were to remain here. It is better that she be raised among her mother's people."

I tried to consider his position. "I think I see your point."

"Do you? Before the settlers came, we lived under the sun. We died under the moon. We preserved our ways. But then the land was taken. The forests were taken. The rivers were taken. Our freedom was taken. But still we have honor. It cannot be taken from us unless we give it away. Can you understand *that*?"

I didn't know what to say. There was nothing I *could* say. He was trying to be fair. He was trying to help his tribe. He was trying to help the baby and the birth parents. Under the circumstances, he was probably right.

The chief asked, "When you found the baby, did you find anything else?"

"A note."

"What did it say?"

"No names. Just, 'Take her as your own.'"

"That is what I think you should do."

Chief Knife Thrower crossed his arms, bowed his head, and refused to say anymore. The audience had ended as abruptly as it had started.

We stood up and went out the door. Those waiting outside watched silently as we climbed into the car, turned around, and drove out of the village. Burton didn't say a word on the drive home. Jonny didn't say anything either. Both of them let me sit and think. I stared out the window and watched the snow-covered trees go by. I looked up into the steel gray sky and prayed. I waved good-bye when Burton dropped us at our front door. Jonny and I went inside.

Janice was in the living room waiting for us. The baby was asleep in her arms, snuggled in a thick blanket. The room was warm and dimly lit in the waning light of the winter afternoon. There was Christmas music playing on the radio, and I could hear Sarah and Jonny whispering in the other room as he told her what had happened. Ruth hovered nearby, waiting for the verdict.

Janice smiled nervously and asked, "So what did you find out?"

She rocked the baby gently, waiting for my answer. I could see redness in her eyes. She had been crying. She was afraid I'd found the father, afraid he'd changed his mind, afraid she'd have to let go of the baby—a baby who had only been in our home for one day but was now in her heart forever. She was afraid I'd tell her to get in the car, afraid of what would happen when we got there. Looking at my wife clutching the baby, that's when I finally understood.

"I found out what happens when you have to make a hard choice because of a difficult situation. The father of the baby, he had to make a choice. The mother and her parents, they had to make a choice. The chief had to choose between *one* of his people versus *all* of his people. And you and I, we have to make a choice too."

Janice held her breath and waited for me to finish.

"I learned something new today. I learned that when you've made a wrong choice, the best way to redeem it is to make a *right* choice."

"And what *is* the right choice?" she asked, almost whispering.

I smiled and said, "I suppose if she's going to stay, you have to pick a good name."

Janice gasped. "You mean it? *Thank you!* Thank you, honey!" She kissed the baby's forehead. "You won't regret this, I promise." Then she kissed me.

Ruth began to cry and I heard Sarah hollering from the other room, "I knew it! I knew it! She gets to stay!" She came running into the living room to celebrate with us. Jonny came in behind her, and even *he* was excited about the baby—even if she wasn't a boy.

Janice said, "I've already picked out a name. I've been thinking about it ever since we saw her on the porch."

"What is it?" we all asked her.

"I want to name her Holly, because her skin is such a pretty red like a holly berry. It will remind us that she came on Christmas. What do you think?"

"It goes perfect with her Hopontop name," I answered. "Before I left, the chief told me they called her Snowbird. He said it was because she flew into our lives in winter."

Janice laughed and wiped at her tears. "Holly Snowbird. I absolutely love it. I don't think I've ever been this happy."

And you know what? To be perfectly honest, neither had I.

CHAPTER 9

The Boomtown Museum

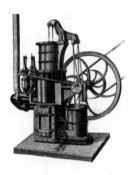

Holly settled into our family like she'd always been there. She was happy, healthy, and loved, not only by our family but by everyone who met her. The church members were delighted. The old women clucked and cooed over the baby. They held a baby shower and sewed little dresses and offered to baby-sit. It's true that some were uncomfortable with Holly's mixed heritage, but for the most part, everyone was gracious and kind.

Once a month the circuit judge, Maria Rodriguez, would come into town. She'd hold court at town hall and hear any cases pertaining to Boomtown; usually there wasn't much for her to do. During this particular visit, she met in closed session with the mayor and Sheriff Ernie to review the progress of the investigation into the mysterious robberies. This was followed by a second closed session with Holly's grandparents—and the baby's mother, who had returned to Boomtown to complete the adoption.

We sat nervously in another part of the building waiting for the news. After about a hour (it seemed more like ten), the judge called us into her chambers. Janice and the three kids heaved a huge sigh of relief when we were told that the mother had not changed her mind; rather, she had wished us well and was happy that her daughter would be raised by a loving family. Many of our friends were there to witness the signing of the papers, and afterward we held a huge celebration party at the Nuthouse restaurant. It was one of those perfect, amazing, life-changing days I will never forget.

A week after the adoption ceremony, we decided to have our first official family outing. It was Saturday, so we took Sheriff Ernie's advice and headed to the Boomtown Museum. Burton had told us all about the museum—actually a mansion that had been *converted* into a museum. It was the largest single residence in Boomtown, located on the east side of town, situated on eighty sprawling acres nestled against the Okanogan River, with gardens, walking trails, workshops, and the Boomtown Power Plant and Water Pumping Station.

It was a three-story Victorian home with twenty rooms, four elevators, a conservatory, a great room, a basement, and a number of sub-basement levels where the inner workings of the house and the exhibits were stored.

Beyond its Victorian facade, however, all resemblance to a "normal" house ended. It had been the property of Dr. Mfana Losotu, the famous South African inventor, philanthropist, musician, archeologist, linguist, business-man, author, and teacher. Dr. Losotu was as well known for his generosity as he was for his inventions. He had also been a close personal friend of Chang. They had collabo-rated on a variety of projects—most that worked, a few that hadn't. He'd been a minority owner of the powder factory and Chang's partner in a number of business interests.

When Dr. Losotu died in 1929, he bequeathed his home, its contents, the land, and a portion of the estate as a perpet-ual endowment to maintain the home as a museum. Burton told us that ever since its foundation, the children and grand-children of Dr. Losotu had managed the property.

When our family came to the door, we were greeted by a stunningly beautiful black woman dressed in the traditional garb of her homeland: a purple turban, an ochre shawl, a bright red skirt, an elaborately beaded *gorget* around her neck, copper arm bands, and woven grass and bead anklets on her bare feet. She bowed deeply as we entered and intro-duced herself as Samora Losotu, the great-granddaughter of Dr. Losotu.

"You're so beautiful!" Sarah said.

"Thank you. So are you," she said graciously.

"I'm Sarah, and this is my baby sister, Holly. I'm ten years old. That makes me the *big* sister."

"Yes, it certainly does," Samora said, with a gentle laugh. "I'm sure you're a very good big sister. And who are these others?"

"This is my mom and dad, and this is Ruth and Jonny."

"Pleased to meet all of you." Samora shook hands all around. "And now let me introduce you to my great-grandfather." She gestured to a large painting of the inventor with a brief printed history of his life and career hanging next to it.

We studied the painting for a moment, and then Janice commented, "It says here that your great-grandfather was a member of the Xhosa tribe from the western cape of South Africa. How did he get from Africa all the way here to Boomtown?"

She smiled and answered in a soft voice, tinged with a distinctive South African accent. "He didn't precisely *come* so much as he was *taken*," she said. "In 1854, he was captured by raiders and sold into slavery. He was only fifteen at the time."

"That's terrible!"

"Yes," she agreed. "Separated from his family and home, he survived the voyage to America—many of the people who were taken did not. He landed in Virginia and from there was sold to a plantation owner just outside of Atlanta. For nine years he worked as a slave in the fields until the owner and his sons left to fight in the Battle of Gettysburg. Mfana decided to escape and make his way north. He was helped along the way by none other than Harriet Tubman herself, who guided him to a safe house of Thomas Garrett in Wilmington, Delaware. He lived there secretly for six weeks."

"We learned about the Underground Railroad in school," Sarah said.

"That's good. If it weren't for Harriet Tubman and Thomas Garrett, my great-grandfather might not have survived. As it was, Mr. Garrett soon learned of Mfana's nimble mind. He taught him how to read and write. Into the wee hours of the night, he studied and prepared himself for the next stage of his escape. Arrangements were made to send him west. While he traveled by train, wagon, or on foot he continued to *read*. He read anything he could lay his hands on. Do you like to read?"

"It's my favorite thing to do," Sarah said. "I love books."

"Excellent! Reading is what you need to do. Then you could grow up to be like Mfana. Because he was so smart, he was able to work his way across the country. With each new job, he mastered new skills. He was an apprentice to a blacksmith, carpenter, wheelwright, cobbler, liveryman, farrier, miller, and so on. He learned about astronomy, philosophy, religion, government, history, finance, metallurgy, geology, chemistry, and mechanics.

"By the time he was forty-two, he'd reached the West Coast and San Francisco. That's where he met my great-grandmother, Nthati. Just like Mfana, she was an escaped slave from South Africa. Isn't that amazing? Two people from the same place meeting on the opposite side of the world! They were soon married and later gave birth to my grandfather; his name is Mendi. But Mfana was restless; he didn't want to stay in San Francisco. He had big ideas. He had a dream!"

Sarah's eyes were as big as full moons. "I have dreams all the time. Did he dream about unicorns? I'm always dreaming about unicorns. And ice cream."

Samora knelt down so she could look Sarah in the eye. "Do you like inventions? Fantastic machines? Unbelievable discoveries? That sort of thing?"

"I do!" Sarah answered enthusiastically.

"Then you would have liked my great-grandfather. When he was working for a blacksmith, he plunged a bar of super-heated metal into a bucket of water and watched the steam rise from the bubbling surface. It made him think about riding the steam locomotive on his journey west. He wondered, was there a way to generate an uninterrupted source of steam power? He could put the steam under pressure, hook it to a steam motor, and hook that to shafts and gears and wheels. All he needed was steam, lots and lots of steam."

"So what'd he do?" Now it was Jonny asking the questions.

"Mfana needed a volcanic region of the country, a place where he could tap into geothermal energy. That place was Washington.

"He arrived here in 1882 and traveled all over looking for the right spot. Boomtown was perfect. It was still called Change at the time; that was when Chang was still alive. They became fast friends, and together they created the wonderful inventions you'll see here in the museum. With the money he made through their patented successes, Mfana built this house. He built his dream."

"It's absolutely amazing!" Janice said. "We can't wait to see what he's done."

"Then let's get started. But maybe you're cold after being outside in the snow? Maybe you'd like some hot chocolate, children? And some coffee for your mom and dad?"

Sarah grabbed Samora's hand. "What are we waiting for?"

We followed Samora from the main entrance, down the hall to the right, and into the kitchen. And what a kitchen it was! Every surface gleamed in bright stainless steel. Overhead lamps illuminated the windowless room with incandescent light. A counter with a conveyer belt wrapped around all four walls; it surrounded a large U-shaped cooking area in the middle of the room.

Just to the left of the double-swinging doors stood a console with various actuator knobs, each of them labeled with the name of their corresponding function. The top row said: LIGHTS, HEAT, WASH, DRY, VACUUM, DISPOSE, LIFT. The second row (breakfast) said: TOAST, EGGS, BACON, SAUSAGE, JUICE, COFFEE, and COCOA. The third row (lunch) said: SOUP, SANDWICH, SALAD, CASSEROLE, FRUIT, LEMONADE, and TEA. The fourth row (dinner) said: STEAK, CHICKEN, FISH, BREAD, VEGETABLE, and DESSERT.

Samora said to Sarah, "Go ahead. Pull the lever that says COCOA three times and the one that says COFFEE twice."

She pulled each of them, and we watched as a small door in the wall across the kitchen opened and three mugs slid out onto the conveyer belt. Right behind them came two coffee cups and saucers. The conveyer carried them along the counter where each of them stopped long enough for hot steaming cocoa and coffee to pour out of spigots that hung over the conveyer belt.

"Cream and sugar?"

"Yes, please."

"Whipped cream?"

"Yes! Lots of it!"

Samora reached over and activated two smaller knobs in

rows along the bottom. Their labels read: CREAM, SUGAR, BUTTER, HOT, COLD, DRESSING, RARE, MEDIUM, WELL-DONE, SALMON, TROUT, RED, WHITE, and so on. I surmised they were modifiers to customize whatever a person might order. We watched as the mugs received a shot of whipped cream while our coffee cups stopped for a squirt of cream and a teaspoon of sugar supplied by dispenser tubes. A small whisk extended from its housing to stir the coffee. Then the cups finished their journey down the conveyor belt and stopped right in front of us. Samora explained the operation of the amazing, self-propelled kitchen while we sipped on our hot drinks.

"You're probably wondering what drives the belts and doors and ovens and other apparatus in this room. It is the same power that drives the entire house: geothermal energy. My great-grandfather's dream is built into the floors and walls and outbuildings. As soon as you are finished, I'll show you the power source."

We finished quickly and placed our cups on the conveyor. Sarah was allowed to pull the WASH actuator, and the dishes disappeared behind another door in the wall. Then it was Jonny's turn. He pulled the LIFT knob and we jumped in surprise. The floor section we were standing on gave a quick lurch and began to slide downward with a loud hissing sound.

"It's all right," our guide said. "I should have warned you. It's a little startling at first."

The hissing noise continued as we headed down. The floor above our heads slid shut while lights in the wall flickered on to illuminate our descent. We passed by several dimly lit openings marked with signs that said LEVEL A, LEVEL B, and so on.

"We won't be stopping at any of the sublevels where the various exhibits are kept and maintained. We're going down to the lowest level, where the power generation system is located."

A few moments later, the elevator stopped to reveal a most amazing sight. As far as our eyes could see, shiny, chrome pipes grew from the floor, up through the ceiling, and into the house above. The maze of pipes surrounded a larger central area, where wisps of steam and the hum of machinery could be seen and heard. A pathway between the pipes was clearly marked with painted lines and was secured by safety ropes on both sides.

Samora led us to the main station. With a wave of her hand, she said, "This is where it all happens—my great-grandfather's greatest invention, and the secret behind all the marvelous wonders in the museum."

"What's that big machine?" Jonny asked.

"Those are the turbines that are driven by the geothermal steam coming up from below the earth's surface. My great-grandfather chose this spot because it is here that the hot magma rises close enough to the earth's crust. It enabled him to drill a shaft deep enough to reach the liquid stone. Water is pumped from the river and poured down a shaft where it vaporizes and returns to the surface as steam under pressure. It is forced through these pipes to the turbines. The steam makes the turbines spin, and they produce electricity to run the house. The steam is also used to heat water for sinks and showers. It drives steam-powered motors and hydraulic systems including the elevators, vacuums, and doors—all activated by the levers you'll see in every room. The used steam condenses into water and is pumped back into an injection well and reused. Some of the excess steam is pumped into condensers that provide rain in the conservatory. You'll get to see that later. But for now, do you have any questions?"

"Dr. Losotu invented and built *all* of this?"

"As I said, he was a tremendous reader. He adapted many of the ideas and concepts invented by others and applied them here. He was the first one to tap into the heating power of the earth and turn it to practical use, that's true, but much of what he did depended on the work of others. Leonardo da Vinci was writing about hydraulics as early as the 1400s. James Watt built the rotary motion steam engine back in 1781. Siemens and Gramme invented the first electric generator in 1870. Archimedes, John Whitehurst, Nikola Tesla, Thomas Edison, Elisha Otis, pioneers of motion and energy, steam, and electricity—all of them were heroes to my great-grandfather. Personally, I think they would have been proud of what he accomplished using some of their ideas."

We spent a few more minutes looking around, but it was uncomfortably warm and sticky down in the "power farm," as Samora called it. We started looking for the exit.

"Over here," she said. "The children are going to enjoy this. I certainly did when I was their age."

She led us over to a niche in the wall where there was an

elevator. It had upholstered seats around three of the four sides with seatbelts and shiny brass handholds. The polished wooden walls had elegant, beveled windows in them, and so did the two doors. The floor was covered with thick, red carpet.

"Get in," she said, "and make sure you use the shoulder and lap belts. It's quite a ride, let me warn you! Make sure you hold tight to the baby."

"I'll just use the stairs if that's all right with you," I said, eyeing the elevator nervously.

"Oh, come on, Mr. Button," said my wife. "Don't be an old poop."

I stepped into the velvet-lined box like it was a coffin. I strapped on my belt and counted the buttons on my sweater. Janice double-checked each of the kids and wrapped her arms firmly around Holly.

"Hold on tight!" Samora warned. She reached over and pulled an actuator switch. We heard a hissing blast of steam the instant before we were launched like a rocket—my guess was about thirty feet per second. The walls of the elevator shaft flew past our eyes. Up through the glass windows of the ceiling, I saw the roof of the house swing open with gray overcast skies overhead. We raced up, up, up, and out into the cold afternoon air, through the roof until we whooshed to a stop about five stories above the house.

"Oh, my goodness!" Janice gasped. To our surprise and relief, baby Holly had slept through the exciting ride.

"Woohoo! Do it again! Do it again!" The kids were thrilled.

"*No!* Please, no," I groaned, turning a little green. My stomach was down in the basement and my head was in my lap. I felt like I'd being thrown through the ceiling like Walter's barber chair. "I'm ready to go back down now—as *slowly* as possible if you don't mind."

"Of course," said our guide. "Nice and slow."

She activated another lever, and with an audible hiss the elevator descended along the telescoping pole it was mounted on. It rotated slightly as it descended, giving us a full view as we slid downward. We could see the spire of our church; we saw the town hall, the fireworks factory, even the smoke rising from the Hopontop reservation over the horizon. Down by the river, past the gardens and apple orchards near the back part of the property, we could see clouds of steam hanging over a windowless, cement building with a spider web of poles sticking out of its roof and wires stretching away from the building toward the main part of town.

"What's that?" I asked, clutching the handrail and pointing toward the strange building.

"That is the Boomtown Geothermal Plant, another one of my grandfather's gifts to the town he loved. It's basically a larger version of the geothermal generator that runs the house. The turbines produce enough electricity to power the entire town—with some to spare. You probably noticed that you don't receive an electric bill at your house?"

"I never thought about it. I guess we don't."

"You won't have an electric bill for the church or anywhere else in town. That's because everyone gets free electricity from the power plant. The Losotu estate pays for any necessary repairs—those are done by my father and brother, who take care of the maintenance for the property. My mother and sister are in charge of the gardens and cleaning, what little there is. They also conduct tours and teach classes. My nephews take care of all the exhibits. It's our family legacy."

Janice said, "It's absolutely wonderful. Free power for everyone?"

"It's even better than that. The power plant is a self-sustaining system. As the steam cools, the water drips down into an underground holding tank where it can be reused. The cloud of steam that hovers over the building mists all the surrounding plants in the gardens. Having abundant electricity means we don't have to cut down trees for fuel or burn oil or coal. It works for everyone without hurting the rivers or forests or the animals that live there."

By the time she finished her explanation, we were passing back through the roof. The clamshell roof panels tilted closed behind us. Samora pulled the STOP lever and the elevator hissed to a halt on the top floor.

"Everyone out!" she said, standing up and swinging the doors open. "Our next stop is a favorite for busy mothers—and children who don't like to do chores."

"That would be *me*," Ruth said.

"And me!"

"And *me*!"

We bundled out of the elevator into the hallway and stopped in front of what appeared to be an ordinary bedroom. Looking through the door we could see a bed, two nightstands mounted on the walls, a chair, a small table, and a wardrobe with a mirror. It was stylishly decorated with heavy curtains over the windows, attractive paintings on the walls, and a crystal chandelier hanging from the ceiling. We could see through a side door into the adjoining bathroom, covered from floor to ceiling with gleaming white tile and chrome. There was a control station just outside in the hallway. There were similar controls for each of the other rooms.

"I know this room doesn't look that special. But Ruth, go ahead and pull one of the levers—anything that looks interesting to you."

Ruth studied the panel and then pulled the actuator marked VACUUM. As soon as she did, the bed, the chair, the table, and the wardrobe slid upward on hydraulic pistons, clearing the entire floor of any obstacles. The baseboard along the right wall popped open and long vacuum heads were pushed across the carpet, dragging hoses behind them. When they reached the far wall, we heard the loud sound of suction come on. The vacuum heads retreated across the floor back into their wall sockets. Within a minute, the entire room was freshly vacuumed and the furniture was lowered back into place.

Janice said, "Oh, I *want* one of those!"

Like most homemakers, Janice hated vacuuming almost as much as she hated washing windows. That's when she saw the WINDOWS knob. When she pulled it, a cloud of hot steam shot onto each of the windows. The top half slid up into the wall and the bottom half went down. When the window closed again, it was clear as crystal.

Janice rubbed her hands together and said, "I want *two* of those."

Samora explained. "There's a rubber blade inside the wall and a drying unit. As the windows go up and down, they're wiped clean and blown dry. In a three-story house, auto-clean windows are a big time saver. No ladders!"

Then Samora turned to Ruth. "Go ahead and pull the BATHROOM lever."

She did, and we watched the door to the bathroom slide shut and heard the blast of steam jets behind the door.

"What's happening in there?"

"The sink, toilet, and bathtub are filling up with super-heated water mixed with disinfectant. Steam jets are filling the entire room with a cloud of hot steam mixed with lemon. That makes everything smell good. Then all the water drains out, and a fan turns on and dries out the room. The entire operation takes about four minutes from start to finish."

Janice was amazed. "A self-cleaning bedroom and bathroom! With a self-cooking kitchen and self-washing dishes. Dr. Losotu thought of everything!"

We heard the sound of a small bell like an egg timer. The door to the bathroom swung open. Every surface sparkled and every fixture gleamed. Clean as a whistle and dry as a bone.

"Over there behind the two small doors in the wall is the chute to the laundry room. The one marked with an H is for hot-water clothes. The other marked C is for cold water. Throw in sheets, pillowcases, shirts, dresses, and under-clothing. They fall down to Basement Level One, where the automatic washers, dryers, and ironing system cleans, dries, and presses your clothes. Open the third door and pull the actuator next to it, and fresh linens are delivered direct to your room."

"Better and better!" exclaimed Janice, glancing in my direction.

"Hey, don't look at me!" I said. "We have to keep doing things the old-fashioned way."

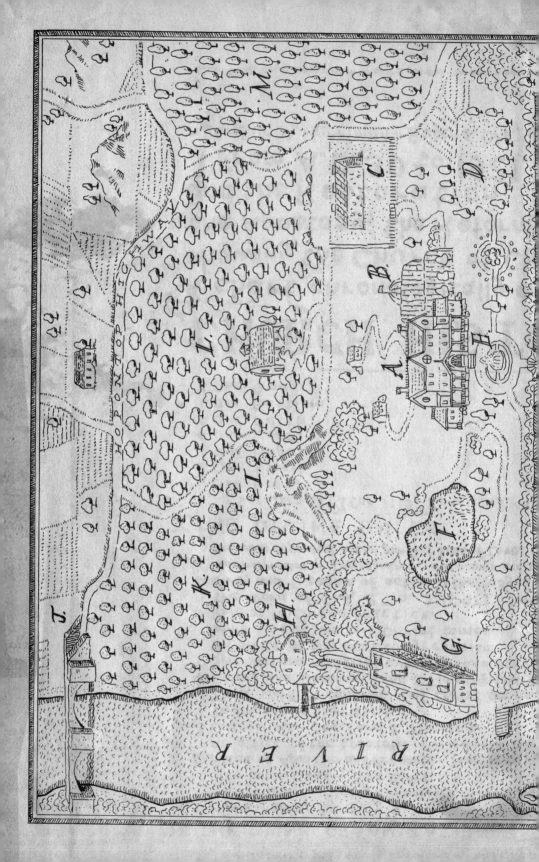

BOOMTOWN MUSEUM

LEGEND

A. Museum
B. Conservatory
C. Nursery
D. Bowling Green
E. Fountain
F. Lily Pond
G. Geothermal Plant
H. Water Pumping Station
I. Telescope Hill
J. Hoponover Bridge
K. Pear Grove
L. Apple Grove
M. Cherry Grove
N. Water Tower

©2005 NOWEN N. PARTICULAR

OKANOGAN

Sarah wanted to stay and clean the room again, but there was still too much to see. We headed back to the elevator. The doors closed, and we descended two more levels to the main floor.

"What next?"

"We have two more things to see," Samora said. "First, the conservatory."

She led us down a hall and around a corner to the back of the house.

"You may want to put on one of those rain slickers hanging on the hooks or grab an umbrella from the stand. It gets pretty wet in here."

We put on the bright yellow coats, and I held an umbrella for Janice and Holly. In front of us were two solid oak doors intricately carved with snakes and lizards and birds and lions and trees. Samora pushed them open and took us into a small lobby. We crowded inside; she closed the first doors and then opened two more.

What we saw on the other side is hard to describe. We were hit with a blast of warm, moist air. Then our senses were assaulted with sights and sounds and smells. It was almost like that scene from *The Wizard of Oz* when Dorothy steps out of her black-and-white world into a full-color tropical paradise. I half-expected to see Munchkins popping up out of the bushes.

The glass roof soared ninety feet over our heads and was big enough to enclose at least an acre. Ahead of us, paths wound their way through the forest of palms, banana plants, lemon trees, limes, oranges, date palms, coconuts, and lychee nut trees. There were mangos, ylang-ylang, plumeria, orchids, and tulips. There were banyan, bamboo, and baobab trees tangled in vines and ferns and flowers and fragrances. Exotic birds nested in the branches. Spider monkeys and lemurs played tag in the trees. Butterflies of every color and description flitted through the air and bees sipped on the nectar of every flower. The temperature was a humid eighty-five degrees, and a steady drip-drip-drip of misty rainwater fell from the ceiling and from every limb and leaf. We could hear the rush of a river from around the bend over the chirping of the parrots and peacocks and finches and flamingos.

"Can we go see, Dad?" asked Jonny.

"Is it okay?" I asked our guide.

She smiled and waved her hand. "Go on. See what you can find. Have fun!"

The three older kids ran off down the path while Janice, Holly, and I took a seat on a nearby bench tucked underneath a canopy of broad palm leaves. Janice retrieved a bottle of formula from her purse and began to feed Holly, who soon fell asleep. I took off my coat and leaned back to enjoy the perfect weather. I could hear the laughter and yells of the kids in the distance.

"How did all of this get here?" I asked Samora.

"Among other things, my great-grandfather was interested in horticulture and zoology," she explained. "His collection started with a small greenhouse with orchids and roses, but his wife, my great-grandmother, missed the flowers from her native land of South Africa. So he had bulbs and cuttings shipped here from the Cape, anything and every-thing she wanted. He built a bigger greenhouse and cultivated agapanthus, antholyza, and belladonna lilies. Then came the Cape Town honeysuckle, gladiolus, grenadilla, and hibiscus, iris, pelargonium, and plumbago. Once he got started, he couldn't stop. He added birds and monkeys and snakes and frogs and fish. The collection became so large he finally had to build this conservatory to hold all the plants and animals."

We sat for a while longer until Samora stood up and said, "Come along. Let's go see what your children have discovered."

Janice cradled Holly while we walked along under the umbrella. We passed through a thick grove of bamboo, and then we could see the large pond with a waterfall cascad-ing down the side of rocks piled high and covered in moss and flowers and vines. The pool was filled with bright fish of every type and description. Up above, on the rocks, we saw Ruth and Sarah laughing and pointing. With a whoop, Jonny flew over our heads and up, out, and over the pond. He was sitting in a chair that was suspended from a cable hooked to the ceiling. It looked a little like one of those swinging chairs at a carnival.

"Look at me! Woohoo!" Jonny yelled as he swung wide over the pond.

"What is he *doing*?" I said, worried.

"Don't worry," Samora assured us. "The entire system is tested and safe. I used to swing on it when I was a girl. Come down the path over here, and we'll go up and see."

The path wandered around to the left, across a small bridge, and up the far side of the rocky cliff. We climbed the steps until we reached a flat, cement platform with guardrails to keep people away from the swing as it came and went. In the middle of the open space was a launcher. It consisted of an open-ended receiving unit that captured the swing by its "tail" and a steel ball on a tether that hung down from the base of the seat. We got there just as Sarah came swinging around. The tethered ball was neatly caught in the receiver.

"You see," said Samora, "the tail has a steel ball on the end that is caught as the swing comes around. As soon as it enters the unit, the brakes are applied and the rider is pulled to a gentle stop. Once it's in the station, the swing is anchored in place. It's all perfectly safe."

We watched as Jonny unhooked the seatbelt and climbed down. Then Ruth took her turn in the swing.

Jonny waited until she was ready. "You pull on this launcher knob and blast her! Watch this, Dad!"

He yanked on the knob. The system retracted a few feet, and with a blast of steam, Ruth and the swing were launched over the pond in a wide arc out and around and back to the platform.

"The system adjusts for the weight of the rider and compensates to bring the swing back to this exact point," Samora explained. "If you look up there at the center point of the roof, you can see where the cable is connected. That's the guidance system. It works every time."

Ruth came swinging onto the platform. "Dad! You've got to try this!"

"Oh, no you don't!" Janice said, handing me the baby. "It's *my* turn!"

I was perfectly content to stand back and watch Janice as she was launched like a rocket over the pond. She screamed and laughed as she circled around and was caught by the launcher.

"Pull it again, Jonny!" and off she went a second time.

They continued to take turns over and over again. They kept urging me to try it—but after all, someone had to hold the baby. Pretty soon, I felt my stomach grumbling. I looked at my watch and realized we'd already been in the museum for more than three hours. Lunch had come and gone. We had been having too much fun to notice.

"Look at the time. The kids are probably starving. We should probably go."

But Samora said, "You can't go yet. You haven't seen the best part—the great room. Please stay. We can have the kitchen make some lunch for us."

"Please, Dad? Please, please, *please*?" Sarah urged.

Janice agreed and we went down the stairs, along the path, out through another set of doors, and into the kitchen. We enjoyed watching our soup and sandwiches travel down the conveyer. Janice and I had iced tea. The kids had lemonade. Holly finished her bottle and fell asleep again.

Then Samora said, "Wait until you see what's next."

CHAPTER 10

The Great Room

From the kitchen, we heard excited voices in the hallway. Since we'd just finished our lunch, we stood up and went out to see. It was a group of about ten children, ages eight to ten years old, carrying instrument cases—violins, cellos, French horns, and so forth. Another graceful woman, almost Samora's twin, led them along the passage.

"My sister, Palesa," Samora said, "taking her class to the music room. My great-grandfather was an accomplished musician—did I mention that? He taught all of his children and grandchildren. We've maintained the tradition and hold regular music classes here in the museum. These children are here to practice for the Spring Fever Festival coming up after the winter thaw. Do any of you play instruments?"

"I can play the flute," Sarah said.

"I play the kazoo," Jonny added.

"I toot a little on the harmonica," I offered.

"That's excellent. You could all play with the Flute Kazoo Harmonica Band in the Fourth of July parade. They're always looking for new people."

After the group moved on, Samora took us down the hall, back through the main entry area, and toward the center of the house. We stopped in front of a large pair of glass doors. The words *Great Room* were etched in careful scrollwork lettering in the glass, surrounded by drawings of prehistoric animals and birds, fossils, hieroglyphs, gears, motors, flying machines, and more.

Samora said, "Through these doors are displayed some of Mfana's greatest inventions—and, to be perfectly honest, some of his worst—along with collections of historical documents, books, city records and archives, photographs, paintings, and drawings. The most unusual is probably the exhibit dedicated to fossils and dinosaurs. And we also have a surprise for the kids."

"A surprise? What is it? Can I see it *now*?" Sarah insisted, pulling on Samora's sleeve.

"If I show it to you now, it won't be a surprise," Samora chuckled. "You'll see, soon enough. Come on inside."

Samora unlocked the door with a silver key and we walked into an empty, windowless room. It was cavernous, as large as a gymnasium and two stories high. The floor was a highly polished oak hardwood. The walls were painted soft beige. Four impressive crystal chandeliers hung from the ceiling. Otherwise, the room was bare from corner to corner.

"There's nothing in here!" Jonny complained.

Samora pointed to a control panel much like the others we'd seen around the house.

"You think so? Four knobs to choose from. Pick whichever you like."

The knobs were labeled DINOSAURS, INVENTIONS, HALL OF RECORDS, and the fourth was blank. There was no discussion. All three reached for the knob that said DINOSAURS.

We gasped when the smooth wooden floor erupted. Like a garden in fast-motion, display cases and exhibit platforms grew up out of the floor. Panels slid open in the walls to reveal maps and photographs and drawings and diagrams. The empty room transformed into a complete museum full of fossils and dinosaur skeletons and ancient pottery and artifacts. There was even a miniature landscape map showing the locations of rivers and mountains and lakes and the sites of various archeological digs.

"The dinosaur exhibit is stored in Basement Level One," Samora explained. "When the actuator is pulled, steam drives the hydraulic lifts and the displays are pushed up into the room. Pull it again and they'll be lowered back down into their designated storage areas. Through a coordinated system of shuffling and positioning, exhibits from each of the four levels can occupy this same space here in the great room. The same goes for the displays in the walls and ceiling."

Dominating the center of the room had to be the strangest-looking dinosaur skeleton I'd ever seen. It stood at least ten feet high and about twenty feet long. It had a long neck and tail, a squat body, and a narrow head full of short, rounded teeth. The strangest thing of all were the three legs—two on the sides and one at the front. The brass plaque on the railing said TRIPODOSAURUS.

"A *tripodosaurus*?" I said. "There's no such thing."

"Of course there is. It's standing right there in front of us."

"That's not what I meant. I mean there's no such thing as a three-legged dinosaur."

"This is the only one ever found, as far as I know. It was Chang who discovered this particular specimen accidentally during one of his mining digs. After he found the skeleton, Chang turned it over to my great-grandfather, and he and his team of paleontologists spent years uncovering what became one of the most important finds in recent history.

"The entire western Washington plain used to be home to millions of ancient creatures, including the tripodosaurus, the only dinosaur on record with three legs."

"But how did it walk?"

"My great-grandfather and his fellow scientists believed

it used its head as a fourth leg. Notice the flat fo[r]
and the long neck. The tripodosaurus would b[e]
down and shuffle forward using its head."

"That's ridiculous!"

"Not ridiculous—just *impractical*. With only th[e]
tripodosaurus couldn't move very fast. It would [be]
natural target for predators. Not too many of t[hem]
have existed. Probably why this is the only one eve[r]

"Is it possible Dr. Losotu made a mistake?
couldn't find the fourth leg when he dug up the [?]

"Don't be silly," was Samora's answer. "Who [?]
of a *four*-legged Tripodosaurus?"

Sarah thought that was very funny. While she la[ughed]
moved along to a glass display case showing vari[ous]
and small animals embedded in blobs of amber. T[here?]
leaves and beetle-like creatures and other fairly
samples, but then we saw something very unusual.

Ruth asked, "What's *that*? It looks like a grasshopp[er]
for the horn sticking out of its head that looks like [a]

"That's another animal you probably won't see [any-]
else. My great-grandfather gave it the Latin nam[e]
orthoptera. In English, it's called the screwhopper. [A per-]
fect name for it, if Mfana was right.

"He believed the screwhopper fed on the wa[ter and]
nutrients found in the stalks of sap-producing p[lants. It]
would hop over to a plant, grab hold of the stalk [with its]
strong front claws and then use its hard, screw [like head to]
gouge a hole in the stalk. Then it would eat the s[ap

oozed through the hole. Of course it's only an educated guess, since this is the only one of its kind ever found."

We stopped to look at the three-dimensional map. It had little stickpin flags showing where some of the more important dinosaurs and fossils had been found. One of the flags was red—that's where the tripodosaurus had been discovered. One of the flags was blue with a yellow star on it.

"What was found there?"

"Come over here and I'll show you." Samora guided us to a glass case that hung on the wall. Inside was the skeleton of what looked like a kite. In the center of the delicate wing structure was the small skeleton that looked almost batlike in its appearance. Next to this was an artist's conceptual drawing of what the "bird" might have looked like. The stretched skin of the wings looked like a dragon's. When they were fully extended, the creature looked like a kite made out of greenish-gray leather.

"This is the *milvus vespertilionid*, or, in English, the batkite. The only three complete skeletons found in the entire world are owned by this museum. The other two are on loan to the Harvard Museum of Natural History and the University of Oslo in Norway.

Sarah said, "It looks just like a kite—without the string."

"That's right. When the wings are folded in, the batkite looks like a closed umbrella, with its small body at the top and the wings extended down toward the back. But in a strong wind, the batkite would rotate its 'arms' forward. The wind would snatch it up into the air like a kite. It sailed back

and forth and caught flying insects for food. When the wind stopped blowing, it would land on the ground or in a tree."

After we finished looking at the dinosaur exhibit, Jonny was allowed to pull the INVENTIONS knob. The displays and cabinets descended into the floor and disappeared into the walls only to be replaced with more displays and cabinets. With a whir and a hum and hiss, we watched the inventions exhibit ascend into place. This time some of the ceiling panels retracted, and several flying machines dropped into the room from above.

Samora pointed up. "You know that the Wright Brothers accomplished the first manned flight on December 17, 1903, at Kitty Hawk. That was more than forty years ago. What few people know is that my great-grandfather was experimenting with flight here in Boomtown as early as 1895. He wasn't quite as successful as the Wrights."

"That one looks like a bathtub with wings," Jonny said, looking up.

"It *is* a bathtub—the wooden one from the old bathhouse here on the property. My great-grandfather added the wood and canvas wings. He mounted a seat inside the bathtub and then installed the gears and pedals from a bicycle and put tires on the side so it would roll. When he was finished, he built a launching ramp and drove it over the side of Rocket Ridge. His wife found him at the bottom of the cliff crashed into the top of a tree. It took four months for his broken leg and arm to heal. She was so upset that she didn't talk to him for a month.

"That didn't stop him, though. He tried a few more designs, but none of them worked. His last attempt is hanging up over there."

She indicated a T-shaped frame with puffy wings on the sides and a propeller in the back. It looked like the pilot would lie down in the middle with his face forward. From that position, he controlled the flaps on the wings and tail and pedaled the mechanism that turned the propeller.

"Mfana thought his earlier designs were too heavy, so he came up with this new idea. You see the baggy balloons in the wings? Those were filled with helium. It was supposed to make the entire airplane lighter than air."

"What happened?"

"It was *lighter* all right! The airplane went *up*, but it didn't come *down*! Not for a whole week anyway. He nearly starved before enough of the helium finally escaped. He landed about three hundred miles southeast from here—in Horseshoe Bend, Idaho. He's considered a bit of a folk hero down there. But when he got back home, my great-grandmother made him sleep out in the barn. He promised to stop after that."

Along the walls were examples of preliminary and final drawings for some of Dr. Losotu's more famous inventions. "Many of these were done in partnership with Chang," Samora explained, "such as the Ding-Dong-So-Long, the Hotcakes, and the Drain Gun. There were also some other inventions that hadn't worked so well. Two of them were the Rocket Shoes and the Shower Bed."

"What can you tell us about these?" Janice asked.

Our guide laughed. "My great-grandfather was always looking for fun ways to use steam power or to make mundane household chores automatic. These were two of his less-than-successful attempts. As you can see from that photograph, the Rocket Shoes had a frame with four small wheels that could be attached and adjusted to fit an average man's shoes. A tank of highly compressed air was strapped to the person's back and tubes ran from the tank to each of the shoes. When the person was ready to go, he pulled on a starter cord. That released the compressed air and propelled the person forward."

"That sounds like fun!"

"It *would* have been fun if it worked. Unfortunately, the wearer would usually flip upside down. His shoes would fly off and land as far as a mile or two down the road. One set of shoes flew across the river and kicked a boat around until it sank! Another pair zoomed down the road and crushed one of our berry fields into grape juice! It was a real mess.

"Mfana had to give up on the idea when a third pair got loose and ran around town for about thirty minutes. They broke into the town hall, chased the mayor up the stairs, and finally ran out of steam, but not before they'd kicked the mayor over his desk."

"Sound like the Rocket Shoes were a problem from the very start," I said.

"Not as bad as the Shower Bed. It worked most of the time—with one small problem. Probably why Mfana couldn't find anyone who was willing to use it."

"What did it do?" Ruth wanted to know, staring at the drawing.

"As you can see, it was a single bed with a tub underneath and surrounded by a waterproof roof and curtain. A person would lie down on the bed, set the alarm, and go to sleep. When the alarm went off, an agitator pulled the blankets and sheets off the bed and down into the tub. The sprayer turned on and the sleeper got a morning wake-up shower—and his pajamas, blankets, and sheets got washed all in one operation."

"Who'd want to wake up like that?" I tried to imagine waking up in the shower wearing wet pajamas.

Samora chuckled. "The real problem was when a person's pajamas got caught in the sheets and he got pulled down into the tub. A small flaw in the design."

Jonny laughed. "We ought to get one of these for Ruth. She has trouble getting up in the morning."

"Very funny," Ruth mumbled, punching Jonny in the shoulder.

Samora continued "Come over here to the center of the room. This is something my great-grandfather invented that *everyone* loves."

She took us over to a flat platform covered in what appeared to be a deflated hot-air balloon or parachute. She bent over and flipped a switch. We could hear the sound of air being pumped and we watched as the balloon began to inflate. As it filled it took on a square shape, like a huge slice of bread, about ten feet square and two feet thick. It quickly rose into the air, trailing ropes underneath.

"Even though the helium-filled wings of the airplane were a failure, my grandfather's one-week trip to Idaho gave him plenty of time to think. Without food or water or a bed to sleep on, he thought how nice it would be to float up in the sky, carrying some basic provisions, with a means to descend at will. That's when he came up with the idea for the Sky Camper. Jonny, hurry up and climb in!"

Jonny scrambled over the edge of the platform and through the door of the camper. Soon the flat balloon rose up to the ceiling, taking Jonny and the expandable room with it. The sleeping area of the camper had been hidden underneath, but was now fully expanded. It was complete with small, net-covered windows and a helium-filled floor. A tether hung down through a hole in the floor and was anchored firmly to the platform.

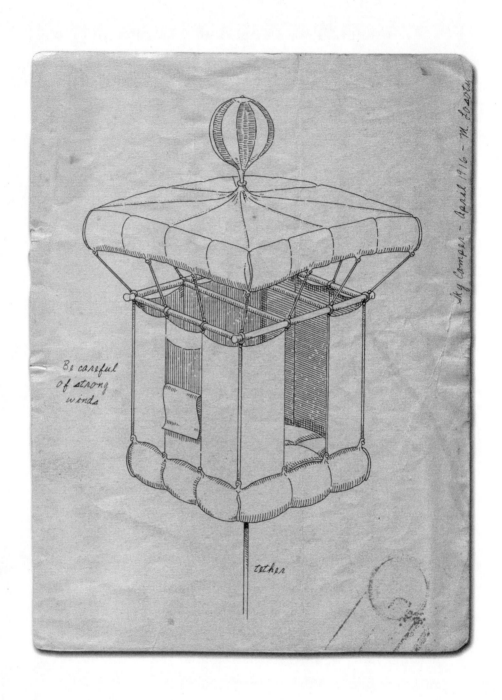

Be careful
of strong
winds

tether

Sky Camper – April 1916 – M. Foster

"The camper is able to hold one average-sized person and enough supplies for one overnight stay. The balloon and helium tanks are portable, so you can travel out to a remote location, fill the balloon, climb aboard, and enjoy an evening aloft. You see the tether coming through the floor from inside? Pull on the tether when you want to descend; release it to return aloft. The windows zip down so you can look out. The balloon acts as a roof to keep you dry in case it rains. It even comes with a battery-powered lantern so you can read at night. Until you've spent an evening camping out in the sky, you haven't been camping!"

Jonny looked down at us from above. "Dad! We've got to *buy* one of these!"

The drifting Sky Camper made me feel queasy. "What happens when it gets windy?"

Samora answered, "That's when it *really* gets exciting!"

"I can only imagine." I shuddered at the thought.

The kids were delighted with the invention and took turns in the floating Sky Camper. But there was still so much to see. Nearby was a long glass case with four strange objects inside. The first one was a dome-shaped box, with latches on the side, a round opening at one end, and a fan unit on top. Samora pulled the deflate cord on the Sky Camper and came over and joined us.

"That's called the Pet Parlor. You put your dog or cat inside. The head fits through that adjustable opening. Once it's closed, you plug in the hose and pump in hot, soapy steam. It's basically a variation on the self-cleaning bathroom. The air fan turns on, and the dog or cat comes out clean and dry."

Sarah said, "Effeneff wouldn't like that very much."

Jonny asked, "Does it come in a sister-size?"

Sarah and Ruth both punched his arm.

"Ow!" Jonny cried.

I pointed at the second object. "What about this?"

"That's the Hair Vacuum. Put it on over your head and attach the hose to a regular vacuum cleaner. It's great for removing dandruff or straightening hair."

"And this?"

"The Naughty Nanny. It's a magnetic belt that connects at the back. If one of your children misbehaves, you put this around her waist and stick her to a metal surface, like a washing machine or refrigerator. That way you can keep an eye on her while she thinks about what she's done."

"Very nice," I said, glancing at Sarah. "Where can I buy one of those?"

"Look in the Sears and Roebuck catalog. They come in three different sizes."

Samora continued. "Next we have the Baseball Bazooka. That was actually invented by my father, based on an earlier design by my great-sgrandfather. Here. Let's take it out of the case, and I'll show you how it works."

She pulled a small key out of the pocket of her dress and opened the glass door. From a cabinet underneath she handed Jonny a baseball bat and Ruth a catcher's mitt and she grabbed a canvas bag filled with rubber balls.

The Stickville Times | WEDNESDAY, APRIL 14, 1948

Hey, Kids! Pitch Like the Pros!

BASEBALL BAZOOKA!

Shoot curve balls, fast balls, sliders, & knucklers!

Martin's Mercantile
ON BANG STREET AT TOWN SQUARE

OVER FORTY PITCHES PER CHARGE!

"Let's put this exhibit away. That will give us the space we need."

We walked to the main door where Samora flipped the switch. The inventions exhibit disappeared into the floor. We moved out into the center of the room while Jonny and Ruth took up positions near the wall. Samora described the features of the bazooka.

"There's a rechargeable canister of compressed air in the stock. Up here is where you insert the balls. They're made of rubber—just for practice—so we don't have to worry about breaking anything. You just point, aim, and pull the trigger."

The gun went off with a loud pop and the ball flew from the gun past Jonny's swinging bat and *smack* into Ruth's mitt.

"I surprised you with that one," Samora said. "Let's see if you can hit this!"

She pulled the trigger and another ball flew across the room. This time Jonny was ready and he whacked the ball off the back wall.

"Home run!" we all cheered.

Samora adjusted a knob on the side of the gun. "If you twist this knob, you can change the trajectory of the ball. Turn it up and it will throw a curve ball. Turn it down and it will throw a sinker. Watch this." She pulled the trigger again and Jonny swung through a diving curve ball.

"My turn!" Sarah shouted as she ran and took the bat.

Samora adjusted the knob again and shot her a slow knuckle ball. Sarah missed, but with a little practice she finally hit a grounder that bounced off the left wall and into the "outfield."

We played for another five minutes, but it was getting late and we still had two exhibits to see. We gathered at the control panel and watched as the Hall of Records rose into view. This time there were shelves of books and drawers full of old newspapers. There were catalogs and maps and photographs hanging on the walls and documents and records and letters behind glass frames. We found several photos of Chang and Dr. Losotu and pictures of the miners in the early days of Boomtown and the picture of President William H. Taft posing with the Hopontops and photos of other famous Boomtownians throughout the years.

Personally, I could have stayed there forever thumbing through the old books (one of my passions) or listening to some of the old music from the record collection or reading the earliest copies of the *Stickville Times*. But the children got bored quickly and kept asking Janice and me to hurry up. They wanted to pull the unmarked knob, the one hiding the big surprise.

"Okay, okay," I said, finally giving in. "Go ahead. I'll come back here on my own some other day." We stood to the side as I watched with some regret the Hall of Records disappear.

Samora said, "By now you must have discovered my great-grandfather's love for children. Kids know how to play and invent and dream big dreams. He got some of his best ideas from children, so he wanted to give them a place where they could come and play, like the swing in the conservatory. And this," she said, pulling the fourth and final activator with a flourish. "The *racetrack*!"

Side compartments in the four walls slid open. Inside were large canvas bags that began to inflate. In seconds, a soft, cushioned wall of air surrounded the perimeter. A short circular wall, also cushioned by air, rose up from the floor to form an enclosed center area with an opening at each end. Four cushioned cars, looking very much like marshmallows on wheels, rose into view. In two corners of the room, a narrow driveway with guardrails on each side slid into place.

"Welcome to the Boomtown Racetrack!" announced Samora with a wave of her hand. "Over here, Jonny, Sarah, Ruth. Come and pick out your car."

They ran across the floor and over to the four parked cars. Each one was marked with a number and had a steering wheel, an accelerator handle and brakes, and a soft helmet sitting on the seat. They hopped in, put on their helmets and seat belts, and waited impatiently for Samora to tell them what to do.

"These cars are driven by steam power," she explained. "Each has a tank with pressurized steam. Squeeze the handle on the steering wheel to make the car go forward. The harder you squeeze, the faster you go, but only up to the speed limit. Release the handle and use the brake to stop. You can only drive in one direction, beginning at the starting line. You have to go ten laps to win, but the cars will only go about seven laps on one tank of steam. That's what the two stations in the corner are for."

Samora gestured and said, "You'll start to feel your car slow down. That's when you want to pull into the station. Drive in the open end, and the station will automatically capture your car and bring you to a stop. A steam hose is guided through a slot underneath each car, and a fresh load of steam will be injected into your tank. It's up to you to decide when to recharge your car—in the fifth, sixth, or even seventh lap.

"But don't wait too long! You'll run out of steam short of the station. If that happens, you have to move the car using the bicycle pedals down there on the front axle. You don't want to have to do that!"

Jonny's mind was racing. "Do you have to wait for a full charge—or can you take off before it's full?"

"Good question. You can take off anytime you want. Just squeeze the handle. Winning a race depends on making good guesses and perfect timing. It's not about how fast you go, but how *smart* you go."

STEAM POWERED RACE CAR.

AUTO-RECHARGE SYSTEM.

Patented April 6, 1922

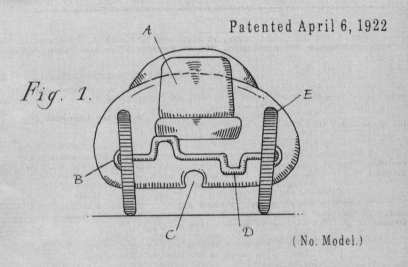

Fig. 1.

(No. Model.)

No. 408,112

Inventor
Mfana Losotu

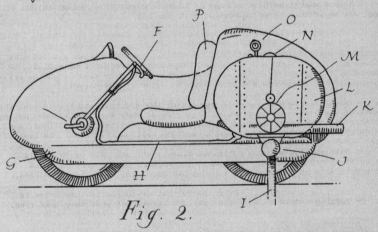

Fig. 2.

We pushed the cars over to the starting line. Samora took Holly into her arms and handed me the starter's flag and Janice the checkered flag.

I raised the green flag and shouted, "On your mark, get set . . . GO!"

With a wave and a shout, they were off. Jonny took an early lead, but Ruth was a close second. They circled the track, once, twice, three times. Jonny and Ruth were neck and neck. Sarah was way behind, but she decided to pull over after only five laps and recharge her car. Ruth pulled over after six. Jonny waited too long, and his car ran out of steam at the beginning of the seventh lap. He was forced to pedal his car into the station. By then, Sarah was way out in front with a freshly charged tank. She easily took the checkered flag.

"I won! I won! I won!" she yelled, jumping up and down. Then she stopped. "What did I win?"

"As the winner of the first race of the day, you've won a mini race car of your very own." Samora went over to one of the walls and opened a cabinet. "Here it is. A yellow one to match your hair."

"Look, Dad! I won a little toy car! How does it work?"

Samora said, "You see the hole here at the back? That's where you insert this little air valve. Hook it to a bicycle pump and you can recharge the small air tank inside the car. Flip this switch and the car will race across the room or down the sidewalk. Another one of my great-grandfather's favorite inventions."

"That's really swell! Thanks!"

They pushed the cars into the stations and recharged their tanks. Then they lined up again. Jonny learned his lesson from the first race and won the second. Ruth took the third. Sarah won the fourth. By then it was almost 5 p.m. and we had to get home. I was preaching in the morning and we had to get Holly fed and put to bed and the children ready for the next day.

"We *really* have to go. Kids, make sure you thank Samora for everything."

They each hugged her and she promised them as we left, "Come back to the museum anytime during the week after school—as long as your homework is done. The kids in Boomtown have races almost every night of the week."

"Thank you, we will!"

Jonny was interested in the music classes, and we promised to talk to Samora's sister that week to get a schedule. I wanted to come back as soon as I could to get a closer look at the Hall of Records. Janice was interested in volunteering in the conservatory. All of us were exhausted, but excited from our visit.

Samora led us to the door and waved as we walked down the sidewalk and into the dark, snowy night. The children chattered happily all the way home, and we all agreed we'd never had so much fun in one day in our entire lives.

Of course, until then, we'd never been to the Spring Fever Festival.

The
GREAT ROOM

Airplanes, Balloons,
Kites, Lighting
System

Ceiling Level
Aerial Exhibits

Tripodosaurus,
Fossils, Petrified
Wood, Maps

Level 1
Dinosaur Exhibits

Baseball Bazooka,
Sky Camper, Naughty
Nanny, Pet Parlor, etc.

Level 2
Inventions

Town Archives,
Books, Journals, Research
Notes, Photographs

Level 3
Hall of Records

Steam Cars,
Race Track,
Recharge Stations

Level 4
Steam Car Raceway

Lifts and Sorting
Mechanisms,
Turbines, Steam
Shafts

Basement Level
Geothermal Plant

CHAPTER 11

Spring Fever Festival

The winters in upper eastern Washington can be long and severe. Nestled up against the North Cascade mountain range in the Okanogan territory and only eighty miles from the border of Canada, Boomtown typically experiences winter temperatures averaging thirty degrees or below. The frigid winds blowing down from the mountains can drift the snow as high as five feet deep. Snow begins to fall in late October and lingers until the last freeze in March or sometimes early

April. A person trapped indoors for five months can develop a terminal case of cabin craziness. That's why the folks in Boomtown look forward to the Spring Fever Festival like a six-year-old waits for his birthday cake.

Janice and I woke up one icy Saturday morning and found a hastily written note explaining where everyone had gone. Ruth was out with her friends working on the Snow Castle. Sarah was out at Fred Cotton's place, and Jonny had gone to meet his buddies at Slippery Slope. Busy was there with seven other boys when he arrived.

"Hey, Jon, watcha got there?"

"It's a rope. Got it from the Reynolds' farm."

"It's really long. What's it for?"

"Let's go on up to the top and I'll show you."

Busy and Rocky and the other guys followed Jonny as they hiked up Slippery Slope. This was a huge hill on Lazy Gunderson's farm. By the second or third day of January, after two weeks of sledding during the winter school break, the hillside would be transformed into a solid sheet of ice, one foot thick, slick as glass, glistening like a jewel in the cold winter sunlight. The ice slide was on the lee-side of a hill and shaded by pine trees. Depending on the weather, it could last well into April and sometimes May.

Most kids in Boomtown couldn't afford to buy sleds and probably wouldn't even if they could. It was a lot more fun to make a sled out of whatever flotsam a kid could lay his hands on. One favorite was to build some runners and a deck out of scrap wood. Mount an old chair on top and away you went! Another popular idea was to take a pair of your father's overalls, soak them in water and hang them on the clothes-line overnight. By morning, you'd have a rock-hard sled with shoulder straps for handles. Take it out to Slippery Slope and you could go as fast as a horse buggy on a windy day. Nothing to worry about; Lazy Gunderson made sure the kids were safe; he always built a wall out of hay bales for the kids to crash into if they sailed off the end of the slide.

At the top of the hill, the boys found an old rototiller up-side down and tied to a tree. The tiller blades had been removed and a rubber tire was in their place. Jonny laid out the rope and asked Busy and Frank to help him loop it between the tire and a bicycle wheel hub that had been bolted to the tree.

"What's *this* contraption for?" Rocky asked.

"It's a ski lift, like they got out at ski resorts," Jonny answered. "You know, one of them rope pullers that can pull you up a hill?"

"That's really swell. You build it? Where'd it come from?"

Jonny glanced around to make sure there weren't any grown-ups nearby. "I got it from *him*. He helped me move it here and set it up. It was *his* idea."

"Oh," Rocky dropped his voice. "So where did *he* get it?"

Jonny shrugged. "Don't know. Probably the same place he got all the other stuff. I didn't ask, and he didn't say."

The boys continued to set up the rope puller. Back at home, Janice and I were putting on our boots and coats and getting ready for the snow. We wrapped Holly in warm blan-kets and a stocking cap and trudged our way out to Slippery

Slope. Several other parents were already there to join in the fun. There was a large bonfire blazing near the end of the ice ramp. Someone had brought along boxes of sticky buns for the kids and folks were passing around coffee and steaming hot cocoa with marshmallows. The sky was blue; the evergreen trees were laced with snow; there was a brisk snap in the air. It was a perfect day.

We stayed at the hill for an hour or so enjoying conversation with fellow town members and watching the kids. Jonny and the gang had built an "ice schooner" out of a sheet of plywood and grain sacks that had been filled with water and frozen solid. These were tied to the underside of the plywood with ropes. There were also ropes on top of the board for handholds. It was big enough for five boys to ride down the hill in one go, which they did over and over again whooping and hollering. Once the rig reached the bottom, they hooked the schooner to a rope puller and dragged it back to the top of the hill.

Quite ingenious, I thought. *I wonder who came up with that?*

On the other side of town at Fred Cotton's place, another group of kids and their parents gathered for the Snow Wars. As with any popular activity in Boomtown, sooner or later it involved explosives, and I wouldn't have been surprised to find Sarah right in the thick of it.

"Let's build our fort right here," she said to her friends. "There's lots of snow and it's on a little hill. That'll be good."

"We'll dig the trenches," Katrina said.

"And we'll build the walls," Sarah offered. "After that, we can all build our army."

That's how it worked. One team built walls and battlements and snow trenches at one end of the field. Behind that they lined up an entire army of snowmen, each about two feet tall, thirty snow soldiers in all. Fred Cotton supervised the opposing team at the opposite end of the field. They were busy making ice balls, about eight inches in diameter, each containing a Hen Grenade. Old bicycle tires were stretched between two trees with a leather pouch in the middle. Ice grenades were loaded into the catapult; the team pulled the tires back as far as they could and took aim; the frozen egg missiles were launched across the field. The game was to see how long it took to blow up the other team's snowman army. Then the teams would switch. There really weren't any winners. Like all boys—and most girls—they just liked to blow things up.

This was the entire premise behind the Snow Castle the kids built every year. Captain Trudeau, a retired captain from the navy, hosted the castle on his property and was in charge of overseeing safety. The children spent months building the castle and its surrounding walls and moat. It took thousands of ice blocks; these were made from snow packed into wooden frames and left overnight to freeze. The bricks of ice were stacked and bonded together with wet snow to create walls, doorways, bridges, towers, stairways, and battlements.

After more than thirty years of this annual tradition, you can only imagine the size and beauty of the castle once it neared completion. Framed against a pink winter sunset or lit by cold beams of sunlight, it was a sight to behold. Still, that was nothing compared to the official beginning of the Spring Fever Festival, when everyone in town gathered in the field to watch the mayor push down the plunger and set off the dynamite and fireworks embedded in the ice. The sky would be filled with glittering fragments of ice and sparkling rocket bursts and shooting flares and booms and blasts and cheers from the crowd.

As much fun as it is to play in the snow, everyone finally reaches a limit—even children. That's why the residents of Boomtown celebrate the annual Spring Fever Festival with such enthusiasm. They gather anxiously at their windows and check the thermostat every day waiting for the temperature to climb above thirty-two degrees. On the day the ice on Lake Caona cracks—the day the creeks and streams begin to run again, the day the steady drip, drip of melting icicles can be heard all over town—the Snow Castle goes up in flames, and the festival begins.

The gazebo in Farmers' Park features performances from local singing groups and musical ensembles such as the children's orchestral group we saw at the Boomtown Museum. Booths are set up where you can buy roasted chestnuts, hot cider, homemade cookies and pies, hot dogs on a stick, and sparklers and firecrackers. Folks gather in knots to catch up on news. The kids have snowball fights in the streets. Music and bands play. Everyone is in a festive mood.

The Slush Olympics are held on the first Sunday afternoon of Festival Week. They feature a variety of events with white, blue, and silver medals given out to the winners (silver being the best). The hardest event is the Slush Swim; the outdoor public pool in Chang Park is filled to the brim with slush, and competitors swim laps in the freezing slushy water. The swimmer who lasts the longest is the winner.

Another big event is the Slush Pull. Competitors build whatever makeshift sledge they can dream up and strap it to the back of a horse. A few use something as simple as a sheet of plywood with rope handles. Others get quite elaborate, like the team who took the hood from a 1936 Buick Century and welded runners and wheels underneath. Another team took an aluminum fishing boat, pounded out the bottom until it was flat, and polished it with wax. They were the winners that year.

Starting in the park at the end of Bang Street, each team of two racers looped around the statue of Chang in Town Square and headed west on Boom Boulevard past the hardware store and the Nuthouse Restaurant. Right on Blasting Cap Avenue, right on Dynamite Drive, and right at the powder factory. The racers finished with a quick dash along the river and back to the park. People lined the streets cheering on their favorite team. They shot off firecrackers and Roman candles at the finish line and bragged about the winners.

Then there were the inner-tube races over at Slippery Slope. The hay bales were moved to the side, and the goal was to slide as fast and as far as your inner tube would take you. There was the Slush Eating Contest, where contestants attempted to eat as many bowls of lime-flavored slush as they could without getting up from the table to use the outhouse. Then the Slush Bucket Relay, where teams of four people scooped up buckets of slush and took turns running back and forth from the starting line until they filled up the bed of a pickup truck. Then the Slushbarrow Race—fill a wheelbarrow with slush, a musher pushing in the back, a slusher riding on top, dashing through a slushy obstacle course. And Slush Hockey—teams of six players with straw brooms trying to score goals by swatting a block of ice past the goalie.

The most important event was the wildly popular Cross-Country Slushathon. It required the use of a modified bicycle that had a studded tire in the rear and a wooden ski in the front. The event called for the participation of the mayor, the sheriff, the fire chief, all the male teachers from the school, and all the pastors in town. As always, I was the last to know. I didn't realize what was going on until Jonny came running over pushing a bicycle. Then he handed me a helmet.

"What's this for?" I asked.

"It's your Slushcycle. And helmet. For the race."

"*What* race?"

"The Cross-Country Slushathon. This is your number . . . 13. Not very lucky."

"I'm not riding in the race!" I protested.

"But you *have* to! *All* the pastors are doing it, Dad. The Reverend Tinker. Even fat old Reverend Platz. The mayor's gonna race. So's Burton Ernie."

"Maybe *they* are, but *I'm* not. I'm a pastor, not an athlete. I'll sit this one out."

Jonny's face fell. "You're *always* saying that, Dad. Why don't you ever have any fun? The other guys, all their dads do stuff. You just sit and watch. You won't even *try*."

Reverend Platz was standing nearby watching the exchange between Jonny and me. He patted Jonny on the shoulder and then took my elbow and pulled me aside.

"Listen, Arthur, don't be nervous. I do this every year. I never finish, but I always start. My people expect it. They look forward to it. Right now they're taking a pool. You're not doing too badly. If you survive, they expect you to come in third or fourth place."

"If I *survive*? Look, I don't know how to ride one of these contraptions. I can't do this. I *won't*."

"Then you'll be the first pastor from Boomtown Church who hasn't ridden in the race for the past twenty-two years. At every festival, if the pastor is alive at the time, he rides in the race and his whole congregation cheers him on."

"But why? What's the point?"

"One of your predecessors, Reverend Andersen—I think he was the one who died in a landslide—was concerned about how the church members were treating him. They didn't regard him as one of them. That's a common problem for ministers and public figures; you know what I'm talking about. People think we're somehow *different*—better, more perfect. So he got together with the other pastors in town, and they talked to the mayor and the other community leaders and found out they were having the same problem.

"That's when they came up with an event that was just for them. It was a way for the people of the town to get a different look at us. This race makes them feel like they can trust us because we're just like them—because we go and make fools out of ourselves and laugh about it. Do you see what I mean?"

He was right. People tended to put leaders, *especially* ministers, up on a pedestal. On the one hand, I secretly enjoyed the attention; on the other hand, I was always afraid of making mistakes. I put a lot of pressure on my family and myself; we had to be careful all the time about what we said and what we did. We weren't any smarter or better than anybody else, but I never knew what to do about it. I suppose if this race had a way of changing the way people thought about us, who was I to stand in the way?

"Okay," I relented. "Give me my number."

"Excellent, wonderful, marvelous—you won't regret it. Why not try out your bicycle for a few minutes and then come and join us on the starting line?"

I tried the best I could. As soon as I started to pedal, the front ski slipped to the right or skidded to the left. The back tire spun on the ice. I got my pants leg caught in the chain.

My foot slipped off the pedal and I banged my shin. This wasn't going to be pretty.

The warning gun sounded, and somehow I managed to slip and slide and slosh through the slush and get myself and the bicycle death machine over to my assigned spot next to the other racers. Burton Ernie gave me a smile and a salute. Reverend Platz gratefully patted me on my back. I could see Jonny, eyes aglow, bragging to Busy and Frank and Lonnie. Everyone else was cheering wildly until Captain Trudeau waved his arms and signaled for silence.

He shouted through a megaphone, "Attention, racers! The three-mile course is marked by red flags along the route. Any deviation from the course will result in automatic disqualification. Observers must refrain from assisting or hindering the racers in any way. Riders may dismount and push their bicycles whenever necessary. The first man to cross the finish line here in Town Square is the winner. Any questions?"

I raised my hand.

"Yes, Reverend Button, you have a question?"

"Has anyone ever *died* doing this?"

The captain laughed, and so did everyone else. "Not so far, Reverend! Don't worry. We'll keep an eye on you. A *thousand* eyes. Just stick to the course."

Then the captain raised the green flag, "On your mark . . . get set . . . MUSH!"

The crowd let out a raucous cheer and threw their hats in the air. Horns blew. Firecrackers went off. People shouted.

"Go, Dad, go!" I heard Jonny shouting from the side-line. "What are you waiting for? You've got to catch up."

With the wave of the flag I'd been left behind in a spray of ice-cold water, standing ankle deep in a puddle of icy slush, unsure of what to do. I was the only one in the race who'd never done this before. I couldn't figure out how to steer or pedal the ridiculous contraption—but I tried. Jonny *needed* me to try. I started to pedal, wobbling and sliding at first. After about a hundred feet, I started to get the hang of it and straightened myself out.

"Good job, dear!" I heard Janice calling as I disappeared down the street. "See you at the finish line!"

The cheering of the crowd quickly drowned her out. I saw several of my church members lining the road and shouting words of encouragement. I heard one say, "That's our new pastor! Look at him go!"

That's when I began to see what this race was all about. My people, out in the slush, cheering me on, for the pride of our church—and for the *fun* of it. I was being such a wet sock. But I didn't have to be. I was going to *win* this race, and even if I didn't, I was going to do the best I possibly could.

In a few minutes, I passed Reverend Platz on the side of the road, his face as red as a ripe tomato. For the first time since I met him he was unable to speak, but he gave me a broad smile of encouragement and a jaunty wave. Next, I caught up to the mayor, who was struggling to keep his Slushcycle upright. Then I passed the math teacher and the school principal and even the fire chief. There was no way, with my late start, that I was ever going to catch up to Burton Ernie, who was in excellent shape—or the Reverend Tinker, whose extra long legs and long, thin body made him especially wind resistant. But I made up my mind; I would ride as hard as I could for my congregation and for Jonny.

The course wound through downtown, out onto Blasting Cap Avenue, and west toward the fireworks factory. All along the way were spectators taking pictures and waving flags. There was a comfort station about every half mile where a rider could stop, exchange his wet socks for some dry ones, get a hot or cold drink, dry his face with a towel, and keep going. By the halfway mark riders were strung out all over the course, but according to one of the station attendants, I was currently in tenth place and not too far behind the rider in front of me. *Not too bad*, I was thinking.

Soon the course climbed to its highest point, out behind Lazy Gunderson's property, and up along slushy, muddy TNT Trail. It climbed the hill and passed through a tangle of trees and bushes at the top. I could see the tire and ski marks from the riders who had passed by ahead of me, and I struggled to avoid the bumps and puddles and rocks on the trail. With my attention focused and head down, I didn't see the strange figure on the trail who was blocking my path. Suddenly, I noticed him. *On no! Where did he come from?* If I didn't turn, I would tear him to pieces with the studded tires of the Slushcycle. Too late to stop, I veered to the right, crashed through a dense thicket, and found myself looking straight down the solid ice surface of Slippery Slope.

"Oh, Lord in heaven!" I cried as I jumped the crest of the hill and started down. Slow at first then faster and faster, unable to stop because the brakes no longer seemed to be working. The front ski slithered side to side as I careened down the hill.

"Oh, no!" I wailed. Down below the hay bales had been moved for the inner tube races a few days earlier. With nothing to stop my headlong plummet down the hill, I picked up speed, flew past the bottom of the hill, then up and over an icy snowdrift. It was just like a ski jump. I was launched thirty feet into the air—head first and hind end toward death and heaven beyond.

A funeral flashed before my eyes. I saw a young widow and four fatherless children. I heard Vera DeFazio leading hymns. I saw Ingrid hanging my photo in the hallway. I saw the search committee meeting to replace their most recently deceased pastor.

"How did he die?" visitors would ask, seeing my picture on the wall.

"Oh, him? He died at the bottom of Slippery Slope with a Slushcycle ski buried in his forehead."

"You don't say?"

"Yep. Too bad. Nice man. Tough way to go."

But miracle of miracles! At the very moment I started my downward plunge, Lazy Gunderson drove underneath me in his pickup truck on his way to dump the slush from the Slush Bucket Relay. *Plop!* I landed smack-dab in the back of his truck without a bruise or a scratch. The Slushcycle, however, disappeared under Lazy's truck with a screeching crunch of twisting metal. It nearly gave him a heart attack. I lay safe and sound in the back of the truck thinking how the mangled Slushcycle could have been me.

"*Yow!* What the hay was that?" Lazy exclaimed, slamming his brakes and jumping out of the cab. "Reverend Button! What're you doin' back *there?* Where'd you come from? You fell out of the sky like a busted kite! You all right?"

I couldn't answer him. I was frightened and freezing and frustrated. All I could do was climb out of the slush pond and stand on my own two frozen feet.

With teeth chattering, I managed to say, "Lazy, I don't suppose you've got a blanket in your truck? And a ride back to town?"

"Sure thing, Preacher. You just hold on."

He hustled around and gave me a blanket to warm myself. He had a thermos of coffee in the cab and poured me a cup. He bundled me into the passenger seat and then backed up slowly to dislodge the mangled Slushcycle from his rear axle. By the time he dumped his load and drove back to Town Square, the race was over. Burton Ernie was the winner for the third year in a row. I was just happy to be in one piece.

The Spring Fever Festival ended without further incident. The spring thaw continued; the streets cleared up, and the snow finished melting. The farmers swung open the doors of their barns and went out for their first spring plowing.

That's when the mysterious mounds were first sighted. Around the whole south and west end of town, in field after field, there were piles of fresh dirt all over the place. Now that the snow had melted they lay in plain sight, like an army of huge gophers had dug up the entire landscape and left their hills behind.

Everybody in Boomtown was talking about it. Burton Ernie went out to investigate. When I saw him that next Sunday in church, he pulled me aside and said, "I got me a theory about what's been going on."

"What do you mean?"

"About the robberies."

"What about them?" I asked, curious about the sheriff's theory.

"At first, I couldn't make a connection between the odd things that have gone missing. You know: the fencing, the truck, the trees, the digging tools, and the lights from the courthouse. And now them piles of dirt."

"What are you thinking?"

"I think somebody's been digging a *tunnel*. Probably a *bunch* of somebodies and a *bunch* of tunnels. You see what I'm getting at?"

"Maybe." I didn't have a clue.

"Think about it. Someone stole the tools so he could dig. He stole the truck to haul the dirt. He stole the wood to shore up the tunnel. He took the lights so he could see where he was going. You get it? It's as plain as the nose on your face."

Burton's theory actually made sense. "I think you've got it, Burton," I told him. "All the pieces fit. Hey, maybe that strange fellow I saw on the trail has something to do with it."

"Who?"

"During the Slushathon this man came out of nowhere. And now that I think about it, I'm pretty sure he was wearing my old coat!"

"You see his face?"

"No, I was too busy trying not to kill myself. But I don't think he was anybody from the town. I can't really be sure; I don't think I'd know him again if I saw him."

"Too bad. Maybe he's the one who's been leaving the dirt mounds. He has to dump all the dirt from the tunnel, if that's what he's up to. That's pretty hard to hide."

"You're right, Sheriff. That's pretty smart."

"Not smart enough. I still don't know *where* he is—or *who* he is."

I shook my head. "That's not the big question."

"What could be more important than that?" asked Burton.

"The most important question of all," I answered. *"Why?"*

CHAPTER 12

The Investigation

Burton was knocking on my front door early the next morning.

"Sorry to bother you at home, Arthur," he said, nodding good morning to Janice. "But I was wondering—if you had the time—would you ride along with me today?"

I thought for a moment. I didn't have any appointments. I was well along with the plans for the upcoming Easter program. My sermon was already outlined and partly finished.

"Sure, Burton. What did you have in mind?"

Burton fiddled with his hat and answered with a sheepish grin, "Well, if it isn't any trouble—I mean, if you think you might be able to come along—of course, if it's all right with the missus and all—maybe we could talk about it in the car." I could tell he didn't want to say anything in front of Janice.

"Okay, Burton. Just let me get my coat and hat."

The sheriff stood nervously in the doorway as I kissed Janice good-bye and told her not to worry. I gave Holly a kiss on the forehead. The other kids had already left for school. I put on my coat and a scarf against the wind and accompanied Burton out the door and down the sidewalk. There was a light drizzle falling from the overcast sky, fairly typical for the last week of March. We climbed into his police cruiser and headed down the street.

"Now tell me, Burton, what's the big mystery?"

He turned right on Bang Street and said, "Let's stop at Mabel's and have a cup of coffee. I'd like to ask her a few questions, and we can make ourselves comfortable while we draw up a plan for today."

"A plan for what?"

"For my *investigation*. I've been putting this off long enough, and with the discovery of the mounds and the connection we made between the digging and the robberies, I've got to get me some results or people are going to start wondering."

"Wondering? About what?"

"About keeping me on as sheriff! They're mostly patient around here, and quite frankly, I think they're more *excited* about the robberies than upset. But now with those mounds of dirt showing up, people want answers. I've got to do something."

"That doesn't mean your job is at stake."

Burton glanced at me as he turned left onto Crumble Street.

"I'm not a policeman," he confessed. "Not a *real* police-man, anyway. I've never had formal training. I used to work down at the powder factory until about twenty years ago. That's when the Bank of Boomtown was robbed. The town didn't have a sheriff up until then because we didn't have any crime—not worth mentioning anyway. People pretty much took care of their own business. But after the bank robbery, the mayor had to find *somebody*, so he asked me."

"Why you?"

"He thought I'd be pretty good at it. He said everyone in town knew me and liked me and trusted me. I had a knack for getting people to talk. Frankly, I was the only one in town who said yes. The mayor asked forty-seven other people before he got to me.

"I'm as good at the job as anybody else would have been, I suppose. I like people. They trust me. I ride around in my cruiser, watch out for trouble, put out the occasional fire (or start a few of my own). It's the perfect job for me, and it makes the townsfolk feel better, even though they've never really needed me to *do* anything."

We pulled up and parked in front of Mabel's.

"So why do you need me?"

"I know we haven't known each other all that long, but I trust you. You're a smart guy, a big city feller, college educated—that sort of thing—and you've worked a lot with people. I thought you might be able to give me some pointers. Keep your eyes and ears open as we go around. We can compare notes at the end of the day. Are you with me?"

I smiled. "Sounds good to me—as long as I don't have to drink Mabel's coffee."

We went inside and sat in a corner booth and waited for Mabel. She had at least fifteen other customers filling the tables. As we came in, most of them nodded in greeting then returned to their conversations. They were probably discussing the latest theory about the crime wave. Mabel swooped in with a coffee cup for Burton—"Nothing for me, thanks"—and stayed long enough to answer Burton's questions.

"Have you heard anything, Mabel? Your customers say anything?"

"Nothing but a bunch of useless gossip and crazy ideas."

"Such as?"

Mabel scratched her head with her pen and pointed. "Ol' Jim Dougherty sittin' over there—he thinks it's space gophers."

"Space gophers?"

"You know, huge alien gophers from outer space. Came down in their gopher space ship, that's what he's sayin'. Thinks they're diggin' around for who knows what."

"Space gophers. Okay. Anything else?"

"Lazy Gunderson thinks it's a government conspiracy."

"What, like spies, CIA, G-men, something like that?"

"Yeah, thinks they're digging a secret base underground so they can conduct secret government experiments. Just the sort of thing Lazy'd dream up while sleepin' on his tractor. Those are the two least stupid ideas I've heard so far."

"Thanks, Mabel."

As Mabel shuffled off to be rude to the rest of the customers, Burton said, "She's up before the crack of dawn to open the diner. I thought maybe she'd have seen something. Whoever's taking stuff and dumping dirt has got to be doing it at night or someone woulda seen him by now."

"You think it's just one person?"

"Could be—though I been hoping it's a whole *gang* of men. Wouldn't that be great? Maybe ten or twenty armed desperados with knives and hand grenades and machine guns."

"I'd think if there were that many strange faces in town, someone would have noticed."

"You're right, sure. You see what I mean—you *are* good at this."

Burton choked down his coffee. We stood up and he went table to table asking each group if they'd seen or heard anything unusual. No one had. We headed out the door and got back in the cruiser.

"Now where?"

"I've got to check in with the mayor," he answered. "He's going to want a report. I haven't the faintest idea what to tell him."

It was only a few blocks to town hall where Mayor Tanaka had his office. I'd met him at the Spring Fever Festival, but never really had a chance to talk to him. I was extremely curious, wondering how a Japanese American could be the mayor of a town only five years after World War II. When we lived back in California, every single Japanese family in the area had been rounded up and shipped off to internment camps. After the war, very few of them returned. If they did, they were treated with suspicion and fear. How did this man ever get elected *mayor* of Boomtown? This would be interesting.

Mayor Tanaka was expecting Sheriff Ernie and graciously shook my hand when we arrived. He was a man of about forty years of age with a strong handshake and dark black eyes and hair. He stood about five feet tall and was dressed in a crisply ironed gray suit, white shirt, and black tie. He had a jagged scar on the right side of his face and deep burns on both of his hands. He also walked with a slight limp, something I hadn't noticed until then.

The walls of his office were covered in photos and signed letters. In one frame was displayed a set of three medals. One was the Purple Heart—I didn't recognize the other two. Next to that was a photo of Mayor Tanaka in his U.S. Navy uniform. He had a miniature battleship on his desk, right next to his name plaque and a tiny American flag.

We sat down and Burton gave his report—such as it was. The mayor was visibly disappointed.

"That's all right, Burton. I'm sure you'll turn up something. Just keep at it."

Then he turned to me and said, "It's very kind of you to accompany the sheriff on his rounds. I'm sure he appreciates the help."

We stood up and shook hands, then the mayor sent us on our way, assuring us we'd come back with more encouraging news. We left his office, stopped to say hello to the mayor's secretary, the janitor, the bailiff, six people in the lobby, and the mailman. Burton wasn't in much of a hurry.

"You've got to tell me how Mr. Tanaka became *Mayor* Tanaka," I said, sliding into the passenger seat of Burton's cruiser.

He turned on the key to warm up the car, but stayed put in the parking space. "Akihiro Tanaka is an honest-to-goodness war hero, no doubt about it. You saw those medals on his wall? The Purple Heart. The Navy Cross. The Silver Star for bravery. Those were all presented to him after the war. There was a special ceremony right here in Town Square after he recovered from his injuries. It was one of the proudest days Boomtown ever had."

"What did he do?"

"Akihiro was already in the navy when Pearl Harbor was bombed. They rounded him up just like they rounded up every other innocent Japanese American they could lay hands on. They were going to ship him off to an internment camp, but he wanted to fight for his country, same as anyone else. So he was allowed to remain on his ship, but only as a dishwasher. It was humiliating for him, but at least they let him stay in the navy.

"Their small battleship ended up patrolling the West Coast near San Pedro, California—not very exciting duty. That is until one day when Akihiro was out on deck, and he looked up and saw a Japanese balloon bomb. You ever hear about one of those?"

I shook my head no.

"Not too many people have. After the Doolittle raid on Tokyo in 1942, the Japanese retaliated by launching some nine thousand silk balloons carrying antipersonnel and incendiary bombs. They were carried by high-altitude winds and traveled six thousand miles across the Pacific Ocean to the coast of North America. Most of them didn't make it, but one day all of a sudden they started showing up in the sky all along the coast. Akihiro spotted one of them and notified the deck officer. The deck officer ran and told the captain. Within a few minutes the ship was firing salvos trying to bring the thing down. And they did, unfortunately, right onto the main bridge of the ship! The amidships was on fire in a flash. The fire spread fast and pretty soon the whole ship was going down. It was bad."

JAPANESE FIRE BALLOON C. 1943

"Then what happened?"

"They were lowering the lifeboats as fast as they could, but the fire was burning so hot a lot of men were just diving over the side. Pretty soon everyone was off the ship, but there were six men trapped down in the engine room. Rescuers couldn't get past the flames. A couple of explosions put a hole in the port side. The ship was filling up with water. It was sinking fast. It was every man for himself.

"That's when Akihiro got a brilliant idea. He climbed up into the aft gun turret. He grabbed one of the powder bags and dragged it down onto the deck. Then he dropped it close to the edge of the fire, hid behind a pile of rope, and waited. *Boom!* The powder blew a neat hole in the deck and cleared away the flames just long enough for Akihiro to throw down a rope and pull the men out of there. He got the Navy Cross and the Silver Star for his bravery above and beyond the call of duty."

"And the Purple Heart?"

"Yep. He got the scar when a piece of flying metal hit him in the face. He got the burns on his hands while the men were climbing to safety. He didn't leave until all six men got out alive. I told you, he's a real hero."

"So how did he end up here?"

"He enlisted in the navy right here in Boomtown; his family owns a farm out on Haymaker's Road. When he got back from the war, the town threw him a parade. Quite naturally, they wanted him to be mayor. Partly because he was a hero. But mostly because he got famous by blowing something up. You know how much we love that sort of thing around here."

"I noticed."

Burton turned off the engine. "Tell you what, let's head on over to the library across the way there. Let's see what we can find out from the librarian, Helga Knutsen. She sees pretty much everyone in town on a regular basis."

We climbed back out of the car and crossed Town Square to the library. It was the largest public building in town, solid brick, three stories high, with classrooms, meeting areas, and a large basement level where newspapers, records, and rare books were kept. It was early Monday morning, but the place was buzzing with activity.

"Pretty busy for a Monday," I commented.

"It's *always* busy," Burton answered. "Most popular place in town. The Arts League meets here twice a month. The Boomtown Historical Society, the Men's and Women's Rotary, the Hug-A-Slug Club, and so on. That group over there is from the Lions Club. This is the place to be when people aren't working."

"At the *library*?"

"Sure 'nough. People in Boomtown read all the time— except when they're working or shooting off fireworks."

"Reading?"

"Everybody in Boomtown *loves* to read. It's one of the two statistics we're proud of in this town—the employment rate and the literacy rate. Both are almost 100 percent."

By then, we were standing at the counter, and the head librarian jumped into the conversation.

"That's right. Like we always say: in Boomtown, everybody has a job and a book."

She put out her hand and introduced herself. "Hello, my name is Helga Knutsen. And you must be Reverend Button. I saw you at the festival, but we didn't get a chance to say hello."

I shook her hand and looked around at all the people. "Very impressive. I don't think I've ever seen this many people in a library at one time."

"It's the usual stampede. Mondays in particular. We have a lot of meetings and classes on Mondays."

While Burton questioned Helga about anything she might have seen or heard from her patrons, I strolled through the rows of books and said hello to some people I knew from the church and town. I saw a group of Hopontops huddled around a table studying a map and waved hello to Flaming Arrow. I bumped into Gramma Edna among the cookbooks and then Mr. O'Malley with his science class in the largest section of the library: "Explosives and Fireworks." Jonny was with his class doing a research project on how to chemically enhance the potency of gunpowder.

Jonny looked over and saw me. "Whatcha doing here, Dad?"

"Sheriff Ernie has asked me to help him with his investigation."

"Really? Can I come?"

"It's the morning of a school day. You can't just skip school."

Mr. O'Malley heard us talking. "Are you kidding? Deny one of my students an opportunity to go with a policeman on a real investigation? He can go. He *should* go."

"Yeah, Dad, I *should* go. I'm sure Mr. O'Malley would want me to."

I studied Jonny's eyes. I couldn't help but think he had an ulterior motive—something in his tone of voice—but I couldn't put my finger on it. Hmm. If nothing else, Janice would be happy if I took him along. "Fine, then. Get your things. I'll have to check with Burton first. This isn't going to get you out of doing your homework, buster."

We rejoined Burton back at the main desk, where he was checking out some books he had on hold. He agreed to have Jonny tag along; they were buddies. Then, as we were saying our good-byes, I thought of one more question for Helga.

"Burton said that literacy and employment in Boomtown is *almost* 100 percent. Who's the holdout around here?"

Helga smiled. "That would be Volodenka Sviatoslavova. Nobody can pronounce the name, so we just call him Denk. He lives down by the river. I'm sure Burton can tell you all about him. Nice meeting you."

As we went out the door and crossed Town Square, I asked, "Learn anything?"

"In any given two-week period, Helga sees nearly every citizen in this town. They check out books and talk about what's going on—the local gossip, current events, upcoming activities—you name it. She's heard all the theories and rumors, but nothing specific. It's a mystery. How could anyone come and go, take what he needs, dig a tunnel, dump dirt, for almost six months as far as we know, without ever being seen? I'm stumped."

"Don't give up yet, Burton. Something's bound to turn up. So where are we going now?"

"Your question about Denk gave me an idea. He's a good one to talk to. He's down by the river and out in the woods near the fireworks factory. Maybe he's seen something. We're going out to his place."

Jonny leaned forward from the back seat and said, "It's by the fireworks factory? Why would you go out there?" Again, I heard that anxious tone in his voice.

"Why *shouldn't* we look there? It's near Lazy's farm, and it's near TNT Trail, where I saw that man wearing my coat."

"What man?" Jonny asked.

"Didn't I tell you about that? There was a man, and I think he was wearing my coat—you know, the one I can't seem to find? He wasn't very tall, now that I remember. The coat dragged on the ground. He had on a wool cap pulled down low and a red scarf. I remember the scarf. But I couldn't see his face."

Jonny leaned back. He seemed relieved. "It could have been anybody."

"Not just *anybody*," I pointed out, studying Jonny in the rearview mirror. "I think it was our mysterious *somebody*."

I was beginning to think maybe someone else in the car thought so too.

CHAPTER 13

Denk

As we drove out past the fireworks factory, Burton filled us in on the details about Volodenka Sviatoslavova. Volodenka, or "Denk" as he was called, lived with his wife and seven children down by the river west of town for as long as anyone could remember, same as his father and his grandfather before that.

Burton said, "They've always been what you'd call mountain men, proud and independent, hunters and trappers and fishermen. There's a rumor that Denk's ancestors can be traced all the way back to the Varangian Vikings, to the three brothers themselves, Rurik, Sineus, and Truvor. No one really knows for sure because Denk's family has always kept to themselves, but you can't look at his seven-foot frame, blond hair and beard, heavy leather boots and animal skins, and not imagine him plundering the coastline of Norway with other Viking marauders.

"Two years ago, his wife died of pneumonia, leaving him to raise seven children alone. He's been on his own ever since."

"Raising seven children by himself?"

"He's got the help of the older kids, but yeah, he's on his own."

I was trying to imagine raising our four kids without Janice's help when we pulled up in front of their ramshackle cabin at the end of a muddy road. The house, if you could call it that, was a hodge-podge of sections culled together under a tin roof and patched with tarpaulin and sheets of bark. A pencil-thin trickle of smoke rose from a river-rock chimney, while a wan light shone through one of the window openings that were covered in thin plastic sheeting.

Two of the children were out in the front yard tending a sow with her piglets. Another stood nearby feeding the chickens. Denk was to the far right of the house splitting wood. An older boy gathered up the pieces after they went flying under the powerful swings of his giant father. He stopped and shouldered the ax and watched us as we climbed out of the car and walked over to where he waited.

"Morning, Denk. Wasn't sure if you'd be home. Thought you might be out hunting."

Denk towered over all of us. Two piercing blue eyes stared suspiciously out of the nest of his long hair and scraggly beard. A puff of steam curled up from his beard in the cool, morning air. He was wearing a cloak made out of beaver and fox skins with a wide leather belt around his waist that held a huge bone-handled hunting knife in its sheath. He had on deerskin pants and heavy boots and a thick, cotton shirt.

He finally answered in a heavy Slavic accent, "Got me a moose two days ago. That's enough for now." He gestured with his thumb toward the animal hanging dead on a hook from a tree.

"That's a big one," Burton said. "No doubt about it."

Denk just stood there like an iceberg. It didn't look like he'd be thawing anytime soon.

Pointing at me, Burton said, "This is the new pastor from Boomtown Church, and this is his boy, Jonny. We were out looking for clues about the robberies—you heard about those? Thought maybe you'd seen or heard something while you were out hunting or fishing."

Denk didn't answer right away. Then he said, "Yeah. I found something."

"You did?"

"Sure. 'Bout a month ago. Down by the river."

"Really? What was it?"

"A letter, I s'pose. You want it?"

"Yes. Of course. I'd like to see it, please."

Denk put down his ax and led us to the cabin. A single kerosene lamp illuminated the dark interior. When my eyes adjusted to the dim light, I could see three more girls sitting on benches and gathered around a sturdy, hand-carved table. One was reading, the oldest was sewing a loose hem on a dress, and the youngest, a girl of about three years old, was perched in a high chair and playing with a rag doll. They stared at us silently and then went back to their activities.

The wood floor was bare but clean and dry. Shelves around the walls held canned goods and other supplies. At the far end was the wood stove and fireplace. A pot of something was bubbling over the low fire. A rifle was pinned to the wall over the mantel. Sitting on the crude mantel was a photo of a beautiful blonde woman—their mother, I assumed—in a rough frame.

Denk tromped across the room and retrieved a single sheet of paper that was propped behind the photo. He handed it to Sheriff Ernie and said, "Can't read it. Don't know what it says. Don't care. You can have it."

Burton took it over near the lamp and studied it for a moment. It *was* a letter—at least, part of a letter in any case. I couldn't possibly know, because it was written in carefully rendered Chinese characters. It was scribed in black ink on a thin sheet of foolscap that was frayed and yellowed with age. Burton held it up to the light and studied it.

"We'll have to find someone to translate it," I said.

"No, I don't think so. I can read it."

"How? It's in Chinese."

"I know. I can read Chinese."

"You can?"

"Sure 'nough. When I worked at the powder factory, my friends down there taught me to read and speak Chinese. I'm a little rusty, but I think I can muddle through well enough to make some sense out of it."

He started to translate haltingly: "*follow directions . . . then I . . . no . . . it says you . . . find hidden . . .* I don't know this word . . . *something is hidden . . . secret . . .* This word means 'secret.'"

"What's secret?" Jonny whispered, leaning over Burton's shoulder to see.

由我給了，你應該沒有的
指揮引起在找出快取方面
的困難，迄今仍然是秘
密。向沒人提及這，雖然
應該你從來做出旅程，你
可能相信我的在變化中的
朋友。我只能希望這件禮
物將補償我的忽略，雖然
沒什麼東西以他的父親的
損失可以償還一個兒子。
我祈求這封信找到朝往你
的手的路徑，懷著最好的
願望，愛和榮譽，你的父親

"I don't know. It doesn't say. But there *is* a warning. Look here: *'Tell no one . . . journey . . . come . . . trust* . . . then it says a name . . . I think it's *Change* . . . it's the old name of Boomtown! Then something about *friends* . . .'"

"What does it mean?"

Burton studied the note for a few more moments. "I think it says, *'Tell no one about your journey to Change; when you come, trust my friends.'*"

I interrupted. "So whoever is writing the letter is telling someone about something that is hidden or secret or both. He wants this person to come to Boomtown—or *Change*—and trust the people who live here, or *lived* here. The letter is obviously very old."

Burton nodded. "I think that's the gist of it so far. Then look at this: *'Gift . . . repayment . . . father . . . lost son.* Then . . . *love and honor . . . father . . . you* . . . and look! Look at the signature and the chop next to it! I *know* that signature. *It's Chang!*"

It was true. At the bottom of the scrap of paper, signed with a flourish, was the unmistakable signature of Chang. Burton read the letter and then read it again, making sure he'd gotten it right. The more he read it, the more excited he became.

He exclaimed, "This was written by Chang! *Our* Chang. It says he was a *father*! No one ever knew that. He lived his entire life as a bachelor, that's what everyone thought. But if this letter is *real*—and it sure *looks* like it's real—this was written by Chang to his *son*."

Turning back to the Denk, Burton asked, "*Where* did you say you found this?"

"By the river. Below the factory. When I was fishing," Denk said.

"And it was just lying there?"

"In a tree. Caught on a branch."

"You didn't see anyone? Any footprints, anything like that?" Burton was visibly eager for details.

"No."

"What do you think, Arthur? Think it has anything to do with what's going on?"

"I suppose it could. The letter talks about something hidden, something that Chang knew about and nobody else. Something he wanted to keep secret until he wrote this letter. To his son, it suggests, who was living somewhere else, probably back in China where Chang was from. That would explain why no one knew about it."

Jonny objected hastily. "But this letter was written a hundred years ago maybe. It wouldn't have anything to do with *now*."

I answered him, "Why not? Our robber or robbers are obviously looking for something. They're *digging* for something. Maybe it's this *hidden* thing, whatever it is, that Chang kept secret. It sounds like he kept a *lot* of things secret. He had a son, which may also mean he had a wife—nobody knew about them. Who can guess what else we don't know about?"

Burton sighed. "We still can't know if this has anything to do with the robberies. Are they connected? It doesn't tell who's been digging or where they've been digging or what they're looking for."

Then Burton had an idea. He asked Denk, "Can you show us exactly where you found this? That would probably help a lot."

Denk shrugged and banged through the front door. He told his oldest boy to watch the other kids and lurched down a trail to the riverbank. We followed behind and skirted the water until we came up on the backside of the fireworks factory. He pointed with a huge finger at a tree branch near the bank of the river. "Right there."

Burton started to look around, and I joined him. Other than our own footprints, there really wasn't anything to see. It had rained so much recently that any signs would have been wiped out. Jonny tried to get us to go further down-river. He kept waving to us. But Burton wanted us to go in closer to the factory.

Just then he glanced down at his watch. "Rats! Look at the time! I completely forgot—we've got to get back to town right now."

"Why? What's the rush?"

"It's 10:46! The bank is going to be robbed in less than fifteen minutes."

"Excuse me?"

"The bank! At exactly 11:00. That's only fourteen minutes from now!"

I didn't get a chance to ask what he was yelling about because we were running back down the trail and chasing Burton on the way to his car. Denk easily kept pace with us through his long strides and was there to watch us leave. His children had finished feeding the animals and stood next to him. They looked so forlorn in their rubber boots and patched coats that I couldn't help but turn around and offer some help.

"Pardon me, Denk. Maybe you don't know about some of the programs we've got at the church. The ladies could help with some food. They could help with the children. We could have some men come out and work on your roof, that sort of thing. Maybe I could come back out and we could talk about it. Maybe tomorrow? How does that sound?"

Denk looked like he would grab my head off its shoulders. He could do it if he wanted to. Instead, with a loud grunt he spun on his heel and stomped back into the cabin with his children in tow. The door slammed with a bang and he was gone.

"Nerts, Preacher! Now what did you go and do *that* for?" Burton cried angrily.

"What?"

"Denk goes and helps us with an important clue, and then you go and *insult* him!"

"What are you talking about?"

"Get in the car. We've got to get going."

Jonny and I hopped in. Burton was steamed.

"What's the problem, Burt? I was just offering help. It's the Christian thing to do."

"You think so? You really think so?"

"Of course I do. The man lost his wife. He's on his own trying to take care of seven children. I saw the way they live. They could use some help. That's all I was saying."

"You *see* the way they live? You don't know *anything* about the way they live. Denk nearly killed himself with grief when his wife died. He had a baby not more than two months old. He had six other children and no wife to help him. He went off into the hills and didn't come back for five months. During that time, his children took care of each other—just like they always do. When he got back, he tried to keep on going—just like he'd always done.

"But . . ."

"Don't 'but' me! Keep your 'buts' to yourself! That older girl in there, Freyja, she graduated as a straight-A student from high school. The older boy, he's tops in his senior class. All the rest of them kids, they're clothed, fed, schooled, and healthy.

"And their father, Denk, he might not be able to read, mostly because he doesn't want to—and he might not have a regular job, mostly because he doesn't need one—but he manages to take care of his family just fine. He hunts and fishes and lays traps. What he shoots, he keeps for food; what he traps, he sells the skins for money. He usually shoots or traps more than he needs; he gives that to Walter, who cuts it up and sells it for him here in Boomtown. He trades extra fish for supplies down at the Red Bird.

"In other words, they don't live in a fancy house or have any fancy things, but they're getting by. They're doing just fine under the circumstances, same as they always have."

I didn't know what to say. I mumbled something like, "I was just trying to help."

"Yeah, sure, just trying to help. Well, next time you can help by minding your own business. Sometimes *that's* the Christian thing to do!"

I spent the rest of the drive with my mouth shut, staring out the window and wondering if I would ever understand the people who lived in Boomtown. Just when I thought I was getting it figured out, something like this would happen and I'd have to start all over again. Maybe I preached about mercy every Sunday, but it was pretty clear—I didn't understand it very well.

But in a few minutes, I had something else to think about. We sped around a corner and screeched to a halt in front of the bank. Burton jumped out and ran around the cruiser.

"C'mon, Reverend! Jonny! It's 11:02. *Let's move it!*"

We got out and stood on the sidewalk next to Burton's car. "What's going on, anyway? How do you know the bank's being robbed?"

"Because it's *Monday*. The bank is *always* robbed on Monday at 11:00 a.m. Same as always, right on schedule."

"But why . . ."

Before I could say anything else the front door of the bank flew open and a man came bursting through it with a bag of money in his left hand and a gun in his right. He looked about sixty-five years old, wearing a jean jacket, a red flannel shirt, gloves, and a black stocking hat and glasses. He didn't seem the least bit surprised to see the police car sitting there or Burton with his gun drawn or the other ten people who'd been standing by waiting for him to come out. The old man threw the bag on the ground, glanced at his watch, and looked at Sheriff Ernie with disgust.

"You're *late*! It's *two minutes* after eleven. I been standing in the lobby of the bank waiting for you!"

"Hey, I'm sorry, Frank. We got tied up down at Denk's place. Really, I'm sorry."

"Well, don't let it happen again." He stood there with his hands on his hips. "So, you gonna arrest me or ain'tcha?"

"Sure 'nough. Just hold your horses. I got the handcuffs right here."

Burton put his gun back in his holster and walked over to the bank robber.

"Burton! Aren't you going to take his gun?" I shouted, pointing at the black revolver still in his hand.

"Oh, right, sorry. I forgot." He reached out to take it and then stopped. "Hey, Frank, that's not your usual gun, is it? The other one's smaller, if I remember right."

"I got my favorite down at Guenther's Gun Corral. Gettin' the sights realigned and the pistol grip recovered. This is my backup piece. Nothin' to worry about, though. It ain't loaded or nothin', same as always."

He pulled the trigger just to prove it. *Bang!* The gun went off and the spectators screamed. Burton jumped back. Jonny ducked behind the car. I felt the bullet whiz just past my right ear. I think it missed my head by a few centimeters. I didn't have a ruler handy so I could measure it. Not that it mattered; I stumbled backward, tripped over my feet, and plopped on the sidewalk. Just over my shoulder, the bullet put a perfectly round hole through the "O" in the No Parking sign.

"Frank, I thought you said it wasn't loaded! Now I'm going to have to arrest you for real!" Burton said.

"It *wasn't* loaded!" the robber insisted, looking at the smoking pistol. "At least, I didn't *think* it was."

He shrugged his shoulders, handed the gun to Burton, put his arms out, and let the sheriff cuff his hands. Then he apologized to me. "Sorry 'bout that, Reverend. Nothin' personal."

I was flat on my backside and leaning against the car and clutching my chest. I counted my buttons—was this the third or the *fourth* time I'd nearly been killed? I couldn't remember. I watched Burton open the car door and deposit Frank in the backseat. Then he came over, stooped down, and asked if I was okay.

"You sure are a lucky buck there, Arthur! What's that? Four times now I declare! You must have one tough guardian angel!"

"My guardian angel is going to put in a two weeks' notice and ask for a transfer. I can't believe this! Who ever thought being a preacher could be this dangerous?"

Burton and Jonny helped me to my feet and tried to brush off some of the mud. "Wow, Dad! Look at the parking sign. That coulda been you."

The crowd had grown to about fifty by this time. People came running at the sound of the gunshot. Others came out of the bank to see what had happened. The initial shock was wearing off, and I was starting to get upset.

"Can you please tell me what *that* was all about?" I asked Burton.

"Sure 'nough, Reverend," Burton explained. "You see that feller over there in my backseat? That's none other than Frank Cavenaugh. Maybe you heard of him, Frankie the Banker? Made a name for himself about twenty years ago."

"Sure, I remember hearing about that. He robbed about thirty banks before they caught him, isn't that right?"

"That's him! He's the one who came to Boomtown twenty years ago and robbed this very same bank—he's the reason

I was made sheriff! He finally got himself arrested doing a job down south of here. He got convicted down there, served fifteen years in the state penitentiary, then got released four years ago with time off for good behavior. He's been living here ever since."

"But why *here*?"

"Frank tells me that when he robbed the bank here in Boomtown, he really liked the place. Nice people and all. He went away for fifteen years, but when he got out, he came back here. The folks were glad to have him. He's what you call a local celebrity, the only man to ever commit a major crime in Boomtown. They let him ride in the Fourth of July parade. And he teaches classes at the library on firearms safety."

"*Firearms safety?* You're pulling my leg, right?"

"No, sir, I'm not. He's usually a lot more careful."

"And now he robs the bank on Mondays?"

"Oh, him and I worked that out a while ago. When he got here, about all he knew how to do was rob banks and make license plates. We didn't need any license plates, so the town agreed to let him rob the bank. Just on Mondays, though."

"You're serious?"

"I told you everybody in town has a job, 'cept for Denk, of course. Frank just wanted to keep himself sharp. We figure he gives our town a little character, and in return the residents pay him a small salary to keep a roof over his head. Pretty fair deal, if you ask me."

I doubted that Boomtown needed to pay anyone to give it any more character than it already had.

Burton took Frank to jail, where he was released the next day, promising to be especially careful in the future. From then on Sheriff Ernie tried extra hard to make it to the bank on time for his Monday appointment.

The No Parking sign was removed and installed in the lobby of the library. Visitors would see it there; someone was sure to tell the story about the Reverend Button, who was *almost* shot by Frankie the Banker.

I stayed inside my house for almost a month after that, except on Sundays. I kept the door locked and my head down. I even gave up shaving—afraid I might die in a horrible shaving accident. But was that the end of it? Not by a long shot.

CHAPTER 14

Fourth of July

March soon gave way to April and Easter week. At Boomtown Church, we remembered the season in typical fashion, starting with the annual children's procession on Palm Sunday. The children marched down the aisle of the church bearing palm branches and singing the hymn "Hosanna, Loud Hosanna!" Then we held a solemn Good Friday service filled with quiet prayers and burning candles. Finally, it was Easter morning; it began with a joint sunrise service in Chang Park sponsored by all three of the town's congregations and was followed by joyful celebrations in each of the three respective churches.

Then, in traditional Boomtown fashion, the real fun began. Everyone gathered on the museum grounds for a community Easter brunch, Easter egg hunt, and other holiday games. Children ran back and forth through the bushes and along the paths searching for eggs. The boys wore jackets and ties, and the girls were dressed in their finest Easter dresses. Parents stood in cheerful groups watching their children and enjoying a delicious breakfast cooked by the museum kitchen.

Even Denk was there with his seven children, and Walter the Butcher put in an appearance; this was the one public gathering a year they both would attend. It was quite a sight to see the two gigantic men standing silently next to one another, arms crossed, scowls on their faces, like two gnarled trees in a forest. But their frowns were unable to dampen the mood. The sun shone brightly in the clear blue sky with not a rain cloud in sight. A cool breeze blew through the blossoming apple and cherry trees. Stomachs were tucked full of eggs and ham and fresh coffee and fruit juice. It was the perfect Easter Sunday.

Still, I don't think I'll ever get used to the traditional Hen Grenade toss, where kids throw egg grenades at a five-foot-high paper mâché Easter Bunny piñata until it explodes and candy goes flying everywhere. It could only happen in Boomtown.

April turned to May, and before you knew it children were out of school. Like other farming communities, Boomtown followed a modified school schedule in order to accommodate families who were busy planting and harvesting crops.

School didn't officially begin until October and continued uninterrupted—except for winter break—until mid-May. Kids would be out for eight weeks until after the Fourth of July and then back in school for part of July and August. May was busy with planting the fall crops; June was set aside for bringing in the winter wheat harvest and cherry picking; August and September for alfalfa, barley, corn, cabbage, squash, turnips, apples, and more. It was always a busy time for Boomtown.

Of course, that didn't stop anyone from making preparations for the biggest celebration of Boomtown's year—the Fourth of July parade. In spite of everyone's full schedule on the farms, they still made time to build elaborate floats, sew costumes, iron uniforms, practice band music, erect grandstands and booths, bake cakes and pies, make caramel apples and cotton candy for sale, and decorate every fence with red, white, and blue bunting. The Hopontop Circus was in town for that week, and so was the Bonitelli Brothers' Traveling Carnival. That meant rides and rodeos to go along with the blasts and booms of the huge fireworks show held on the shores of the river in Chang Park at sundown on the Fourth of July.

Of course, Chang's Famous Fireworks Factory had been producing full tilt since January in order to meet the demand for fireworks. They were busy filling orders for as far away as New York and Florida. They also had to supply the nine *tons* of rockets, shells, firecrackers, Roman candles, girandoles, cherry bombs, spinning wheels, whistles, snakes, bottle rockets, fountains, sparklers, smoke grenades, gerbs, firefalls, and set pieces needed for the residents of Boomtown.

BOOMTOWN

52ND ANNUAL

FOURTH of JULY PARADE

FIREWORKS

IN CHANG PARK AT SUNSET

COME and JOIN THE FUN

BANG STREET ❧ BOOM BOULEVARD
STARTING AT NOON SHARP

Every season, Chang's would unveil something new and exclusive just for the townspeople: a more spectacular fountain, a louder firecracker, or a specially colored sparkler. This year Han-wu and his team had modified the rocket they'd been testing. It stood six feet high, two feet in diameter, and was filled to the top with hundreds of fireworks. It would fill the sky with a magnificent finale of shooting stars, fiery rainbows, dazzling sparkles, and ringing blasts. The huge rocket joined the rows and rows of cannons positioned on Left Foot Island. Workers checked and double-checked the arrangements while the whole town counted the hours until the big blastoff scheduled for a few days later.

Sheriff Burton Ernie was busy with his own concerns. The day after the Monday bank robbery, he was back down at the river below the fireworks factory trying to find more pages from the mysterious letter. He looked for footprints and tire tracks. He tried to find signs of digging. From there he traveled all over town searching high and low for the opening to the tunnel that *had* to be somewhere, but he couldn't find it. New mounds appeared every now and then. Wood posts and boards came up missing from the Straightline Lumber Mill. Food was taken—freshly baked pies from Gramma Edna's windowsill, eggs from Lazy Gunderson's hen house, and a side of ham from in front of the Red Bird. No one was seen. Nothing was heard. It was driving Burton crazy.

Everyone else was too busy to notice. There were crops to harvest, dresses to sew, food to prepare, stands to build, circuses to attend, broncos to bust, rides to ride, and a parade to plan. Janice and the kids were caught up in the fervor. Janice was helping some of the ladies sew banners and bunting. Jonny and Sarah were wrapped up in their secret class project, a special float built by the children of Boomtown School. Ruth, as Slug Queen, would be riding with Waldo Wainwright, the Slug King, and her entire court of Slug Princesses. I had been recruited, along with Reverend Platz and Reverend Tinker, to serve as masters of ceremonies for the parade.

The floats would gather at the west end of Boom Boulevard, wind their way around the statue of Chang in the center of Town Square, and then head north along Bang Street accompanied by bands and cheerleaders and dancers and marching teams. Bringing up the rear would be the annual Founders' Day Float, a plaster re-creation of the old city on a hill that would be blown up from the inside. This was scheduled to happen just as it reached the center of town. It commemorated the founding event of Boomtown and was always a parade favorite.

As one of the three masters of ceremonies, I was assigned a position in front of Chang's statue where a public address system was installed. It was our job to announce each float and group as the parade passed through Town Square. I was nervous—*very* nervous—being surrounded by stuff exploding in my face every two seconds.

Ruth came to my rescue. "Here, Dad," she said, handing me a Slug football helmet.

"What's this for?"

"I knew you were nervous about all the fireworks. Waldo let me borrow this from the team."

"Thanks. I need all the help I can get."

"Did you want some football pads too? I can probably get some of those."

"No, the helmet should be enough, sweetheart," I said, giving her a quick hug. "Burton promised to keep an eye on me. And the two reverends, of course, they'll be guarding my safety. It's like having my own security detail." I hoped I wouldn't need it.

The morning of the parade finally arrived. Helga the librarian was in charge of getting everyone lined up. She hustled up and down the line, handling last-minute emergencies, encouraging the musicians, straightening ribbons and bows, and telling everyone to smile, smile, *smile*.

Mayor Tanaka and his wife, Kyoko, rode in the lead car waving to the crowd. A float that re-created his heroic act during the war—a battleship on fire—followed behind. Akihiro's son stood on the back of the float firing a small, brass cannon. The blasts echoed off the sides of the buildings and rattled the glass in the windows. It was a fitting display for the start of the parade.

The Stickville Slugs marching band followed right behind, playing the school fight song. Next came Ruth and her court standing on the Slug Queen float. The float was flanked by two huge slugs covered in ivy and flowers and featured a slug "grotto" where Ruth sat on her throne. Her king, Waldo, stood on the front, holding a football, commemorating the historic win over the Giants. The three princesses in their slime-green silk dresses blew kisses and waved to potential boyfriends in the crowd. The entire Slug football team, wearing muddy uniforms, marched in their shadow.

Folks from all around—Stickville, Ainogold, East Wallop, and as far away as Wahalawamawampa and Updown—lined the sidewalks ten deep on both sides. They waved American flags and shot off toy cap guns and party favors. They cheered when the Slug Queen and Slug King rolled by and chanted Waldo's name.

They cheered even louder at the appearance of the Hopontop trick riders, decked out in feathers and face paint and doing handstands and backflips on the backs of their horses. Archers and drum players and dancers followed nearby. Chief Knife Thrower was there, juggling four spinning knives, accompanied by the acrobats and tumblers, each wearing colorful masks and spinning around like dervishes. Eye of the Eagle shot clay pigeons and Hen Grenades as they were tossed into the air. Children from the tribe threw lit firecrackers under the feet of the dancers as they danced.

Next came Sheriff Burton Ernie waving from the front seat of his cruiser, honking his horn and sounding his siren. He preceded the proud and solemn faces of the war veterans dressed in their respective uniforms and marching in front of their VFW float. Everyone clapped and cried as the color guard of the navy, army, air force, and marines marched past. They said a silent prayer of gratitude in honor of their fallen heroes and remembered again how grateful they were to live in such a wonderful country.

I was able to look down the long procession to see the approach of the Boomtown Museum Float—always a crowd favorite. The steam-powered float was piloted by the grandson of Dr. Losotu, who took great pleasure in yanking on the steam whistle and blowing huge gouts of steam into the air. Hovering overhead were three Sky Campers. I could see Samora and her sister and brother in each of them throwing bubble gum and penny candy down to the kids in the crowd. Some of the children from the museum's music classes rode on the float, blowing trumpets and whistles and beating on tin-can drums and otherwise creating quite a racket.

Next came the Farmers' Float, pulled by Fred Cotton and his tractor, stacked fifteen feet high with alfalfa hay. A banner hung on each side that said BOOMTOWN FARMERS and HAPPY 4TH OF JULY in large, bright red letters. Some of the farmers hoisted children up into the wagon where they took turns waving to the crowd through windows cut in the hay bales.

Clown cars and clowns from the Bonitelli Brothers' Traveling Carnival whizzed around in circles just behind the farm wagon, followed by the fire engine driven by the fire chief and his crew. The marching band from East Wallop High marched by playing "God Bless America" and "The Star-Spangled Banner," followed by their cheerleading squad and baton twirlers. The bell choir from First Presbyterian chimed their way down the street. Right behind them was the

Hog Callers Club, calling *SooooWHEE! SoooWHEE!* They had ten sows on tethers—each was decorated with red, white, and blue ribbons.

Reverend Platz, Reverend Tinker, and I took turns announcing each float and performing group as they came near. When it was my turn, I said into the microphone, "Please turn your attention to our next float, sponsored by the Ladies Rotary Club, inspired by the famous painting by Emanuel Gottlieb Leutze, *Washington Crossing the Delaware.*"

The float was actually a rowboat borrowed from Dusty Winslow and outfitted with wheels. Dusty himself stood proudly in the middle of the boat dressed as George Washington—powder wig and all—while his fellow passengers shot bottle rockets and exploding helicopters into the air. The helicopters were a stiff, cardboard propeller on a stick attached to a spinning firecracker that lifted the helicopter into the air until it exploded. I had no idea what bottle rockets and helicopters had to do with George Washington and the Battle of Trenton, but the crowd seemed to appreciate it nonetheless.

The Miners' Float came next, a tribute to Chang and the miners who had helped build Boomtown. The current president of Chang's Black Powder Plant, Lin Chow, was dressed up as Chang. Some of his employees were dressed as miners. They walked behind the float handing out bright red, cinnamon-flavored candy to the crowd. The candy looked like small sticks of dynamite with a black licorice "fuse" coming out of the top.

Next came the Root Beer Float. The members of St.

Bernard's Lutheran Church served ice cream and soda to the crowd as fast as they could scoop and pour. It was followed by the Back Float, sponsored by Carlson's Chiropractic; the Goat Float, by Fannie's Fleece and Feathers; the Coat Float, by Kellogg's Clothiers; and the Note Float, by Boomtown Music.

The noise of the crowd was soon overwhelmed by the banging, clonking, clinking, bonking sound of the Bangonbuckets Band, led by Gus Odegaard, owner of Gus's Gas-N-Go. His "band" was open to anyone who wanted an excuse to march in the parade, regardless of musical ability. All a "musician" was required to do was bring a bucket or a frying pan or a tin can and something to hit it with. I could see Gus marching proudly at the front of his band, beating on his collection of metal containers with a huge ladle.

If that weren't loud enough, along came the folks from Chang's Famous Fireworks Factory. Strings of firecrackers burst underneath the feet of the lion dancers in their brightly feathered costumes. The women were dressed in traditional silk robes. Some wore masks or had their faces painted white or were costumed as ancient Chinese deities. They rang chimes and bells and waved to the appreciative crowd. Their children ran back and forth shouting, "*Gung hay fat choy!*" which meant "Wishing you prosperity." They threw sample packs of fireworks to the spectators and small bags of candy wrapped in silver and pink ribbon.

The parade group consisted of about sixty Chinese men, women, and children, about half of the Chinese Americans who lived in Boomtown. From the platform I caught a glimpse of Fie-tann, manager of the fireworks factory. He and Lin Chow sat on the town council and were among those who continued to maintain Chang's companies following his untimely death.

They had built a tightly knit Chinese community around the factories. They always put on a great show during the annual parade, and they sold herbs and teas and rice and fireworks at the Saturday Farmers' Market. Everyone applauded as they passed by, knowing that these families were a lasting part of Chang's legacy and essential to the success of the town.

As the parade drew to a close, the noise level grew louder and louder because everyone anticipated the grand finale, the destruction of the Founders' Float. Just in front of it were the floats built by the students from Boomtown School, another highlight of the parade. Jonny had been the prime instigator of the design of the school's float.

"How about a fire-breathing dragon with fire coming out of its mouth and everything?" he had suggested.

"Yeah, that'd be swell!"

"It could have smoke come out of its nose—and we could drop firecrackers out of its rear end."

"And sparklers burning on its back and tail!"

"And we could make it roar—just like a real dragon!"

Busy and Rocky had the solution for that: "We could borrow the sound system from the school and hook up speakers and make it really, really loud."

Jonny suggested, "What about wings? How about huge wings and a tail that moves and a mouth that opens and closes?"

"The boys could dress up like knights and have swords and shields and try to slay the dragon."

"And the girls can dress up like princesses. They could run down the street crying because dragons like to *eat* princesses."

So that's what the kids had done. The crowd was so impressed by their float that they started to follow along behind the dragon's tail as it went by. The Founders' Float crawled down the street just behind the crowd so that everything and everyone began to converge on Town Square in a rolling sea of people and floats and animals and children and noise and confusion—with me standing smack-dab in the middle of it all. I tried to get everyone to stand back and make room, but the noise was too loud.

The Founders' Float stopped about ten yards in front of our stage, where Burton Ernie stood directing the crowd. He waved for people to spread around in a circle to make room.

"Stand back!" he shouted. "Farther back! At least fifty feet. *Back up!*"

While he directed traffic away from the float, the crew manning the rig prepared to destroy it. Three men scrambled around the truck that held the display and began to string fuses. Two others checked the blast packs positioned underneath the deck.

I nudged Reverend Platz and asked, "Do they have to park that thing so close to us?"

He studied the situation and answered, "It's about the same as last year. You have to watch out for that one fellow, though. You see the gangly gentleman under the truck there? Tends to overdo it on the gunpowder."

Before I could object, the men scrambled for cover. Sparks raced along the length of the fuses. I caught a glimpse of Sarah and Jonny standing on the edge of the circle. I waved but they didn't see me. Too late to have them stand back. The noise of the crowd swelled. Loud shouting and cheers. Hands on ears. *Kaboooooom!*

The plaster mountain and the tiny village disappeared in a cloud of smoke and flying debris to the delighted cheers of the spectators. Bits and pieces flew in every direction. I think I saw the model of the Boomtown Museum head toward Farmers' Park. The miniature Boomtown Library landed on the roof of Top's Soda Shop. The mini town hall shot straight up in the air and kept on going. The entire *floor* of the truck shot straight down and punched a crater in the street.

Reverend Platz said, "Exactly what I was talking about. Too much gunpowder."

The hole under the truck opened up a crack in the street. It was small at first, but got bigger as it went along. It raced across the asphalt and quickly reached our platform. Along with it came the sound of splintering, ripping, and cracking cement as the road began to give way. The crack split left and right. We watched it disappear around the far side of Chang's statue.

Reverend Platz was the first to feel the ground shift. Reverend Tinker felt it second. As the crack raced around the perimeter of the curb surrounding the statue, they both jumped. The short, round preacher rolled to the left. The tall, thin preacher jumped to the right. His flailing arm knocked me backward into the statue of Chang, where my shirtsleeve snagged on the beak of one of the bronze chickens.

I heard a roar and a loud cracking noise. I felt the whole world tip upside down. I saw the bright blue sky overhead. I seem to remember someone shouting my name. After that, I don't remember much. It was all a blur.

Later that day, after I regained consciousness and was lifted up out of the hole, my family was there to explain what had happened.

"Where am I?" I asked groggily.

"You're in Dr. Goldberg's office, dear," Janice answered.

"How'd I get here?"

Jonny piped in. "Sheriff Ernie carried you down—after they dragged you up out of the hole. Don't you remember? All the people in Town Square. You remember that?"

"Um, I think so." My memory was pretty fuzzy.

"The crowd kept getting bigger and bigger. Musta been more than a million people!"

"It was more like two thousand," Janice corrected him.

"Sure, maybe. Sheriff Ernie thinks the vibrations from all the marching and the weight of all those people with all the floats and then the Founders' Float blowing up, that's what did it."

"I can't really remember what happened," I admitted. "What did I miss?"

"You got caught on one of Chang's chickens. Grabbed

you with its beak, that's what it did! And then *crash!* Down you went! *Whomp!*"

In bits and pieces, I finally managed to get the whole story. Basically, I'd been sucked down into a gaping sinkhole. Panic ensued. Children wept. Women prayed. Men called for ropes and shovels. Burton Ernie blew his whistle. Dr. Goldberg grabbed his bag. The fire chief brought a ladder. The search committee from Boomtown Church checked their calendars. Janice and the kids just stood next to the hole waiting for the dust to settle.

When it finally did, there I was twenty feet down in a hole sitting right in the middle of Chang's bronze lap, covered in dirt and debris, bruised and battered, with a sprained wrist and chunks of cement in my lap. Otherwise, I was all right, thanks to Waldo's football helmet and the most overworked guardian angel in human history.

Still, that wasn't the biggest shock of all. No one could have prepared for what they saw next. Looking up out of the shadows of the hole, standing in the opening of what was clearly a tunnel, covered in dust and wearing a hard hat on his head, was the living, breathing, mirror-image of Chang himself—back from the grave. His face was filthy from the cave-in; his clothes were torn and tattered; his eyes squinted from the dust and the sudden bright light pouring into his underground hiding place—but the resemblance was unmistakable. If this wasn't Chang, then it was his twin brother.

He looked at me. I looked at him.

"Oh my," I said, recognizing the face.

Then I fainted.

PARADE GOES BUST IN BOOMTOWN

4TH OF JULY CAVE-IN REMAINS A MYSTERY

BOOMTOWN — The citizens of Boomtown remain stunned over the unexplained cave-in that followed the climax of the town's annual 4th of July parade. The crowd, estimated in the thousands, stood by for the explosion of the Founder's Day Float which apparently opened a crack in the street surrounding Town Square. The statue of Chang, founding father of Boomtown, plunged downward into a hidden, underground chamber. Pulled along with it was the most recent minister of the Boomtown Church, the Reverend Arthur Button, who has already survived five other spectacular accidents over the past ten months, includ...

Town Square remains cordoned while a full investigation continues. Sheriff Burton Ernie is in charge and has since dispatched volunteers to trace the tunnel back to its origin. So far, nearly all of the stolen items (recently reported missing by this newspaper) have been recovered.

This is what is known for certain. The entire scheme was carried out by a single man working alone. Digging during the day and dumping dirt under the cover of night, he single-handedly dug a tunnel from Chang's Famous Fireworks Factory, approximately two-miles due east to the underground chamber.

As to the identity of the "Mysterious Mole" as he has come to be known, reports allege that his name is Xian, the great-grandson of Chang, although his true iden-

MAN
TWO
GET

GO...
surprisi...
John Fis...
with two...
announc...
undergo...
reverse...
doctor...
George...
agreed to...
controvers...
When finis...
will have o...
back leg.

When a...
motivation,...
he was tired...
around in...
natural resul...
having two l...
travel const...
direction....
can't wait...
things norm...
ing back a...

"People...
walking for...
he said....
trying to wa...
mailbox and...
to go around...
tire block jus...
there."

Mrs. F...
was very e...
the future ho...
regains the...
straight line...
was quoted a...
now on, whe...
the store, h...
and down...
ket with a s...

CHAPTER 15

The Trial of the Century

The town was buzzing like a swarm of bees in a rose garden. All anyone could talk about was the upcoming trial scheduled for exactly three weeks from the Fourth of July. A *trial*—with an actual jury and judge and everything!

Of course, every able-bodied citizen in Boomtown wanted to be on the jury. Mayor Tanaka's office was bombarded with phone calls and letters and a line of people at his door demanding to be selected. In other towns, you couldn't *pay* people to stand jury duty. But this was Boomtown's trial of the century.

Since the town didn't have its own prosecutor or defense attorney, it had to borrow both of them from Stickville. Likewise, the circuit judge, Maria Rodriquez, would have to sit in for the trial; she was given a temporary office down the hall from Mayor Tanaka. She couldn't get a moment's peace either.

The immediate problem was where to hold the proceedings, since all eleven hundred seventeen residents of Boomtown wanted to attend. Not more than fifty would fit in the regular courtroom downstairs; only two hundred in the main room of the library if all the tables were removed; only about four hundred in the great room of the museum, even if everyone stood up; only three hundred and fifty could fit into the gymnasium of the school.

The problem was solved when the Hopontops offered their main circus tent as a courtroom. It seems that even the socially distant Hopontops were suffering from a severe case of "trial fever." They graciously rearranged their summer travel schedule in order to make the tent and grandstands available. The tent was staked out in Chang Park and a makeshift judge's podium and jury box was built. The Hopontops offered their public address system, and that pretty much settled it. Everyone in town was welcome to attend the trial and would be able to see and hear the entire proceedings.

News updates about the trial were on the radio day and night. It made the papers in Stickville and Ainogold and as far away as Spokane and Seattle. Soon we had eight newspaper reporters and even a film crew staying at Mitterand's Boarding House. Everywhere you turned, a reporter was pushing a microphone into someone's face. They were as common as cow pies in a cornfield.

Not that anyone seemed to mind. It was the only thing anyone wanted to talk about—except for me, that is. They learned about my other five "near misses" and how I was the one who'd almost been killed by the mysterious "Mole" (as they were calling him). They heard I had helped Sheriff Ernie with part of the investigation. They heard I would be called as a star witness for the prosecution. After that I wasn't given a minute's rest. They kept asking the same ridiculous questions over and over again:

"Were you surprised when the street caved in?"

"Did you have any idea who was behind the tunneling?"

"Are you going to sue the Mole for damages?"

"Is it really true that you've nearly been killed six times?"

"Is there any way you can sneak us into the jail for an interview with the Mole?"

They hounded me for the slightest tidbit of information that could be added to the very little that any of us already knew—which wasn't much. By now we'd determined that the "Mole" was in fact Xian (pronounced "She-On"), the great-grandson of Chang. His previous existence was unknown; he was currently a permanent guest at Burton's station house. Men had climbed down into the hole and traced the tunnel back to its origin. It headed west toward the river, passing just to the south of Lazy Gunderson's house, and then straight on to the north side of Chang's Famous Fireworks Factory. Hidden by the thick trees and heavy overgrowth was an abandoned warehouse. Inside the basement of the building was where we discovered the entrance to Xian's excavation.

Everything that had been stolen was found in the tunnel. Wood and boards were used to shore up the ceiling and walls. Various parts from farming equipment, bicycles, wheels, wires, belts, gears, and whatnot had been culled together to build a digging machine—rather ingenious, and strong evidence that Xian shared his famous ancestor's knack for invention. The lights stolen from in front of the courthouse were tapped into the electricity from the factory and strung along the tunnel to light the way. The motor from my lawn mower was cleverly rigged as the drive unit for a rope and pulley system to pull cart-loads of dirt down the tunnel. A conveyor belt lifted the dirt up to where Fred Cotton's truck was parked inside the warehouse. Xian had devised a special sort of muffler for the truck so it could be driven in absolute silence around town at night so he could dump the dirt. The entire setup was quite remarkable. It was hard not to be impressed by Xian's ingenuity.

Beyond that there were a thousand unanswered questions, especially the question of who would sit on the jury. Town hall was swamped with phone calls, and a line formed down the hall and out the front door morning, noon, and night.

It was Helga the librarian who finally came up with an agreeable solution. Every eligible juror in town had a library card.

She took all of them (except those on the witness list) and put them in a basket, and Judge Rodriguez drew out twelve names. Fair, impartial, and fast. Boomtown had its first official jury in history. Unfortunately, the jurors who were named now became fodder for the newspaper reporters. The judge had to sequester the jury before the trial just so they could get some sleep.

Fortunately for the jurors, the trial was scheduled only three days after the selection. Everyone on the witness list spent that time being interviewed by Xian's defense attorney, George Rigdale, and the prosecuting attorney, Horatio Hooke. The former was quiet and efficient and kept his questions to a minimum. He wanted to help his client with as little trouble as possible. The prosecutor, however, was a horse of a different color.

it remains to be seen what the outcome of the trial

Horatio Hooke has been retained by Okanogan County as prosecuting atto... in the case. He has been practic... in the city of Si...lville...

The venerable Horatio Hooke was an ambitious lawyer from Stickville positioning himself for a future career in politics. He made no secret that the trial was his opportunity to get away from prosecuting parking tickets; he wanted to step up to the big leagues. He seized every opportunity to push his face in front of the cameras, to offer his latest theory of the case, to get his picture in the paper, and to pontificate about his strategy for the upcoming trial and his plans to get the maximum sentence for the Mole.

He stood on the steps of the town hall dressed in his black suit and white shirt, his dark hair slicked back, waving his arms, punching the air with his fist, and decrying the rapidly rising rate of crime in the county. He blamed Sheriff Ernie. He blamed the mayor. He blamed the county government. He blamed Congress. He blamed the Supreme Court.

Stomping his foot and pounding his fists, he cried out, "The only way to stop the deterioration of decent society and clean up our streets is to elect new representatives who can restore sanity to the towns and villages of Washington!

"We need *better* leaders—*stronger* leaders—*courageous* leaders! You need a man who will seize the reins of government and do whatever it takes to save our women and children from the degradation that threatens to destroy our way of life!"

He humbly announced his intention to run for governor of the fine state of Washington as soon as the trial was over. Until then, his entire life would be strictly focused on the trial and the conviction of Xian, "the most notorious and dangerous criminal of the twentieth century."

Horatio Hooke continued to bang the drum until the very morning of the trial, 9:00 a.m., July 25, 1950, a date that would go down in Boomtown history. As expected, everyone was in attendance. The circus tent was filled to capacity and overflowing with people trying to catch the smallest glimpse of the action. With a few loud bangs of her gavel, Judge Rodriguez called the courtroom to order and the trial began.

Horatio Hooke stood before the jury to deliver his opening statement. The pompous lawyer stuck his thumbs in his vest, puffed out his chest, and marched back and forth like a peacock. Dramatically he crowed, "Ladies and gentlemen of the jury, today we have before us, sitting over there next to his defense attorney, a man who has no defense. A criminal of the most despicable sort! A man who, unbeknownst to the citizenry of Boomtown, snuck into your small town under the cover of darkness and began to steal whatever he could lay his hands on. While you slept, he took whatever he needed—food, supplies, equipment—and then he began to dig a tunnel underneath your very feet!"

I sat toward the front with Janice and Holly on my left and Ruth, Jonny, and Sarah to my right. I glanced down the row and received a smile of reassurance from Ruth. Sarah fidgeted in her seat. Jonny wouldn't look at me. His eyes were riveted on the drama unfolding in front of him. He was pale and gripped the edge of his folding chair with white knuckles. Why was he so nervous? What was going on with him?

Horatio Hooke commanded attention with his thundering voice. "*Why* did the defendant do it? *What was he up to?* That is what we are here to find out!

"It is my purpose in this trial, as the prosecuting attorney for the fine county of Okanogan in the wonderful state of Washington, to prove, beyond a shadow of a doubt, that Xian, the great-grandson of Chang, intended, without regard to the safety or well-being of the residents of this fair city, to dig a tunnel underneath Town Square until he reached the Bank of Boomtown, where he planned to rob the bank by digging under the vault and making his getaway, taking with him every nickel and dime that the citizens of this town have slaved so hard to earn and save! When I have finished presenting evidence and testimony, you will most certainly return a verdict of guilty, guilty, *guilty* for attempted bank robbery, not to mention the other daring crimes he has committed! You will sentence Xian to the maximum sentence, twenty years in prison, which he so richly deserves!"

When he was finished, Mr. Hooke wiped his sweating face with a handkerchief and marched back to his table where he plopped down in his chair and stared triumphantly at Xian and his lawyer, George Rigdale.

The lawyer stood, walked over to the jury, smiled, and calmly said, "Xian is guilty of everything for which he has been charged."

Everyone in the tent gasped in surprise and started talking at once. The photographers flashed pictures. The reporters jotted down notes as fast as they could write. Horatio Hooke crossed his arms and smiled in victory. Judge Rodriguez banged her gavel and demanded silence.

As soon as order was reestablished, George Rigdale continued. "It doesn't *matter* that he's guilty. As soon as you hear what he has to say, the bank will drop the charges against him and let Xian go free." With that, he turned around, went back to his table, and sat down.

The courtroom exploded a second time. Everyone was shouting. Reporters ran for the exit to go and call their newspapers. The judge banged her gavel again and again to no avail. Burton Ernie and the bailiff stood up and tried to get the situation back under control. In spite of everyone's best efforts, it still took at least five minutes for the pandemonium to subside.

Once it was quiet again, the judge said, "One more outburst like that, and I will move this trial back to the courthouse and *no one* will be allowed inside—*especially* the reporters. Just because we're in a circus tent doesn't mean this is a circus. It's far too hot in here for funny business. Be quiet, or I'll *end* this thing!"

The assembled audience quieted down, chagrined by the judge's harsh words. Then she gestured and said, "Proceed, Mr. Hooke. Call your first witness."

The prosecuting attorney called Fred Cotton to the stand. He waved to his wife from the jury box and saluted some of the farmers he knew out in the crowd. He'd come straight in from the field, dressed in his boots and overalls and a wide-brimmed hat. He removed his hat as he took the oath to tell the truth, the whole truth, and nothing but the truth, so help him God.

Mr. Hooke approached and asked the first question of the trial: "Please state your full name for the court."

"Fredrick Lawrence Archibald Cotton, named after my granddad on my mother's side and my uncle on my father's side."

"Yes, thank you. Please refrain from any unnecessary embellishment. Just stick to the questions."

"Yes, sir."

"As I understand it, your truck was stolen during a rain-storm in mid-September of last year?"

"More like it came up missing. Floated down West Chang to be precise."

"However it turned up missing, isn't it true that it ended up in the hands of Xian, who used it to haul dirt from his secret digging site?"

"That's what I've been told."

"You're aware of the muffler system he installed so he could sneak around town without being detected?"

"I am. Very clever. Never would have thought of it myself."

"Be that as it may, you must be furious knowing that your truck was being used in the commission of a crime."

"No, not really. Quite the opposite in fact."

"No? May I remind you that you are under oath? It doesn't bother you, not even in the slightest, that your precious truck, used in the daily conduct of your farming business, was sto-len and secretly used by the defendant in a desperate plan to rob the bank, which, may I remind you, included the money *you* had on deposit?"

"Why should it? My truck is *famous* now. The Boomtown Museum wants to put it on permanent display. This is the most exciting thing that's ever happened to me!"

Everyone burst out laughing. Even the judge smiled before she tapped her gavel as a reminder. Horatio Hooke was stunned. This wasn't what he was expecting. He wanted outrage. He wanted indignation. He wanted demands for justice—not this.

"No further questions for this witness," he grumbled and sat down.

"Mr. Rigdale?"

"No questions, Your Honor."

"Mr. Hooke, call your next witness."

Next to the stand was Gramma Edna. She'd had three pies stolen by Xian. The prosecutor tried the same approach as he had with Fred Cotton. It didn't work any better than it did the first time. Gramma Edna wasn't upset. Instead, she smiled sweetly at Xian sitting at the defendant's table and said, "I hope they tasted okay. Sometimes I use too much nutmeg and cinnamon with the apples. And I overcooked one of the crusts. I'm sorry, dear."

Horatio Hooke paraded five more people through the witness box, witless "victims" of Xian's terrifying crime spree: Tom O'Grady, Captain Trudeau, Matthieu LaPierre, Ellis Brown, owner of the Red Bird, and Lazy Gunderson. None of them were angry. Instead they were curious as to when Xian had arrived, how he managed to move around town without being seen, and why he hadn't simply asked for help.

Lazy Gunderson said, "Xian did me a *favor*. My wife has been after me to fix the front fence for years. If he hadn't stolen the posts and wire, I would have been out there busting my back for a week!"

Sheriff Burton Ernie was next on the stand. Horatio Hooke had no idea what he'd gotten himself into.

"Please state your full name for the court."

"Burton Albert Ernie."

"And what is your current position in Boomtown?"

"I'm the sheriff here."

"You've been sheriff for how long?"

"Twenty-one years this past June."

"And in that period of time, how many crimes of any significance have occurred here—crimes of a federal nature?"

"Just one. Frank Cavenaugh robbed the Bank of Boomtown back in 1929. Frankie the Banker. You can say hello to him. He's right there in the front row of the bleachers. Hey, Frank!"

"If you don't mind, please refrain from addressing anyone besides the officers of this court."

"Sorry. It's just that I didn't get to arrest Frank this week because of the trial and all. I'll let him rob the bank twice next week to make it up to him."

"Exactly! That is *precisely* what I wanted to ask you about. As the sheriff of this town, you seem to have a complete disregard for law and order. You spend your days drinking coffee and wandering around town and wasting taxpayer money with your malingering habits. If it weren't for the cave-in, your neglect and incompetence would have allowed the Bank of Boomtown to be robbed a *second* time! What do you have to say about that?"

Burton stared at the pompous lawyer. "I say you don't have to be so *rude*, that's what *I* say about it."

The crowd clapped and cheered. "You tell him, Burt!"

The judge rapped for order in the court.

Burton continued. "You come strutting into my town with your fancy suit and expensive shoes and big-city swagger and talk to my friends like they're a bunch of greenhorns. You don't understand Boomtown at all. I may not be the best investigator that ever was, but you forget that in more'n twenty years, we've only had *one* real crime. That crime was solved and most of the money was returned. And you see Frank over there? We helped *rehabilitate* him. That's more than most towns can say. And finally, when it comes to Xian, your theory is that he was heading for the bank, but you don't know that. All you know is that he's a means to an end—a way for you to make a name for yourself. We don't have much patience for that sort of thing in Boomtown."

When Burton was finished with his speech, the crowd let out another roar. This time the judge didn't stop them. You could tell by the look on her face that she was in agreement with Burton; she didn't like ambitious lawyers any more than he did. Horatio threw up his hands and returned to his seat. George had no questions for the witness. Judge Rodriguez called for a lunch recess. I would be called as a witness following the break. The relief was welcome; it had to be almost ninety degrees inside the tent.

Following lunch, court was reconvened and the bailiff called the court to order. The jury filed in and took their seats. Judge Maria Rodriguez instructed the prosecuting attorney to call his final witness. As soon as I was seated and sworn in, Horatio Hooke confidently approached the witness box and began his questions. I could tell from his demeanor that in spite of the unexpected testimony from earlier in the day, he thought I was just what he needed to turn the tide and get the guilty verdict he wanted.

"You are the current minister of Boomtown Church?"

"Yes, I am."

"And how long have you served in that capacity?"

"My family and I arrived in town August of last year."

"And as a minister, as a man of the cloth, as a man who has dedicated his entire life to the propagation and defense of the truth, can I depend on you to be perfectly honest and accurate as you answer my questions?"

"Of course."

"Thank you. Is it true, then, that your brand-new lawn mower was stolen from the front yard of your home?"

"Yes, it is."

"Is it also true that your lawn mower was found in the tunnel under Town Square, where it was being used to ferry dirt out of the tunnel?"

"Yes."

"And it was you, the owner of said stolen lawn mower, who nearly plunged to his death when the street gave way and you were pulled downward into that yawning pit where you nearly died, as I understand, for the sixth time in less than a year?"

"Yes. That was me."

"And when you briefly regained consciousness, you saw the defendant, Xian, standing near you in the tunnel?"

"Yes. I saw him there."

"So there can be no doubt in your mind that it was Xian who was responsible for the theft of your lawn mower, no doubt that he was the one responsible for stealing Fred Cotton's truck, Lazy Gunderson's fence, the lights, the digging tools, who knows what else, and no doubt in your mind whatsoever that it was Xian who nearly caused your death by cave-in?"

I hesitated. I looked at Janice. I looked at my children. I looked at all the townsfolk who were gathered there. Finally, I looked into the eyes of Xian sitting a few feet away from me. I really had only one thing I could say.

"There is no doubt in my mind. Xian is the one who has done all these things."

"Aha!" shouted Horatio Hooke. "I've *got* him!" The lawyer began to hop up and down in joy. Visions of fame and fortune danced in his head.

"With all due respect, sir, just what do you have him *for*?" I asked.

"For theft. For malicious mischief. For attempting to rob the bank! For nearly killing *you*, my fine fellow! He's guilty of all charges. *Guilty!* I've got him dead to rights."

"You're assuming, of course, that by the end of this trial, you'll still have someone who wants to press charges. I'm not so sure I'll be among them."

"What? What are you talking about? He nearly *killed* you!"

"I've been through worse."

Horatio Hooke didn't know what to say. He sputtered. He stammered. He steamed. He stomped back to his table, wiped the sweat from his brow, and took a long drink from his glass of water. He stopped to flip through his notepad. He seemed to be searching for something, found it, and then turned back to face me with a knowing smile. There was a strange look in his eye, like a cat that had already eaten the canary and was looking for dessert.

The lawyer addressed me with a patronizing tone. "You're

being quite *liberal* when it comes to dispensing forgiveness, Reverend, but that's the business you're in, I suppose. But would you feel the same if you knew how this criminal had duped your *son* into helping him?"

"My son? How does my son have anything to do with this?"

"You don't know?"

"Know what?" I glanced over at Jonny, who was avoiding eye contact with me.

"That all these months, behind your back, your son and his friends have been supplying Xian with food and water. That they, in fact, could be charged with aiding and abetting a suspected felon."

A loud murmur passed through the crowd.

"What are you talking about? Why would you *say* something like that?"

Horatio pointed a fat, stubby finger in Jonny's direction. "Maybe we should ask your *son!*"

Every eye in the courtroom turned to look at Jonny, who was sinking lower and lower into his chair. He tried to cover up his head with his arms. I could see three or four of his friends doing the same thing up in the bleachers. I even saw Busy try to slip under the bleachers and head for the exit, but Lazy caught him by the sleeve.

"Jonny?" I asked, staring at my son in dismay. He looked back at me wide-eyed and trembling. "For heaven's sake, Jonny, what have you gone and gotten yourself into *this* time?"

CHAPTER 16

Jonny's Testimony

Before things could get out of hand, Judge Rodriguez took charge.

"Reverend Button, I'm going to ask you to take a seat. The prosecuting attorney reserves the right to recall you to the stand. Isn't that what you'd prefer, Mr. Hooke?" The lawyer nodded in agreement.

As I stepped down and walked over to where my family was sitting, the judge continued. "Jonny, I'm going to have you come up here for a minute. I need to ask you a few questions."

Janice put her arm around Jonny to protect him, but he stood up and said in his bravest voice, "It's okay, Mom. I'll go." He scooted down the row of chairs and walked toward the judge's bench. He kept his eyes down—he wouldn't look at me.

"Jonny, I want you to sit there in the witness stand. I'm not going to swear you in—you're not on trial here. But I *do* need to talk to you. Anything you say won't get you in trouble—well, maybe *some* trouble—but I'm on your side. Don't worry."

Jonny sat down and answered nervously, "Okay. If you say so."

"Yes, I say so. Now, I'm going to ask you something. Don't be afraid. Don't worry about your father for a minute. Don't think about the lawyers or anything else. I want you to pretend it's just you and me. Do you think you can do that?"

Jonny glanced over at me then back at the judge. "I'll try."

"That's good. Okay. Now, is there anything you need to tell me? Something to do with Xian over there?"

"Yes."

"I can't hear you. You need to speak a little louder."

"Yes, ma'am," he said.

"What can you tell me about Xian?"

"We saw him."

"*Who* saw him?"

"My friends and me. On Halloween. We *saw* him. In Town Square."

"What do you mean?"

"We wanted to go trick-or-treating together. Busy and Lonnie wanted to meet in the square."

"Just the three of you?"

"No," Jonny hesitated, glancing around at the bleachers. "Sorry, guys. It was me and Busy and Lonnie and Rocky and Frank and Bobby and Steve."

"The seven of you got together as planned. So then what happened?"

"We all had our flashlights. We were talking about where we wanted to go first, and we were shining them on the statue of Chang. That's when we saw him—I mean, Xian—standing there looking up at the statue."

"Xian was in Town Square? Why?"

"We don't know. We just knew we were *scared*, because they looked so much alike. It was like Chang's ghost was standing there! Then he saw us looking at him and he ran down the street past the library. So we followed him."

"You followed him. Where did he go?"

"We were sneaky about it. We stayed in the shadows and hid behind bushes so we could watch him. He went down the road and then out into Lazy Gunderson's field. He kept going until he got to the fireworks factory. That was *really* spooky 'cause Busy said it *proved* it was Chang's ghost; he was going back to haunt his factory. And then, all of a sudden, he disappeared! We didn't see where he went."

"He disappeared?"

"Yeah, like he sort of vanished. Lonnie says that's what ghosts do. Bobby said he saw one once in their attic. It was like that. *Poof!* He was gone."

"Was that the end of it?"

"No. The next morning we wanted to go back and look around. We didn't see anything at first, but then Rocky spotted some footprints near the river and a candy wrapper next to some trees. We decided to come back that night and see what happened. That's what we did. Me and my friends hid in the bushes and waited.

"About midnight we heard some branches moving and saw a flicker. Then here comes Chang—we thought it was Chang— right out of the dark carrying a lantern. Bobby screamed, 'It's the ghost!' We all screamed, not just him. That's when he caught us hiding in the bushes."

Horatio Hooke was looking at me with a smug grin on his face while Jonny was talking. I wondered how he'd figured it out—how did he know about the boys? Why hadn't *I* figured it out? I was his father. Suddenly a lot of things were starting to make sense. *How could I be so blind?* The judge prompted Jonny to continue.

"We could tell he was cold and hungry. So me and my friends decided to help him. I took some food from our pantry at home. Rocky got some from his house. Bobby rustled up a few things around town—so did some of the other guys. After that, we all took turns going out to the tunnel at night. We took out some blankets and spare clothes and whatever else we could find."

So *that's* why things had started disappearing from around the house—little things like my coat and the food. It's why Jonny had seemed so tired all the time. I knew he was up to something, but I never figured he'd been sneaking out at night.

"Was that all? Just some food and clothes?"

"At first. But then we got to know him a little bit. He told us his name was Xian. It sounded like 'Sean' when he said it, kind of like *my* name, Jon, so I wanted to help. He didn't tell us who he was, just that he was digging for something. He said it belonged to him; it was lost a long time ago and he came to find it."

"So you helped him *dig*?" The judge sounded shocked. I, too, found that hard to believe; I couldn't get Jonny to pick up his dirty socks; I sure couldn't imagine him digging a tunnel.

"It made the work go a lot faster," Jonny admitted. "We

took turns, two of us at a time. Xian did most of the hard work, but we helped him put up the beams to hold up the tunnel. And while we helped him, he helped us. He was the one who came up with the rope puller, the one over on Slippery Slope."

"I see. And how long did it take to dig all these tunnels?"

"I don't know, a long time. Several months, I guess."

"You're telling me that you and your friends helped Xian dig more than a mile's worth of tunnels in less than nine months? That hardly seems likely."

"They weren't *all* caved in," Jonny explained. "A long time ago, Boomtown blew itself inside out. A lot of the tunnels collapsed, but not all of them. We found one that was almost half a mile long. That was about two months ago."

"In May?"

"Yeah. Then school let out and we had more time. It went pretty fast after that. We were worried, though."

"Worried?"

"Sure. Sheriff Ernie had found the letter by then, and people had figured out that Chang maybe had a son. We asked Xian about that. He told us Chang was his great-grandfather. We figured it was something like that, anyway. Chang and Xian were practically twins."

"Is that it? What about what happened on Fourth of July?"

"Xian was pretty upset. Not about the cave-in. A couple of days before that."

"What was he upset about?"

"Because we found the chamber. You know, the one

underneath the statue? That's what Xian had been looking for. But it was *empty*."

"It wasn't supposed to be empty?"

"No. He never told us what to expect. But he found the chamber where it was supposed to be. When it was empty, Xian almost cried. We all did. All we found was some Chinese writing on the wall. Xian said it was a note written to Chang's wife, but he wouldn't tell us what it said. It sure made him sad, though. The next day the street caved in. You already know about that."

Jonny stopped talking and glanced around the tent. As soon as he saw me looking his way, he hung his head and stared at his shoes.

The judge frowned. "Jonny, you should have *told* somebody. It's good that nobody got hurt, but they *could* have. This could have been worse. You should have told your father! Or Sheriff Ernie. You should have *trusted* them."

Jonny answered sheepishly, "I know. But we were just trying to help."

"*Help?*" thundered Horatio, leaping up from his seat. He had been sitting quietly, listening to Jonny's testimony and taking notes, but now he was on fire again. He'd been patient long enough. "Help a *criminal*? Help a wanted man get away with his crimes? You call that *help*?"

"We didn't know what he was doing!" Jonny cried. "He wouldn't tell us why he was hiding or what he was looking for. He said it was *his*, whatever it was."

"He said it was his—and you *believed* him? That's *all*?" The lawyer waved his hands at the jury. "You see this boy sitting here? *All* he did was give aid to the enemy. *All* he did was hide the truth from the authorities. *All* he did was make sure that the man who was robbing you didn't get caught! *That's all!*"

He turned and pointed a shaking finger in my direction. "And what about *you*, Reverend? What do you think *now*? Now that you know how this desperate man duped your son and his friends into helping him? Isn't it obvious? Your son helped dig the tunnel—the one that nearly killed you! Are you so generous with your forgiveness *now*? What do *you* think about all of this?"

I looked at Janice. She flashed me a look of hope. I looked at the assembled townsfolk, sitting on the edge of their seats waiting for my answer. I saw Xian regarding me with sincere regret and apology in his eyes. Finally, I looked at Jonny sitting in the witness box and digging a hole in the ground with his toe. I looked into his eyes that were full of tears and fear. He was *afraid*—but not of the judge or the trouble he was in. He was afraid of *me*.

I stood up and walked over to Jonny. In that moment, I finally understood. That was *me* sitting there. Jonny was turning into *me*. Why should I be surprised? *I* was the one who was afraid all the time. I was the one who was always afraid of what people would think. I forced my family to live under that same cloud. They had to be careful about what they said and what they did. I wanted everything to be under control, *especially* my wife and kids. This was what fear did to people. Jonny had been sneaking around behind my

back, but *I* was the one who put him there. I'd been sneaking around for years.

It was just like the story in the Old Testament. I was like
cowardly King Saul. My boy was like courageous Prince
Jonathan. The nation of Israel had been in trouble, just
like Boomtown was in trouble now. It was too late for Saul
and Jonathan. But maybe it wasn't too late for us.

I turned to face Mr. Hooke. He stood there wearing his
expensive three-piece suit and silk tie. He stared at me triumphantly with his arms crossed over his chest waiting for
an answer. He didn't care if he was driving a wedge between
me and my son. All he cared about was *winning*. But suddenly
I cared about something a lot more important than that.

I looked him square in the eye and answered as loudly as
I could so everyone could hear me. "You want to know what
I think? Here's what I think! I think there has never been
a father who is more *proud* of his son than I am at this very
moment. *That's* what I think."

The entire courtroom burst into cheering followed by
a thunderous round of applause. Janice began to cry. Ruth
and Sarah were smiling at me. As I faced him, I saw Jonny
heave a huge sigh of relief, and he smiled at me.

"Really, Dad? You mean it?"

"Really, Jon. I really mean it."

Horatio Hooke couldn't believe his ears. "You're proud?
How can you be *proud* of your son?"

I knew the answer to that question. "I'm proud because
my son *proved* to Xian what his great-grandfather had tried

to tell him—what *I* should have been telling him. He should have *trusted* the people of Boomtown. Xian was having trouble doing that—he probably has a good reason; you'll have to ask him. I can certainly sympathize because *I've* been having the same problem. I haven't trusted anybody. So whatever Xian has been up to, maybe *all* of us can learn something about trust. Even *you*, Mr. Hooke!"

The lawyer was coming unglued. "I can't believe this! I can't believe *you* or any of the people in this crazy nut house of a town. What a bunch of saps! You're all a bunch of back-woods Pollyannas! Don't you see what's going on here? *Xian was going to rob your bank!* He was going to steal all your hard-earned money! He was going to steal from the members of your church!"

"You don't *know* that," I shouted back. "Sheriff Burton made the same point—weren't you listening? The only one who knows what he was really doing is Xian. Why don't you ask *him*?"

"That's *exactly* what I'm going to do—if his lawyer has the guts to put him on the stand! Judge, I have no further questions for this witness. The prosecution rests."

Horatio sat down in a huff, folded his arms, and glared as Jonny and I embraced. Side by side, we made our way back to our seats. Janice greeted me with a warm hug and a kiss of relief. Folks up and down the aisle patted me on the shoulder and whispered words of encouragement and gratitude.

Judge Rodriguez pounded her gavel and said, "The prose-cuting attorney has turned the case over to the defense. It's hot in here—too hot—and I think we've heard more than enough for one day. If Mr. Rigdale is in agreement, we'll adjourn until tomorrow morning? Yes? Good! That'll do it then." She slammed down her gavel and we were dismissed.

We went home that night as happy as we'd been in a long time. Exhausted, we went to bed early, excited about what would happen the next day. Of course, we didn't *all* sleep that night. One of us stayed very busy.

CHAPTER 17

Xian Takes the Stand

That night, a rainsquall passed through the area. By morning, it was a cool sixty-eight degrees and very comfortable in the tent. Every seat was taken; every inch of standing room was occupied and then some; the reporters and film crews were standing by. Everyone expected this would be the day the mystery would be solved.

Everyone except for Jonny, of course, who was not in his bed when we got up that morning. We searched the house and the backyard. I made a few phone calls. When we got to the courtroom, I took a quick survey of the bleachers and checked with Lazy Gunderson and Jim Dougherty; both of their boys were missing too. That could only mean one thing—they were off on another one of their adventures. That spelled trouble; we'd have to wait and see how much.

I didn't have any more time to track him down. I was on the witness list; I had to be available in case I was called back to the stand. How could Jonny miss the show? Where *was* that boy? I hoped he was okay.

As soon as the judge had taken her seat, the trial resumed. George Rigdale stood up and said, "Your Honor, I will be calling only one witness this morning. I call Xian, the great-grandson of Chang, to the stand." Horatio Hooke watched as the defendant rose. The lawyer grunted in satisfaction now that the final showdown was set to begin. He was looking forward to this like a dog waits for a bone.

Xian made his way carefully to the witness stand. Like his famous ancestor, he was a diminutive man, barely an inch over five feet tall. He had a smooth, unwrinkled face that defied age, though he was forty-nine years old at the time of the trial. He wore the simple, black linen jacket and pants common to his people, slippers, a black hat, and the traditional *queue* (ponytail) running down his back. He glanced nervously at the assembled crowd as he settled into his seat, expecting to see anger and indignation, but all he could see were amiable faces and encouraging waves. His face was an inscrutable mask, though I sensed surprise behind his dark eyes. A warm welcome from the people he'd stolen from was the last thing he was expecting.

Defendant: Xian   Defense Attorney George Rigdale

George Rigdale crossed the grass floor and approached the witness. He stopped for a moment to regard the members of the jury, trying to calculate the mood. He saw twelve townspeople eagerly awaiting testimony from Xian—not a hostile face in the bunch. They were fascinated and intrigued. The lawyer hadn't faced that many juries in his career; those he'd faced were often predisposed to convict. What he saw in front of him was a jury that embraced Xian, regardless of what he had done. They thought of him as the reembodiment of their town's hero and founder. It almost didn't matter what Xian had to say. The jury was ready to throw him a parade.

Mr. Rigdale turned and faced Xian. A hush fell over the assembly as he adjusted his tie and prepared to question the defendant. The tension was electric, but not nearly as excit-ing as the story Xian began to tell.

"Would you please state your full name for the court?"

"My name is Xian, son of Kang."

"Kang was your father. And your grandfather?"

"His name was Wang."

"And *his* father?"

"Chang, my great-grandfather."

His voice was a barely audible whisper, aided only by the sound system and the microphone positioned near his mouth. His accent was distinctly Chinese, and he spoke in halting English, although his pronunciation was impeccable and his grammar correct. As he began to talk, everyone leaned forward so they could hear.

Mr. Rigdale continued, "So you *claim* to be the great-grandson of Chang. That is one of the primary issues this fine jury and all the people of Boomtown wish to pursue. You bear a striking resemblance to Chang, that is unmistak-able; but how is it possible that you are his direct descendant when he was a man who was thought to be unmarried and without family until his death?"

"That is not a mystery. My great-grandmother, Sang, was pregnant when Chang escaped from China in 1846; he was only seventeen years old at the time. He did not know his wife was carrying a child when he left. If he did, he never would have gone."

"You say he *escaped*? From what was he trying to escape?"

"Chang was born in 1830, during the latter days of

the Qing Dynasty, which ruled my country for more than three hundred years. It was overthrown in 1911 after many years of struggle. After that the nation became known as the Republic of China; more recently, the People's Republic of China, governed now by socialism at the hands of Mao Tse Tung. It is a sad and evil time for my country.

"But no more or less than it was in days of my great-grandfather, who lived to see the uprising of the White Lotus Sect. This paved the way for invasion by foreign capitalists, leading to what was called the Opium War in the twentieth year of Daoguang, a ruthless and corrupt emperor who persecuted intellectuals such as Chang's father. He was both a professor of history and a gentleman, unused to war and unwilling to fight."

While he spoke, Xian kept his dark eyes focused on the jury, although every now and then his gaze drifted over to where we were sitting. He told his story with bridled emotion. He seemed relieved to finally get all of the secrets out in the open.

"The cruelty of the emperor bred rebellion like mushrooms after the rain. He was always at war—with neighboring countries and especially his own people. When Daoguang sent his troops to forcefully draft all the young men of my village, Chang faced a horrible decision. If he yielded to them, he'd be forced to do what was being done to him. If he refused to join the army, they would have him killed or imprisoned. Chang's father encouraged him to run away.

"He said, 'Go to America, my son. Make your fortune there and then call for your wife. We will send her to you.' And so he went, planning always to send word of his whereabouts and to send for Sang as soon as it was reasonable."

George Rigdale frowned. "But Chang never sent for her, not as far as we know. He never mentioned having a wife—*or* a son."

"He could not have known what happened after he left," Xian explained. "The emperor, Daoguang, was so angry with Chang's father that he had him arrested and thrown into prison. From then on he sent spies into our village to seize any letters that Chang might send. He wanted to prevent any of our family from leaving to join him.

"During that time Sang gave birth to Wang, but Chang never knew she was pregnant and never learned the fate of his father and his family. Not until much later."

"Tell the court, if you will, what happened next."

"My family continued to live as prisoners in the village, even after the death of Daoguang and the fall of the Qing Dynasty. His agents in the government made sure that the policy against Chang and his descendants continued. His letters were taken. Our letters to America were seized.

"But then something happened. A friend of my father was traveling to America on business. He agreed to search until he discovered what had happened to Chang. He would send word to us through his network of business associates. Years went by and we gave up hope of ever hearing from him, until one day there came a knock on our door. It was an agent bearing news."

"What was this agent able to tell you?"

"It was just as we had feared. Chang was dead. But now we knew what had become of him. He lived in Washington and died in Boomtown. He'd invented many wonderful things during this life and was considered a friend to many and an honorable man. Beyond that, the man was unable to say."

"So that was the end of it?"

"No. There was more to come. My father had an acquaintance in China who was working as a minor clerk in the government archives section in Beijing. He agreed to do what he could to find any records referring to my great-grandfather and smuggle them out of Beijing and bring them to us if possible. It was a very dangerous mission for which my family will be forever grateful. Five more years passed, but we continued to wait. One day a bundle arrived on our doorstep. Tied to the bundle was a note."

"Do you have that note with you today?"

"I do."

"Your Honor, I wish to enter into evidence this note written by an associate of Xian's father."

Judge Rodriguez asked, "Any objections from the prosecution?"

Horatio Hooke approached the bench and took the letter from Xian's hand. "This note is written in *Chinese*. How can we verify what it actually says? As far as we know, it could be a fabrication by the witness, a fakery to go along with all of his other lies."

The judge answered, "For the time being let us assume it is genuine and that Xian will read it accurately. If you find anything damaging to your case in the letter, you may object at that time. Agreed?"

Mr. Hooke reluctantly withdrew his objection and marched back to his seat.

"Please continue, Mr. Rigdale."

The defense attorney faced his witness. "Will you please read the letter at this time?"

Xian began to read:

"Dear friends, after many years of careful searching I was finally able to locate the sealed records of your ancestor, Chang. They were locked in a basement vault where until recently I was forbidden to go. Buried among the other documents, I discovered a collection of

letters written by Chang and sent to his family over the years, seized by the government and locked away until now. I was afraid to take them all at once. So each week for a year I secreted a single letter inside the lining of my hat and carried them one by one out of the government building and to my small apartment where I have kept them hidden until now. I am risking my life delivering these letters to you, so I ask that you remember me with favor if the letters should prove to be of any value. Until then, I remain your friend, anonymously."

Mr. Rigdale waited patiently while Xian took a moment to take a sip of water and collect his thoughts. After a few moments of tense silence, the lawyer continued his questioning. "Did the letters prove to be of any importance?"

"Yes, they did. Our family finally learned what had happened to my great-grandfather. The letters told us about his escape from China and how he sailed to India and how he went from there on foot across Europe. He sailed from France working as a cook aboard a tramp steamer bound for America.

"He arrived in New York, where he learned of the Gold Rush. Like many Chinese, he was hired to help build the railroads to the West. The people of Boomtown know this part of his story—how he worked his way across the country, turned north when he reached California, and arrived here in Washington. His letters described a beautiful place of mountains and streams and wonderful, kind people who adopted him as their own son. He wrote about his many friends here, and I am ashamed that I did not trust them as he told me I should."

Mr. Rigdale held up a sheet of paper. "You are referring, of course, to the last page of the letter that was found down by the river by Denk and turned over to Sheriff Burton Ernie?"

"Yes. I dropped the page during one of my nightly raids."

"Do you have the rest of the letter in your possession?"

"I do."

"Are you prepared to read the letter here and now in front of this jury?"

"Yes, I am."

"Before you do, I have a few more questions, just for clarification. You said you did not *trust* the people of this town?"

"This is not their fault. I should have announced myself as soon as I arrived in Boomtown. I see now that I would have received a graceful welcome. I have been treated well as a guest of the sheriff in his very pleasant jail cell. Many admirable people have visited me every day. They have given me a comfortable bed to sleep in with fresh linens every morning. Mabel from the diner brings me terrible coffee for breakfast; Mrs. Kreuger brings me delicious sandwiches for lunch; the women from the Boomtown churches bring me supper at night. My Chinese countrymen have visited me frequently from the fireworks factory. I could not have been treated more kindly or with such courteous respect if I were a visiting king."

"And your justification for stealing supplies and equipment from around town? Your reasons for involving the boys in your secret activities? What could that be?"

"This is the thing I am most sorry about. I shouldn't have stolen anything. I shouldn't have gotten the boys involved.

"But you must understand. My family has lived under the cloud of suspicion for generations. We were afraid of the government, afraid of the spies, even afraid of our neighbors who might accidentally whisper our secrets to the wrong person. We have lived as virtual prisoners in our own village and had forgotten how to trust. When I made my way here to Boomtown, I did not know what else to think. So I hid myself away and came out only at night to gather supplies and equipment and to dump the dirt from the tunnel. The boys brought me food. Their help and trust should have been enough to convince me that the people of Boomtown would have done the same. I am very sorry."

Mr. Rigdale nodded. "Yes, it's true that a considerable amount of trouble and misunderstanding could have been avoided if you had simply announced your arrival and asked for help. The tunnel you mentioned could have been dug in *days*—not months. And the Reverend Button could have avoided yet another death-defying adventure in his considerably dangerous life."

"I see that now."

"Very well. That brings us to the nature of this most interesting tunnel you have worked so hard to dig. What can you tell us about that?"

"When I came, I did not expect that I would have to dig. You understand, Chang died in the explosion that turned this town inside out. He was not able to send another letter explaining what had changed, because he was *dead.* The map he sent along with his last letter gave instructions, but those instructions were based on tunnels that no longer existed. They were buried in the explosion. I had to dig out the old tunnels, starting from the fireworks factory and leading toward Town Square, as you already know. This took far more time than I had planned; even though some sections were still open, much of the tunnel had collapsed and filled in. I expected to find what my great-grandfather left behind. Instead, it became necessary for me to dig—something that has taken almost nine months to finish."

"So you admit that it was you and *only* you who should be held responsible?"

"Yes," Xian confessed. "Don't blame the boys. I was the one who took the truck. I was the one who took the wood and the wire and the tools and the lights and more. None of it would have been necessary if I had asked for help. I have never known people like the ones who live here."

Horatio Hooke didn't seem to care about the generous citizens of Boomtown. By the look on his face, you could tell he was congratulating himself. The defendant had just confessed under oath in front of a thousand witnesses. The judge and the jury had heard him say it. As far as he was concerned, a conviction was guaranteed and so was his future as governor of Washington. After that, who knows? A senator and maybe even president of the United States? I watched him rub his hands together as he dreamed about the possibilities.

Mr. Rigdale continued. "Then it was never your intention to hurt anyone? Never your intention to harm Reverend Button? Never your intention to rob the bank, as our illustrious prosecutor has suggested?"

"No! Never! I was not digging the tunnel to reach the bank. I was looking for something else."

"Does the letter tell us what that might be?"

"The map and the letter. Yes, they do."

"Please read it for the court."

Xian reached into his pocket and pulled out the letter. Mr. Rigdale handed him the lost page. It matched the others, wrinkled and yellowed with age, folded many times but otherwise lovingly preserved. For Xian, it was the final link in a chain that connected him to his famous ancestor—a man, as it turned out, no one really knew or understood. Chang had been a man with a thousand secrets and a deep sadness that he'd never shared with his friends in Boomtown. Xian held the pages in his trembling hand and began to read the letter:

"My dearest son, a man came to town today. He came from China, from a village near our own. He told me about the arrest and death of my father. He told me that my beloved wife has died. Then he told me about you, my son Wang, about whom I knew nothing until now. If I had known, I would have crawled back to China on my knees to be with you.

"The man warned me of how the government has seized my letters and spied on our family. They have waited for my return to

arrest me as an enemy of the state. I am ashamed of my fear but have decided to gamble on your ability to escape as I did. The man has agreed to carry this letter and a large sum of money back to China. I have paid him handsomely to help you and your wife and children to buy safe passage to America. Here you may finally find freedom from tyranny. Come as soon as you are able.

"Should I die before you arrive, it will be with regret and tears. But all is not lost. I have drawn a map that shows the way to a secret chamber. Hidden there is a treasure—half is for your family; the other half must be shared equally with every man, woman, and child of my adopted home. I love them as if they were my own—in the same way they have loved me.

"If you come and I am gone, you must follow the directions I have given. Find the treasure that remains secret to this day. Mention this to no one on your journey, though you may trust my friends in Change. I can only hope this gift will make up for my fearful neglect. Even so, nothing can repay a son for the absence of his father. I pray this letter finds its way to your hand with love and honor, your father, Chang."

The assembled crowd remained frozen like statues during the reading of the letter, but as soon as Xian finished they burst like a thunderstorm in spring. Everyone was talking at once. Photographers snapped flash photos. Reporters yelled into their microphones. Film crews recorded the pandemonium. Horatio Hooke shouted his objections. The judge pounded her gavel. George Rigdale smiled in satisfaction. Xian sat back in his chair and sighed with relief.

"Order!" cried Judge Rodriguez. "I will have order in this court!"

But no one listened. The bailiff shouted. The reporters reported. The jury clapped. Horatio Hooke called for a mistrial. Even the usually reserved George Rigdale stood up on a chair and tried to shout over the uproar, but even he was unable to regain control. More than five minutes passed before Judge Rodriguez restored order.

She pointed her gavel at Xian and asked the question that was uppermost in everyone's mind. "This so-called treasure, Mr. Xian, the one mentioned in the letter, the one for which you have so diligently searched—did you find it?"

Dead silence. Followed shortly by his disappointed answer, "No. It is just as Jonny said. I didn't find it. It wasn't there."

Shocked silence. Followed shortly by a shout coming from the back of the tent, *"He* didn't find it—but *we* did!"

At the sound, everybody's heads spun around to look. In marched a parade of boys, covered with dirt and mud from head to toe, about ten of them marching up the center aisle directly to the witness stand where all could see. Leading the way was Jonny, bent over at the waist and struggling to carry something heavy, wrapped in a muddy strip of canvas. He stumbled to the front, dropped the bundle on the railing of the witness stand, and nearly collapsed from the effort.

Horatio Hooke bellowed over the tumult of murmuring spectators, "I object! I object! These boys have no official business in front of this court. The case goes to the jury! Xian is guilty! I win! Get these filthy urchins out of here!"

But no one cared what Horatio had to say. Because at a nod from Jonny, Busy reached over and unwrapped the package sitting on the rail. After that there was nothing left to discuss. Lying on the rag, gleaming yellow in the late-morning sun, was a solid bar of the most beautiful gold you've ever seen, as big as two fists and worth a small fortune. It looked like it could weigh as much as fifty pounds!

Then Jonny shouted triumphantly over the ensuing chaos, "There's more where *that* came from! A *lot* more!"

The judge smiled and banged her gavel. "Case dismissed!"

CHAPTER 18

Farewell for Now

About a month later, we were packing to leave for Seattle. I'd been offered a pulpit in the city and accepted—but not before days and days of crying and complaining on the part of my family.

I could hardly blame them. In the short time we'd been residents of Boomtown, they'd fallen in love with the people just as the townspeople had fallen in love with us. This is where Holly had joined our family. This is where Janice had found so many new friends, but not half as many as Ruth, Jonny, and Sarah. They didn't want to leave; *of course* they didn't want to leave! Boomtown was a playground, the perfect place for a kid to grow up. Every day was a new adventure.

No, it wasn't Janice or the kids. *I* was the one with the problem. It was during a morning in late August when I made up my mind. I stood in the window of our front room staring blindly at the turning leaves. I counted the buttons on my favorite sweater, over and over again, absently repeating the poem I made up in my head:

> *One*—This isn't any fun;
> *Two*—What should I do?
> *Three*—Why is it me?
> *Four*—I can't take any more.
> *Five*—I'm lucky to be alive.
> *Six*—I'm in a tight fix.
> *Seven* . . .

I stopped and looked down. The seventh button on my sweater had popped off. It was lying in my hand, staring up at me like an omen of things to come.

"Seven," I murmured. "Time to go to heaven." That was the final straw.

The next morning we held a family meeting. I sat at the head of the table with my temples throbbing and surrounded by hostile faces.

"Dad! We *can't* go. What about my friends?" Jonny was almost on the verge of tears.

"You'll make new friends in Seattle."

"I graduate from high school this coming year," Ruth said. "I just got a job at the Boomtown Bookstore. I was saving money for college."

"I know that, dear. I'm really sorry."

Sarah kicked my shin under the table.

"Ow! *Sarah!*"

"It's not fair! I'm starting the sixth grade. I get to build a rocket this year."

"Janice, help me out here."

"What do you want me to say? I've made a lot of friends too. That's always been hard for me, being the pastor's wife, to make any real friends. People always treat me differently, especially other women. But not here in Boomtown. They've helped me fit in. I love it here. So do the kids."

"But just look at me! Red circles under my eyes. Face as white as a sheet. I can't eat. I can't sleep. I'm afraid to go outside. I'm afraid to stay inside."

I held out my hand. It twitched like the last leaf on a winter branch.

"Just the other day, I was in my office at the church and

Ingrid dropped a stapler. A *stapler*! I hid under my desk like a frightened rabbit. It took Ingrid thirty minutes to coax me out of there."

Janice was sympathetic and patted my hand. "I know, dear. Things have been hard on you. But look at the bright side. Other than a sprained wrist, you've never really been badly hurt."

"*Are you kidding?* I've been knocked unconscious *twice*. You've almost been a widow *six* times! We've got a new baby and three other children. What are you going to do if a tree drops on my head? What if I fall down the stairs and break my neck? What about a tornado or a stampede?"

"Now you're just being silly. Boomtown has never had a tornado."

"There's always a first time."

We spent hours arguing about it, but I wouldn't listen. I wanted to tell them what I was really feeling, but I didn't know how. I thought after the trial things would be different for me, but as the days went by, I regressed backward into my earlier trepidations. What could I say? I was *embarrassed* by my fears.

I was supposed to be a man of faith; I preached about courage and facing life's troubles; but all I could think about was running away. So when a congregation in Seattle called, I jumped at the chance. They'd heard about me because of the publicity surrounding the trial and begged me to accept. Of course, the search committee from Boomtown Church was very upset. I met with them after my final Sunday and we talked.

"I'm really sorry. It has nothing to do with any of you. We love Boomtown and all the members of our church. But I've got to leave—before I *can't*."

"But, Reverend, we were just starting to get used to you! It was hard at first, but now we can't get along without you. We've *never* had this much excitement in our church before."

"That's exactly why I'm going. Too much excitement! I was chased by a rocket, nearly crushed by a barber chair, blown up by Santa Claus, mangled by a runaway bicycle, shot by a bank robber, and buried alive in a cave-in. My heart can't take it anymore!"

"But what are we going to do?"

"Look at it this way. You shouldn't have any trouble finding a new minister, not with all the fame and fortune you're enjoying. Besides, you'll have broken the curse. I'll be the first minister in seventy years who's *walked* out of the building instead of being *carried* out! Just think what that will mean to the next minister you find."

"Hey, you're right!"

As soon as they started thinking about it that way, they felt much better and were ready to start looking. They finally hung my picture up in the hallway with a plaque underneath that said "Served 1949–1950, Still Alive and Kicking." They threw a going-away dinner in the park attended by nearly every person in town. All of our new friends were there: Burton Ernie, Helga, Gramma Edna, Matthieu and his thirteen kids, the Beedles, Fred Cotton, Lazy Gunderson, Walter the Butcher, even Denk and his children. They all came out to say good-bye. Reverend Platz and Reverend Tinker said a prayer. Everyone shook hands and we all cried and laughed and told stories about everything that had happened.

Of course, I've forgotten to say what happened after the trial, what Jonny found in the tunnel, and what happened with Xian. So here are the final details, and then I'm finished.

All charges were immediately dropped against Xian; that should come as no surprise. After the gold was found, no one was willing to prosecute. Xian was set free, and Mayor Tanaka gave him the key to the city.

Horatio Hooke gave up his dreams of a life in politics and went back to Stickville to prosecute parking tickets. I don't think he ever got over the humiliation and disappointment. He nursed a grudge against Boomtown from that day forward. It came back to haunt the town, but that happened years later.

George Rigdale tried to fade back into anonymity, but the newspapers and radio stations wouldn't leave him alone. There was talk about nominating *him* for governor. A parking space was reserved with his name in front of the Boomtown courthouse for whenever he stopped by for a visit. He was a frequent visitor at Mabel's Diner.

Burton Ernie became famous as the lawman who cracked the case, even though the only thing he'd really done was drink bad coffee and drive around town looking for clues. He did, however, organize the digging crew that pulled Chang's statue out of the hole and clear all the debris from the chamber that lay hidden underneath. All those years, and no one knew a massive fortune had been right under their feet waiting to be discovered.

Xian explained what some of the other letters had revealed, that Chang had stumbled across a large vein of gold while digging for sulfur. He kept the discovery secret because he knew what would happen if word spread that gold had been found under the streets of Boomtown. It would trigger another gold rush. Fortune hunters would flock to the area like crows in a cornfield. They would bring guns and liquor and gambling and corruption along with their insatiable appetite for wealth—something Chang would not allow. So he kept his discovery secret as a way of saving the home he loved.

He sealed off the entrance to the tunnel and allowed the trees and bushes to overgrow the abandoned warehouse. He told no one about his discovery. Instead, over the years he continued to mine the gold and refine it in secret, storing the growing treasure in the hidden chamber.

When Chang found out he had a son and grandchildren

living in China, he dreamed of the day they would come to claim his family's fortune—but he didn't live to see it. He was killed in the explosion that turned Boomtown upside down. It buried the tunnel and his secret. It lay hidden for almost sixty years until Xian came and tried to dig it up.

Jonny explained what had happened on the night of the first day of the trial.

"Busy and me wanted to take one more look in the tunnel, just in case we missed something. We got all the guys together and decided to sneak out that night."

"I really wish you'd stop doing that, Jon, I really do," I sighed.

"Sorry, Dad, but it worked out, didn't it?"

"That's not the point."

"Okay. So anyway, we used Chang's statue like a ladder and climbed down into the hole. We were looking for maybe another door, maybe another place where Chang could have hidden the treasure. It was dark, but we had flashlights and shovels if we needed them. But we didn't find anything and pretty soon it was morning.

"When the sun came up, it shone on the back side of the hole, right on the note Chang had painted on the wall. We couldn't read it, but we saw something we hadn't seen in the dark. It was covered in mud until we wiped away some of the dirt. It was a gold medallion with a picture of Chang on it."

"Busy had a jackknife and he tried to pry it out of the wall, but instead it *pushed in*, like a button! The whole wall opened up—swung open like a gate! And that's when we found it!"

The "it" Jonny and his friends had found was a huge pile of gold bricks—more than a person can even imagine. Over the years, Chang had managed to assemble nearly five *tons* of gold—almost two hundred gold bricks weighing fifty pounds apiece. In 1950, gold was selling at an average of $35 an ounce; that's about $560 a pound. That made the total fortune worth more than five million dollars!

Xian honored Chang's wishes. He kept half of the money for his family; they were already on a ship to America to join their incredibly wealthy father. The rest of the money was divided evenly among the remaining eleven hundred seventeen residents of Boomtown. It put a total of $2,506 into the pockets of every man, woman, and child who lived in the town. My family collected more than $15,000. It was the money we used to move to Seattle, buy a house, and put Ruth through college. Needless to say, things were booming in Boomtown!

The day finally came for us to say good-bye. Burton Ernie and his wife, Laverne, and their young son, Vernon, were the last to see us off. We stood next to the car exchanging hugs and handshakes. Vernon was nice enough to hold Holly while we did.

"Here, Vernon, give her to me," Janice said, holding out her hands. But Holly wouldn't let go. She kept clinging to Vernon, both of her little arms wrapped firmly around his neck. Holly cried when Janice tried to take her.

"That's strange," she said. "She doesn't usually act like that. She must really like you, Vernon."

Vernon smiled happily. "I like her too. I wish she didn't have to go."

"We'll come back for a visit," I said politely. I meant it at the time, I really did, but I never kept my promise. But *Holly* did—she and Vernon—it's strange now that I think back on it. Strange how things come full circle. It was almost like Holly *knew* something we didn't, something that drew her back to Boomtown—and it's a good thing that it did. But that's another story.

We decided to take the long way around as we left. We cried as we drove down Boom Boulevard, past the hole in Town Square that had changed our lives forever, past Lazy Gunderson's place, past the powder plant and the fireworks factory, across Ifilami Bridge, and on to our new life in Seattle.

As we drove, my mind raced through all the unbelievable things we'd seen and all the impossible things that had happened—I still think of them after all these years. My memory wanders down the streets of Boomtown and I remember that remarkable and wonderful place. I wonder how Burton Ernie is doing. I wonder if Mabel ever learned how to make coffee. Is Frankie the Banker still robbing the bank? Is Walter still terrorizing his customers? I wonder how Xian's family has adapted to their new home. I wonder if Fred Cotton's truck is still on display at the museum. I wonder if the new pastor at the church has survived.

And I wonder if people will ever learn to live like the people of Boomtown already know how to live.

I wonder.

Boomtown Timeline

1830   Chang born in China.

1839   Mfana Losotu born in South Africa.

1846   Chang escapes China; Sang gives birth to Wang.

1848   California Gold Rush begins.

1850   Chang arrives in Okanogan Territory, Washington.

1854   Mfana Losotu taken as a slave to America.

1863   Mfana escapes during the Battle of Gettysburg at age twenty-four.

1872   Chang establishes the Black Powder Plant and Chang's Famous Fireworks Factory.

1878   May 18, Founding of Change, Washington, by
        Mayor Alden Purdy.

1882   Mfana Losotu arrives in Change.

1889   November 11, Washington achieves statehood.

1892   Chang dies in Hen Grenade explosion.

1894   The town of Change changes its name
        to Boomtown.

1899   Groundbreaking for the town hall.

1909   Stickville Slugs begin forty-year losing streak.

1911   President William H. Taft visits Boomtown.

1912   Boomtown Power Plant up and running.

1914   First Slush Olympics is held.

1929   Dr. Losotu dies and bequeaths his home and its
        contents as a museum.

1949   Reverend Button and his family arrive.